The Laureate

A Nico Argenti novel

Ken Tentarelli

AC1H Publications Newbury NH

ISBN: 978-1-7331773-0-6

To Lizzie

Introduction to Nico's World

Renaissance Florence abounded with opportunities for law school graduates. Each branch of government had a tribunal where lawyers negotiated legal issues. Other lawyers served on special commissions where they ruled on various administrative and legal matters. Each of the city's twenty-one guilds had lawyers overseeing guild regulations.

Many who practiced law in Florence were schooled at the University of Bologna. Founded in 1088 it is the world's oldest university in continuous operation. Under the protection of Holy Roman Emperor Frederick Barbarossa, students flocked to the university from more than 30 'nations' throughout Europe. Bologna offered programs in both civil and canon law. At least four Popes studied canon law at Bologna. Many of Bologna's law students also made major contributions in other fields. Its alumni included humanist, writer, and poet Petrarch, architect Leon Battista Alberti, and Archbishop of Canterbury Thomas Becket. At the height of the Renaissance in the 1460s, the University of Bologna had 40 professors on its law school faculty.

The de Medici family was established in Florence for over two centuries before Cosimo de Medici began his 30-year reign as leader of the Republic of Florence. His power derived, in part, from the wealth of the famous Medici bank founded by his father, but he also gained public support through his policies, such as a tax imposed on the wealthy, including himself, to support the poor. He was the greatest private patron of his time who used his wealth to foster a new era of art and learning. His tenure marked a time of peace and prosperity in the Florentine Republic. When Cosimo de Medici died on August 1, 1464, his passing left a political vacuum in the Republic and unleashed a struggle for power. The ensuing turmoil touched all citizens of the Republic, including a new graduate of the University of Bologna law school, Nico Argenti.

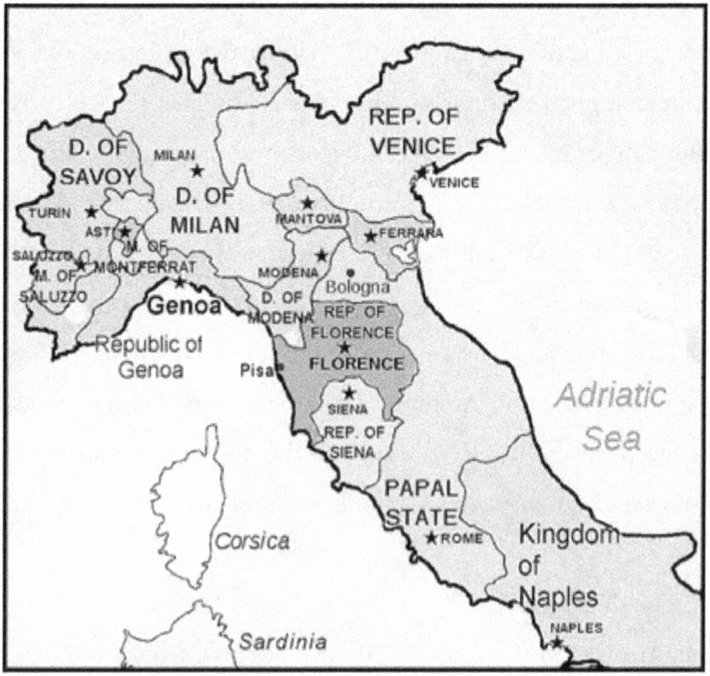

Chapter 1 Saturday, August 4, 1464

We eased our horses to a stop at the crest of a small knoll. "We're getting close" I announced. "That's the dome of the cathedral in the center of the city."

Simone drew his mount abreast of mine and scanned the sweeping vista before us. "Where?" he asked.

I pointed to sunlight glinting from an object poking above treetops in the distance. "There. That is definitely the cathedral."

Hot August sun made our journey from Bologna a tiring ride. The feeble breezes were too warm to be pleasant and merely added to our discomfort by raising clouds of dust from the dirt road. Our hope for relief came in imagining cool drinks awaiting us in Florence. With our destination in sight, we were eager for our journey to end.

We loosened the reins letting the horses move forward down a gentle slope onto a section of road bordered by scraggly brush. Where the road crossed a small stream and curved sharply to the right, a large boulder alongside the road masked the view ahead. As we passed the boulder, a figure stepped out from the brush and into our path. His sudden appearance startled the horses. They reared, their forelegs reaching high into the air, throwing me off balance. I pitched backward and pressed my knees tightly against the saddle to keep from falling.

The figure was a short man, with straggly hair, dressed in a dirty laborer's smock. He held aloft a long wooden staff. A short distance behind, a second man stepped from the brush, but this one remained near the side of the road. He too held a wooden staff, but his was held lower with one end resting on the ground.

The short one barked in a rough voice, "All must pay a toll to enter the city."

I walked my horse forward then pulled back on the reins bringing it to a stop directly in front of the short man. Travelers say that encounters with bandits do happen on frontier byways, but never on the main road from Bologna nearly within sight of the Florence city gate.

The short brigand had hair dangling in greasy dreadlocks and an odor that reached me long before I came near. He was clearly someone who did not value cleanliness.

He spoke again, this time to his companion. "These travelers dress fancy. They can pay many ducats."

His companion did not respond. If these were truly highwaymen, why were they holding wooden poles rather than swords or daggers? Their demand might succeed with travelers on foot, but surely not with riders on horseback. They were no threat. If I were to urge my mount forward, it would either push the little man aside or trample him underfoot.

We could have simply ignored their threat and ridden past, but after six years of rigorous study, I was eager to use my legal training. I thrust my hand toward him to display my shiny new ring. "There is no toll on this or any road of the Florentine Republic. I am a citizen of the Republic, and, as this ring signifies, I hold a Doctorus Juris degree from the University of Bologna. I know all the laws of the Florentine Republic including the ones you are breaking by assaulting us. Now step aside and let us pass."

I may be merely a new laureate, but I smiled inwardly feeling my words were worthy of even a seasoned magistrate. The short man stood motionless looking up at me, his mouth open but unable to find words. Had he never been challenged before, or was he new to the highwayman trade?

Law professors drill into their students that reading the expressions of adversaries is an advantage in the courtroom. I had practiced that skill in the classroom, and now I could use it to press the diminished confidence of these would-be highwaymen.

"I repeat, move aside and let us pass or I will have the Guardia arrange prison cells for both of you."

Hearing my words the taller man cast his eyes downward and shuffled away slightly opening the space between the two men.

The short one scowled at his retreating accomplice and shrieked, "Stop you cowardly pig. Leave me and you will rot in hell!"

I guided my horse around the small man ignoring his

continuing rants. Simone followed close behind me. We stopped again when we came abreast of the tall man. By the time I reached him he had moved to the side of the road and did not attempt to intercept us. Physical size wasn't the only difference between him and his companion. Brown and purple stains on his hands suggested that he worked in one of the city's many tanning or wool dyeing shops. He gripped the wooden staff awkwardly using only his thumb and two fingers. One finger of his left hand was missing. The smock he wore was clean, although it showed the same stains as his hands. His hair had been brushed, and I detected no odor encircling him.

Laborers like him suffer long hours at grueling, dangerous jobs where injuries, or worse, are not uncommon. Each day for them is the same as the last with little hope of escaping to a better life. Pity, and maybe a touch of guilt that only a fortune of birth separated us, had me reach into the leather pouch tied at my waist to gather a few silver coins. I studied him as I probed for the coins: his hands large and rough, his frame sturdy as well as tall, and his arms heavily muscled. The shop owner surely gets more than a full day share of work from this one I thought.

Despair in his eyes told me that coins were not the answer to his problem; he needed help. I withdrew my hand from the coin pouch and asked, "What is your name?"

He replied simply, "Orsino."

Orsino, little bear, a fitting name for someone built like a bear.

"Do you work in a tanning shop?"

"A wool shop. I did work there."

"Orsino, thievery is not a good path to a better life. Do you know the place called the Uccello?"

"Yes"

"If you are willing to work, go there tomorrow. Ask for Nico."

I loosened the reins and rode on.

Chapter 2

Simone, my fellow traveler, followed closely behind me. He said nothing during the encounter, but his athletic build was evidence that he could take care of himself when necessary. If the incident had resulted in an altercation, I would have been well served to have him at my side. Simone Pisani is a handsome fellow with deep gray eyes and the soft facial features that distinguish Venetians from Florentines. He had just finished his fifth year at the University of Bologna. After one more year at the law school he too would earn a Doctorus Juris degree.

To his professors, Simone is the perfect student who studies with passion and probes legal issues more deeply than any of his classmates. His skill in applying precedents in any legal situation was envied by all his fellow students. We had become close friends while studying together, so to celebrate the completion of my schooling I invited him to spend part of his summer holiday with my family in my home city. It was intended to be an enjoyable experience spent with a trusted friend. Encounters with bandits were not the kind of experience we anticipated. I hoped this did not bode further misfortune during his visit.

As we distanced ourselves from the thieves and rode on toward the city wall, now within view, Simone eased alongside and gave me a questioning look as if expecting an outpouring of wisdom, or at least a thoughtful comment about the incident. I had no wisdom to offer; in fact, thinking back on the episode, my actions may have been more foolish than wise.

During the journey we had not spoken about my family. Doing so now might get our thoughts away from the episode so without any preamble, I began. “Once, at the university, I told you that both of my parents perished along with thousands of others when the Black Death swept through Florence. I was ten years old when that happened. My father had been in the military, and everyone expected that I would follow him and make my career in the military as well.

“He was a nuncio whose function was representing the army in diplomatic missions. He often traveled to Milan and Rome, a few times to Marseilles in Francia, and the Kingdom of Naples; that’s where he met my mother. His missions were ones of peace, not war, to build better security for the merchants of the Republic. Later he returned to Florence and represented the army at proceedings of the Tribunale di Esecutore, one of several tribunals in Florence.”

I glanced at Simone pleased to see that he was focusing on my words and no longer thinking of the bandits, so I continued. “No child should be without his parents, but I was fortunate to have wonderful and caring relatives. One of them, my uncle Nunzio, took me into his home and treated me as his own. His son, Donato, who is six years older than I, became like an older brother to me. We will be staying with Donato and his family when we arrive in Florence.

"Uncle Nunzio was a successful businessman. For many years he apprenticed to an innkeeper where he learned the trade and eventually saved enough money to buy the inn. What he bought was merely an old building with seedy furnishings. Uncle made improvements over time, as his funds allowed, and the popularity of the inn grew accordingly. The biggest change he made was converting the inn into a dining club, the first of its kind in Florence."

Simone looked puzzled so I paused to let him collect his thoughts. The rhythmic slap of horse hoofs on the hard-packed dirt roadway filled the silence briefly until Simone asked, "I don't understand what you mean by dining club. If that is where people go to have a meal, how is it different from any other restaurant?"

"Restaurants offer only food; Donato's dining club offers more than just food. It is a place where men can relax on a comfortable couch to enjoy a glass of wine, or they can meet with friends to talk, or play cards. Often men spend entire evenings there socializing with others. Uncle's club became an instant success, especially among men who wanted a place to escape for an evening from a nagging wife."

Simone nodded, "I'm sure we have nagging wives in Venice too, but we don't have any dining clubs as you describe them, or if we do, I have never heard of them." He asked, "You call them clubs, does that mean only members are allowed?"

"Yes, members and their guests... male members and their male guests."

I continued speaking without giving Simone time to ask why the club was restricted to members, or why women were excluded. "Several years ago uncle Nunzio decided that his son, my cousin Donato, could manage the club better than he could, so Nunzio bought a vineyard outside the city and passed ownership of the club to Donato.

"Donato proved to be a genius with ideas for expanding his club in ways no one had ever imagined. First, he arranged to have entertainment by musicians, storytellers, singers, and other improvvisatori. Then he added separate rooms where men could meet to discuss business or share their views in private. The private rooms even have hidden entrances so men can arrive unseen by carriage. Members of different guilds often meet in those rooms to enjoy a fine meal while they complain about taxes or someone in the government. Women are welcome to attend functions in the private rooms as guests of members.

"Next Donato sought ways to expand the menu. Fruit and spices from foreign lands that are sold at the Mercato, the central market in the city, come to the port of Pisa by ship and then make their way to Florence. To expand the fare offered at his club,

Donato traveled to other port cities, Naples, and your home city, Venice, to procure unusual produce. That gained Donato's establishment a reputation for having unique and exotic items on its menu. Donato's ability to find unusual food items led one wealthy shop owner to ask that Donato arrange a special birthday celebration for his daughter at the owner's palazzo. It was an extraordinary success which prompted other prominent people to ask for Donato to arrange events with food and entertainment. It seems that each person wanted to host a more memorable celebration than his rival.

"Donato's friendships with foreign traders helped him satisfy even very unusual requests. Once an important official wanted troubadours to serenade at a celebration for his French wife, so Donato had poets and musicians brought from her hometown in Provence. The wife was ecstatic, especially when she learned that two of the musicians were distant cousins of hers.

"On another occasion a banker wanted figs served at a dinner for his mistress, so Donato had succulent brown figs imported from Turkey. All of this has earned him election as a consul of the Innkeepers Guild. In addition, he has become known throughout the city as il Festatore, the festival maker."

Chapter 3

By the time I finished my story the magnificent dome of the cathedral, Santa Maria del Fiore, loomed ahead. We had reached the northern gateway and were passing through Porta San Gallo into the city of Florence.

We left our horses at a stable near a parish church and walked the short distance to the house of il Festatore. I hit the boar's head door knocker against the bronze striker plate to announce our presence and was greeted quickly by Carlo, a long-time member of the household staff. In the three years since I'd seen Carlo, his hair had gained more gray, and lines had emerged on his thinning face. Before I could utter a word, he wrapped his arms around me with a welcoming hug proving that his strength hadn't left him.

Carlo escorted us through the loggia to the interior courtyard. It was kind of him to lead us, but unnecessary as the house had been my home until I left to attend the university. As we passed through the logia, I glanced around looking for changes but I noticed only the increased height of the lemon trees in the courtyard ahead.

We gave our duffels to Carlo, who would bring them to our rooms, then Simone and I climbed stairs to the second level following our noses toward the tempting scents flowing from the dining salon.

Servicing the needs of clients often forces Donato to spend evenings away from his family, so it was a pleasant surprise to find him, his wife Joanna, and their son Giorgio, at home and seated at a large table preparing to eat their evening meal. They all rushed to embrace me as soon as I passed through the doorway leaving no doubt that they were as happy to see me as I was to see them. My studies at the university kept me from returning to Florence for the past two years, but their warm welcome made me feel as though I had never left.

Engulfed in a four-way embrace, we moved away from the doorway to make it possible for Simone to enter the room. Despite being a newcomer, he too was pulled into the embrace.

"We didn't know if you would be arriving from Bologna today or tomorrow. It is a long tiring journey. You must be hungry," Donato said.

Without waiting for me to answer Joanna set out two plates filled with her delicious pappardelle al cinghiale. Conversation and hearty Tuscan wine flowed throughout the evening.

They were eager to hear about my life at the university, but they were even more enthralled by Simone who told of life in Venice. They peppered him with a seemingly endless stream of questions: Do you have brothers or sisters? Do you play sports? Have you sailed on any of Venice's great merchant ships? Do you have a girlfriend? What do you hope to see in Florence? How long can you stay with us?

Upon hearing about the city of canals, Giorgio's eyes widened and he asked, “If there are no roads do you get around by swimming instead of walking?”

Everyone laughed, then Simone answered, “I suppose we could, but no, we use boats to travel around the city.”

“Wow, that would be fun.” Giorgio turned to his father, “Just think papa, we could have our own boat.”

Donato ran his hand through Giorgio's hair and said, “Yes, I imagine we could. Maybe you would even have a little boat of your very own.”

At that Giorgio’s eyes grew even brighter. He turned back toward Simone, “What about houses, do the houses float, or do you live in boats?”

“Venice is filled with small islands, dozens of them, and the houses are built on the islands.” Simone reached into a pocket, pulled out a silver coin having an image of boats on the Grand Canal. He handed the coin to Giorgio.

Giorgio studied the coin, showed it to his mother and father; then reached out to pass it back to Simone.

“That’s yours to keep. Maybe someday you'll visit Venice and you can use it to buy something nice for yourself - or some lucky lady.”

When the exchange of stories and banter finally waned, Joanna decided it was time to put Giorgio to bed. Fatigue from our long journey and the stressful encounter with the highwaymen made Simone opt for sleep as well. Joanna led him up to the sleeping area on the third level where a room had been prepared for him.

Donato and I refilled our wine glasses and turned our conversation in a more serious direction. Donato began, "Surely knowledge of Cosimo de Medici's passing last week has reached even to the academic quarter of Bologna."

"Yes, even students who are not from Florence were wondering about his successor."

Donato continued, "Most Florentines believe he has been good for the Republic. His power and influence have been growing for decades, causing many people to believe he had become too powerful. Even some elected members of the Signoria have been reluctant to speak against him."

"But we have laws," I interjected, "Surely he must have followed the laws."

"Oh, he follows the laws. However, if the laws become an obstacle to accomplishing his goals, he has them changed."

Donato leaned back in his chair and took another swig of wine to drain the glass before continuing.

"Don't misinterpret my words, Nico. Cosimo was a great man. Everyone agrees that he deserved the title 'Father of the Republic.' But now, with Cosimo gone, others think it is time to end the Medici dynasty. They want to grab power for themselves."

It struck me that Donato was more attuned than usual to the happenings of Florentine politics.

"Is Cosimo's son Piero willing to step aside?" I asked.

"Piero has suffered from gout for many years and his condition is worsening steadily. He will certainly try to follow in Cosimo's path, but he spends most of the time convalescing at his villa at Careggi. He rarely even comes to Florence."

Donato poured another glass of wine before continuing, "Displeasure with the Medicis has been growing among some members of the Signoria and among leaders of the guilds. Several of them, the opposition leaders, have been invited to a gathering next week at the house of Luca Pitti. I know this because they have engaged my services to arrange a dinner for them. I sense that they hope to enlist others in putting an end to the Medici dynasty."

No rumors of a challenge to Piero de Medici had reached Bologna, so the situation described by Donato was new to me. Disputes had always existed among the leading citizens of Florence. Even Cosimo himself was once imprisoned by his adversaries, but that was nearly thirty years ago, and since then his political grip had not wavered. I asked, "Which of these positions do you support?"

Donato chuckled, "I am not a politician. They play their power games so the winners can preside at official functions wearing fancy robes."

Showing my cynical streak, I inserted, "The winners also get to dip into the city treasury."

"Sadly, that is true. For me though, and for all other hard-working, honest businessmen, it hardly matters who wins. My worry is not about victory, but that turmoil from the power struggle will spread to everyone. When big men throw rocks at each other, small men get hit with stones."

Donato finished his wine, leaned back in his chair, and closed his eyes. Sharing his concern with me seemed to relax him, but I could think of nothing that either of us could do to change the outcome. Sleep was calling me. As I rose to leave, Carlo entered the room and handed me a folded sheet of paper. "This message just arrived for you."

I unfolded the sheet and read, "Can we meet tomorrow?" It was signed Bartolomeo Scala.

Bartolomeo Scala was the second Chancellor, one of the most important positions in the government of the Florentine Republic. Why would someone in his position want to meet with me, and how could he know that I had just returned to Florence?"

I looked again at the paper. It was a plain sheet with no official seal or government emblem. As I puzzled over a possible reason for the invitation --or summons -- Carlo asked, "Do you wish to respond? The courier who brought the message is waiting."

"Yes. Tell him yes. And ask when and where he would like to meet."

As Carlo turned to leave I called out, "No. No, that won't do. I'm sure the Chancellor will say when and where he wants to meet. Just say I will be honored to meet with him."

Chapter 4 Sunday, August 5, 1464

Sun streaming in the window meant that I slept late despite spending a restless night. Whatever ghosts might have poked at me during the night fled with the darkness. Donato deserved a share of responsibility for my restive sleep, as he had been diligent in keeping my wine glass filled, although I should have been emptying it at a more measured pace. During my early years at the university I, and my fellow classmates, regularly consumed generous amounts of wine without being dulled in classes the following morning, but as we moved into the more intensive law courses, we found it necessary to scale back consumption to more modest levels. Now, I found a single glass of mulled wine in the evening to be sufficiently relaxing.

The main reason for my fitful sleep was concern over the message from Chancellor Scala. At the foot of the bed, I bent down and raised the cover of a small wooden chest that contained my greatest treasures, favorite items accumulated in my youth, including priceless remembrances of my parents. From the collection I removed two items.

The first, wrapped in a protective cloth was a small portrait of my mother and father made on their wedding day. There, after I removed the item's covering, was my mother's tender smile. The painting could not recreate her soft voice, but I could hear it nonetheless, as clearly as ever. In the painting she stood, elegant in her wedding dress, next to my father, who was beaming proudly in his military uniform. Moving across the room to the far wall I found a bent metal hook I had fastened to the wall many years ago. I reached up and restored the painting to its proper home on the hook.

The second item was a small carved wooden dog. From time to time my father was a guest lecturer at the University of Florence, and on a few of those occasions he let his young son accompany him. I sat in the first tier next to an attentive student who absorbed every word my father spoke.

At the conclusion of the lecture, the student turned to me, "You must be a new member of the class and certainly our youngest. Welcome. Attending classes here is something I do every day, but this is surely a special day for you, a day to be commemorated."

He told me his name, but I did not remember it at the time. Then he placed into my hand the small carved wooden dog, not saying whether the animal had any special significance to him or was simply a trinket that had come into his possession. Truthfully, I cherished the little carving more because it reminded me of a special time spent with my father than because of the student who gave it to me. In fact, it wasn't until several years later that I asked my father the student's name and he told me it was Bartolomeo Scala.

That was the only time I had met Messer Scala. A short time later, funding problems caused the University of Florence to suspend operation. Scala and his fellow students were forced to complete their studies elsewhere, with Milan being the destination chosen by Scala.

The ringing of the bells at nearby Basilica Santa Croce interrupted my thoughts. I dressed quickly, listening for any sounds that might tell whether Simone was awake. Hearing nothing, but detecting the faint aroma of a morning meal, I headed down to the dining salon.

A large meat pie sat on a warming tray in the middle of the dining table. From its aroma, I judged it to be rabbit with pork belly and prunes, a specialty of the Argenti kitchen. A few slices were already missing so there should be no objection to my cutting a generous slice for myself. As I was reaching for a knife two arms gently wrapped around my waist from behind. "Dottore Argenti," a gentle voice said.

The fragrance of her perfume reached me an instant before her words, and I knew immediately that it was Alessa. I spun around, hugged her close, kissed her lightly on both cheeks, and then stood back to look at her. She had the same warm smile that I remembered from three years ago when I saw her last. Then she was a young girl; now the loose smock she wore could not hide the attractive figure of a woman.

A flash of movement at the corner of my eye drew my attention to Simone who had just stepped into the doorway. Still holding Alessa by the hand I beckoned Simone to join us. "Simone, this delightful young woman is Alessa. Isn't she as lovely as a flower with a smile as bright as the sun itself?"

Simone moved into the room to face Alessa, and said, "Ah, the beauty of Neroli, the brilliance of Khepera."

To me Simone's words were baffling. Alessa startled but she recovered quickly and responded, "Neroli, yes, but Morocco not Egypt."

Her words did not help my understanding at all. "You two just met and already you are speaking in a code that I fail to understand."

To avoid being excluded from the conversation entirely I changed the subject. "We should eat before this pie becomes cold and before I faint from hunger. Later you can share with me the meaning of your cryptic phrases."

As we sat to breakfast on rabbit pie, fresh pecorino cheese, and a variety of fruit, Alessa asked Simone how he knew of Neroli, her fragrant Egyptian perfume made from orange blossom flowers, and Khepera, what Egyptians called the morning sun. He responded only by saying, "I live in Venice," as though that would be a sufficient explanation.

I elaborated with, "Simone, a star student at the University of Bologna; indeed, he is one of its brightest stars. He will graduate next year, no doubt in the first rank of the law class. He is from The Most Serene Republic of Venice where his father is a member of the government's ruling body, the Council of Ten."

Alessa looked toward Simone and said, "Interesting facts but they don't explain your knowledge of Khepera, and how did you know I am wearing Neroli perfume?"

"Venice is a seafaring republic whose wealth is totally dependent on our merchant fleet. Our ships are constantly bringing us goods, - and legends, - from Egypt and the Levant. My father was elected to the Council because he knows that the success of our Republic depends on understanding our trading partners. I credit him with giving me that appreciation as well. Through the years I have become acquainted with Egyptian beliefs and their products."

"Does that extend to recognizing Neroli solely by its fragrance?"

"It is a unique, memorable fragrance, a favorite fragrance also preferred by another lovely woman. Perhaps if ... when you come to Venice you will meet her."

"A girlfriend?" Alessa asked.

"My sister," Simone answered. "She has light skin while yours is the color of hazelnut. She has grey eyes; yours have the hue of fine chocolate. But you both share the smile that brightens any room."

Alessa stood motionless, warmed by Simone's words. Had she been made of butter she would have become a puddle on the floor. That she was taken by Simone's words was no surprise to me. At the university, I had witnessed him charm the girls of Bologna, and do so by merely expressing his feelings honestly.

"I should stop lest you believe I have an unnatural obsession with my sister. Now you must tell me of the sun in Morocco, the sun that matches the brightness of your smile. Merchants from Genoa and Naples command the trade routes to Morocco. They do not welcome intrusion by our Venetian ships, so I have little knowledge of Western Africa."

Alessa was not comfortable talking about her past so I told her story to Simone. As I began speaking, she drifted from the table to a nearby pantry to distance herself from the unpleasant memory.

"On one of his journeys to Naples to purchase African grains, Donato noticed a cabin girl aboard one trader's ship. She was a small waif with bright eyes. Donato watched as she did her work with care, always knowing what needed to be done without being told. Donato learned she had been purchased by the shipowner on one of his voyages to Morocco. Donato thought that being a cabin slave on a merchant ship held no future for an intelligent and industrious youngster. He made a generous offer to buy the girl, and the shipowner readily agreed, always happy to make a profit, and saying he could find a replacement on his next voyage. Donato brought her to Florence as a free child, not as a slave. She was an eager worker who helped Joanna with many household chores. In time Alessa became like a daughter to Joanna and Donato, and a sister to me."

Before I could add details of Alessa's past, Giorgio scampered into the room, ran to me and held out a folded sheet. "This just came for you," he said, "a messenger brought it. He said I should give it to you immediately."

I unfolded the sheet and read it aloud, "San Salvi at hour fourteen." It was not signed but there was no doubt that it was sent by Chancellor Scala.

Turning to Simone I said, "I had planned to spend today showing you around this great city, but this morning I must meet with the Chancellor." Then to Alessa, I said, "Would it be possible for you to show Simone around the city this morning?"

At first, she just said yes. Then after a short pause, she added a sisterly teasing, "I had planned to do many things today, but for you, Nico, I suppose my plans can be changed. It will mean much extra effort tomorrow but there are times when a girl must endure pain to help her brother."

There was no need to ask Simone if the arrangement suited him. His expression showed he would be delighted to have Alessa as his escort. He pulled me aside and asked, "You and Alessa?"

I answered quickly, "No, there is nothing between us, as I said she is like my sister."

He was visibly pleased with that response. Perhaps too pleased so as he turned to leave, I grasped his arm and repeated, "Remember that, she is my sister."

Chapter 5

Bartolomeo Scala chose an unusual place for our meeting. The monastery of San Salvi has been home to Benedictine monks for hundreds of years. It was built long before any of the defensive walls that encircle the city. It sits on the flat plain of the Arno river valley outside the walls. That morning the air was unusually crisp and cool, so I welcomed the long walk and the warming sun. Although it felt like early morning to me, when I passed the cathedral and headed east on Borgo dei Greci, the city was already alive with workers headed toward shops and women bringing baskets of dough to the nearby bakery. It is a ritual the women repeat every day, leaving their dough with the baker in the morning and then returning in the afternoon to collect warm loaves of bread for their evening meal.

I passed out of the city through Porta Pinti, one of the oldest gates in the city wall and continued a short distance down a dirt road. At the end of the road, I turned into one of the fields surrounding the monastery where a few brown-cloaked monks were carrying pails of water to a small flock of sheep. The cloudless sky signaled that the day would be hot, a typical August day, so the monks would need to repeat that chore again later, perhaps several times.

In the distance, a figure paced in the shadow of the cloister alongside the church. Not until I reached the church grounds did I recognize that the figure was Chancellor Scala. He wore the rumpled smock of a laborer and old leather sandals. I had not expected to see him in his official Chancery robe, but a stylish tunic would have been more befitting of his stature. Seeing him in peasant garb was surprising.

He paced as though agitated by impatience, but the church bells had not yet rung for Terce prayers, so his distress was not caused by my being tardy. Another matter must have been causing him concern.

Scala maintained a loose friendship with my father after their initial acquaintance. Since my initial encounter with him at the University of Florence, I had seen him occasionally at festivals and sponsored government events, but we never had reason to speak.

I had no contact whatsoever with Scala while studying at the university in Bologna. At times his activities, and his elevation in Chancery status entered into the casual conversation of the Florentine students, but no more so than did talk of any other government functionary. It is well known that Scala is a capable administrator. He was highly regarded by all members of the Signoria, and thus regularly appointed to various commissions and given important government assignments in addition to his customary tasks as second Chancellor.

Coming closer I announced myself, "Chancellor."

He acknowledged by nodding and gestured toward a horse path that led through a field away from the monastery. He began walking in that direction. I turned onto an intersecting path and joined him. We crossed a small grassy field still wet with morning dew and entered a large garden where monks grew produce in abundance, more than enough for their needs. Much of the excess was given to the needy, the remainder sold in the markets of the city.

For a few moments he looked at me saying nothing, then, "You have the same intense dark eyes as your father. When I last saw you, you were smaller. You have grown tall, again like your father, and you carry yourself with assurance as he did. Your coloring is lighter than his, perhaps that is from your mother. Unfortunately, I never had the opportunity to meet her."

Without further pleasantries, the Chancellor began answering the questions I was waiting to ask. "You must be wondering why we are meeting here, rather than at the Chancery, and why I am hiding in this old peasant smock. Some words need to be said where there are no extra ears to hear and no extra eyes to see."

"Mostly I am wondering why you wish to meet with me. We

haven't even seen each other in many years."

Scala chuckled. "Yes, I have no doubt that my invitation to meet was unexpected. When you applied to the University of Bologna, your tutor sent a recommendation to the university. A copy of that letter was also sent to the Chancery... to me. When I saw your name, I immediately remembered the time when you attended one of your father's lectures. You listened intently and even took notes. You sat near me, near enough for me to be able to read the notes. They were questions about the topics your father had mentioned. I was impressed to see a boy of nine years do that."

His recollection made me laugh. "Your memory of that day is better than mine."

Scala continued, "While you were at the university, professors sent evaluations and progress reports to the Chancery."

That revelation was a surprise to me. Neither the university nor the professors ever mentioned that practice. "They send reports without informing the students?" I queried. "Do they report on all students?"

"As a courtesy to the Chancery, they send reports on any students we request." He added slyly, "Whether they inform the students or not is between the university and its students. It is not a matter for the Chancery to decide."

Then without waiting for my reaction, he returned to the central topic of the meeting. "Cosimo was a great leader, a force that held our Republic together. He was admired ... loved by almost all. True, the House of Medici profited greatly during his tenure, a reason for some to envy, even despise him, but for more than thirty years the Republic has prospered, and we have been at peace with our neighbors. It is no secret that Cosimo's death leaves a vacuum. Under other circumstances, his son, Piero, would step into Cosimo's shoes, but I am certain that will not be so. Even supporters of the Medici are concerned about Piero's illness; however, illness is not the greatest concern surrounding Piero. He lacks the esteem and confidence of his father. There are powerful men who see a vacuum of authority and an opportunity to seize the reins of government."

He waited for my response to gauge whether I understood the import of his words. "Yes," I said. "My brother, Donato, told me that he too is worried that there might be unrest."

"He is right to worry but unrest is too weak a label. Certain members of the Signoria have already made known their intention to use every means available to gain influence and advance their positions. Those who do so following the laws are no threat; indeed, that is as it should be."

Then, placing emphasis on every word, he added, "Others, however, are prepared to employ violence and bloodshed to achieve their goals."

It was a bold statement for the Chancellor to assert with such certainty that leaders of the Republic were preparing to usurp power through violent means. That expectation was a reason for him to be concerned, but it did not explain the reason for our meeting. The role of the Chancery is to administer relationships between the Republic and all foreign states. Internal affairs of the Republic, including maintaining civil order, are the jurisdiction of the Onesta, not the Chancery, so why, I asked him, is the Chancery concerned.

"One concern is that internal unrest could make the Republic vulnerable to external pressures. Our wealth makes us a valuable prize that is coveted by many foreigners. There are speculations that certain powerful men within the Republic intend to actively solicit the assistance of foreign powers to advance their goals. It is crucial to the stability of the Republic that we learn the names of these men and the details of their plans. The Chancery needs trustworthy people who care deeply about preserving the Republic, people without a political bias, who can move freely among the circles of power to gather facts. I am hoping that you can be one of those people. That is the purpose of this meeting.

"The Chancery has many well-placed sources both inside our Republic and elsewhere, but there are still gaps. We need a source that can move about to gather information in different places as the situation demands. We need someone with sharp observational skills and a logical mind who above all loves our Republic. The person we need, Nico, is you."

I stood motionless, stunned by what he was asking of me. "You honor me beyond my ability to express, but I am hardly more than a student, I am not a ...." My voice trailed off because I couldn't think of a single word to summarize the function he described. "I have been away from Florence in an academic community. I don't have contacts among the elite of the Republic."

Scala scanned the ground of the Campo ahead of us and spotted a single small yellow flower growing in a patch of green. He walked to it and pointed. "The seed that made this flower had no connections among these weeds, yet it is able to flourish here. Had it been planted in other soil it would have flourished there as well. I knew your father, not well but well enough. If you possess his instincts and dedication, then you are like that seed able to flourish among business leaders and government officials as well as among academic orators and peasants."

He did not ask for any commitment nor did I give him one. He knew it would take me time to process his request. Thinking back to that meeting, I believe he was certain, even then, that I would accept.

Chapter 6

To emphasize the urgency of the situation, Scala began revealing sensitive information. "There is other news you do not know. The Holy Father is gravely ill. A confidential source at the Vatican tells me that the Holy Father may pass from this Earth within a month." Scala's words came as a total surprise. Donato has contacts everywhere and is usually among the first to know important news, yet he had not mentioned hearing even a whisper about the declining health of the Pope. My thoughts drifted back two years when I watched the Pope consecrate the Duomo in the town of Pienza. He was not a young man then, but he was strong and healthy. My reflection was interrupted by Scala asking, "Do you know what the death of the Holy Father will mean?"

I wasn't sure how best to answer. The practice of summoning the Cardinals together to elect a successor to the Holy Father is common knowledge, but doubtless, the Chancellor was expecting a more insightful reply. When my silence finally outlasted his patience, he answered his own question. “Four years ago Pius obtained vows from representatives of all the Christian States and the princes of all Christian Duchies to mount a crusade against the Turks. Those vows have helped preserve peace on the Italian peninsula by giving the Florentine Republic and all our neighbors a common adversary, the Turks. Thus far the vow exists only as signatures on a paper because nothing has actually been done to mount a crusade against the adversary.”

I began thinking aloud, “The Papal States are not a republic like Florence with an elected body like our Signoria to maintain a continuity of policy. When a pope dies his policies may die with him. If his successor chooses to act differently, the crusade against the Turks may never happen.”

“Exactly,” Scala exclaimed and smiled broadly, delighted that I grasped the significance of the situation and that his time talking with me might be well spent after all. He encouraged me to continue, “Go on. Go on.”

“If the republics and duchies do not have a common adversary they may turn against each other. Peace would be lost.”

“And if the leaders of Florence are already bickering amongst themselves?” he asked.

“Then our neighbors could take advantage of the situation.”

“Exactly, but again the phrase 'take advantage of'' is too weak. If internal bickering were to make our Republic a tempting target, there is a strong possibility that dissolution of the Papal commitment would make us the prey for every republic, kingdom, duchy, and empire."

Now I understood his concerns but I didn't see how he, or especially I, could help the situation. As if reading my mind, he shared a final piece of news. "It saddens me deeply," his voice cracked with emotion, "that another great man and good friend is also in worsening health, the First Chancellor of our Republic, Messer Accolti."

I did not know Benedetto Accolti personally, but I certainly knew his accomplishments, as did every other Florentine citizen. First Chancellor is the highest administrative appointment in the Republic. Because the position of Chancellor is not an elected post, it is free from political squabbling. Only competent men of high integrity are appointed to that post, and once selected they usually remain in the position for life. Appointments are made by a vote of the Signoria so in principle the Signoria could remove a chancellor, but that rarely happened. By itself, the death of a First Chancellor is a significant event. Coupled with the recent demise of Cosimo de Medici the combined strain could undermine the Republic.

Scala's revelations made my head spin. I would have welcomed a place to sit for a moment but there were no resting places nearby. We had passed out of the garden, out of the monastery grounds, and walked a considerable distance to the area known as Campo di Marte, a training ground of the Florentine militia. That morning though there were no military exercises. Scala and I were alone in the vast field. We walked a few more minutes then he suggested that we retrace our path and head back toward the monastery. I took his suggestion to mean that his tale was complete, but I was wrong. We returned only a few steps when he stopped and said, "The Signoria has already decided who will succeed Benedetto as the next First Chancellor. Following Chancellor Accolti's recommendation, they have asked me to fill the post and I have accepted.

"As you know, the First Chancellor has many duties and responsibilities. Most important among them is protecting the security of the Florentine Republic from all outside threats. It is also the most difficult responsibility because the First Chancellor controls neither the police nor the militia. The only weapon available to him for discharging this responsibility is information. He must gather information about all forces, thoughts, ideas, and plans that might harm the Republic. And without question, that information must be truthful. From that knowledge he must put forth policies and information to cause events to occur for the good of the Republic."

His phrasing, 'cause events to occur,' was both intentional on his part and surprising to me. By law, the Chancery is empowered to set policies, make treaties, and litigate disputes with foreign governments. In six years of legal study, none of my professors had ever mentioned that Chanceries have an authority to initiate events. What kind of events might a Chancery initiate? Has the Chancery launched clandestine activities in the past with such skill that the public never learned of their involvement?

While I puzzled over Scala's last statement he continued, adding in a slightly softer voice as though sharing a secret, "Unlike information sought by the Chancery, the information it disseminates need not always be truthful."

Another topic not covered in my courses: falsehoods issued by Chanceries.

During the remainder of our return walk to the monastery, he revealed other information vital to the security of the Florentine Republic. When our discussion ended, I was still unsure whether I could help him, but we agreed to a test. He described an event being held that very evening and my test was to find a way to attend the event as his eyes and ears. That sounded easy enough.

Chapter 7

After parting from Bartolomeo Scala at the monastery I needed a long quiet walk to collect my thoughts. I headed south, leaving the meadow along a dirt path that paralleled the city wall. Since its earliest days when Florence was part of the Roman Empire, Florentines relied on walls like this one to secure their city. The wall rising above me was the sixth stone barricade to encircle our growing city. In its 130 years it defended us against invading armies many times, but in times like these when neighboring communities are at peace the walls are taken for granted. People expect that peace will continue forever. However, it could be that harmony will endure only as long as people like Bartolomeo Scala work at it.

I passed into the city through the Porta alla Croce gate. By the time I approached the center of the city the sun was high overhead baking the stone fronts of the buildings that lined the wide Borgo la Croce. Even before I entered the city proper, the bells at Santa Croce had sounded for the midday Sext prayers, meaning my stomach was justified in complaining that it was neglected. To satisfy its craving I pointed myself toward the Uccello where one could always find good food. Unlike early morning, roads were nearly empty now as people sought indoor hideaways from the intense heat.

The long walk gave me time to reflect on the things Chancellor Scala had told me and to scan the shops and side streets in the hope that I might encounter Alessa and Simone, although the chances of doing so were small. The first place Alessa would take a new visitor to our city would be the impressive Santa Maria del Fiore cathedral and the baptistery of San Giovanni with its magnificent bronze doors, doors so beautiful that they are considered by some as the gates to Paradise. Every visitor to Florence is awed by these two impressive buildings, even Venetians who are justly proud of their Basilica San Marco. There is so much to see in Florence that it is impossible to guess what order Alessa might have chosen for Simone to visit all the other marvelous sites.

The rear of the building where the Uccello is located can be reached through a carriage track used by vendors making deliveries. The path ends at an open area behind the Uccello where there is a smoker for curing meat, a covered pit for storing ice brought from the mountains, and space for loading and unloading delivery carts. Stepping from the path into the open area, I could see members of Donato's staff already preparing for the event that he would be serving in the evening. Two women were placing table coverings, serving trays, utensils, and other items into a cart for delivery so setup could be done early at the event location. Other carts would deliver food and drinks later.

I entered directly into the kitchen at the rear of the building where workers were busily preparing food for the event dinner and for the Uccello's dinner menu. Two workers were chopping vegetables, one was butchering a hog, and the head chef was preparing a salsa. Despite the bustling activity, Donato stood to one side observing but making few comments to the competent workers who needed little direction. When Donato saw me enter the kitchen he called out, "Wipe your shoes!" then he reached into a cupboard, withdrew a bottle of local Tuscan wine and two glasses, and led me to one of the vacant small dining rooms where we could talk in private.

I began speaking slowly while deciding how much could be revealed without breaking the Chancellor's confidence. "Chancellor Scala believes as you do that Cosimo's death might lead to unrest in the government." I stopped abruptly and corrected myself. "No, he is quite vocal in saying that 'unrest' is too kind a word. His words were 'violence and bloodshed.' In fact, he believes there are several possibilities where violence could be a likely outcome."

"He could be right," Donato agreed, "but what was his purpose in meeting with you? He knows little about you. You haven't even seen him since you went to Bologna, have you?"

"No, I never saw him while I was at the university, but I was surprised to learn how much he does know about me. He keeps himself well informed. He knows what courses I was taking, and he even mentioned some of the legal precedents that I cited during the oral examination for my jurisprudence degree. He knew so much of my experiences at the university that I began to wonder if his sources might include a spirit hovering invisibly above my head in all my classes."

Donato raised an eyebrow. "Don't you find it unnerving that the Chancery tracks all Florentine students who attend the University of Bologna?"

"It doesn't trouble me that the Chancery monitors students, but I believe the university should make students aware that it is happening."

Donato leaned forward placing both elbows on the table. He rested his chin on his clasped hands, his eyes narrowed, and his brow furrowed as he spoke. "Scala is an important member of the government, although the extent of his role is sometimes clouded in mystery. Laws clearly define limits to Chancery authority, but at times its activities have extended beyond its official charter."

"What activities are you referring to?" I asked.

"The one you just mentioned is a good example, tracking students while they are enrolled at a university in another Republic."

Our conversation became difficult because I had promised the Chancellor that I would tell no one of the First Chancellor's illness, of Scala being selected to succeed him, nor of the Holy

Father's failing health. These facts helped me to understand the Chancellor's thinking, but they were unknowns to Donato. Just one short conversation with the Chancellor, barely an hour, had left me with a collection of issues that could not be spoken of. Were these only a few threads of a larger web entangling the Republic?

"What does Scala expect from you?" Donato asked, "You are a law student who has been living in Bologna for the past five years. You should be devoting your energies to establishing a career. In any case, you have no knowledge of anyone who might be vying for power."

"Scala believes that being disconnected from those in power is what makes me well suited to help him. I am no threat to the power seekers so they would have no reason to shield their intentions from me."

Donato clapped his hands together and laughed. "So, you are to become a Chancery spy whose innocence will gain you access to the innermost secrets from those plotting against the Republic. Do I have that right? He expects you to mingle among the powerful elite and uncover their evil intentions?"

Scala's request had sounded plausible when he voiced it, but Donato painted it like a nearly impossible task. I could only leave his question unanswered and move the conversation in a different direction.

"The Chancellor's immediate concern," I continued, "is that the strong relationship between our Republic and the Duchy of

Milan is due in large part to the personal friendship between Cosimo de Medici and Duke Francesco Sforza, meaning the death of Cosimo might weaken the relationship between Florence and Milan. The Florentine militia is a proud troupe, but it is considerably smaller than the armies of our neighbors. The Signoria sees the continuing peace with our neighbors as the reason to cut funding for security. They let the militia dwindle relying instead on the use of mercenaries. If we lose favor with the Duke of Milan, and he withdraws the protection of his army, our Republic could become an easy target."

This thought was new to Donato, so he spoke at a measured pace as he considered it. "That's true, the military support we enjoy from Milan is a result of the relationship between the Medici and the Sforza. But their relationship was not based so much on friendship, it was more of a business arrangement. The Medici bank provides financing for the Duke's escapades, and in return, he lends his army as a security blanket for our Republic."

"Has the Duke indicated whether he will continue the same agreements if Piero succeeds his father as the controlling director of the Medici bank?" I asked.

"The Duke says publicly that the banking relationship serves him well," Donato answered.

"Privately he might be saying something else?" I speculated.

Donato nodded in agreement and provided possible evidence of duplicity. "Some bankers, officers of the Bankers and Moneychangers Guild, met for lunch at the Uccello two days ago.

They spoke openly about the Duke's money problems. According to them, he needs large sources of funds to pay for his army and bands of mercenaries who keep France and the Duchy of Savoy from nibbling at his territories. Thankfully, the peace treaty arranged by the Holy Father has prevented states from waging war, but it hasn't stopped minor disputes over territory."

I held my tongue at Donato's mention of the Holy Father, but I wondered: Will a new Pope be able to keep the peace treaty from dissolving?

"How does Scala expect you to discover the Duke's private thoughts?" Donato asked, his voice dripping with skepticism.

"The Chancellor and I devised a test case to see whether I can gather meaningful information. As you know, the Milanese ambassador to Florence is hosting a reception this evening for officers of the bankers and money changers guild. Members of all the wealthy banking families have been invited. Scala thinks Milan is using the reception as a guise to explore other means of financing should the relationship with Piero de Medici unravel.

"Chancellor Scala wants me to attend the reception to learn what is discussed there. Surely anyone with a criminal scheme won't discuss it openly, but he might accidentally expose clues to his plans. The problem is that I'm not sure how to gain access to the event since I'm neither a banker nor a diplomat. I have no connection to ambassador di Pontremoli and I can't just show up uninvited."

Donato banged his fist on the table and laughed loudly. "That clever fox! Scala must know that ambassador di Pontremoli has retained me to arrange his reception. No doubt Scala expects me to be your key.

"My people and I will be there to set the tables and serve the dinner. We will be passing among the guests constantly refreshing their drinks. I can always use more help," Donato flashed a smile before adding, "especially help that works without pay. If you can keep wine glasses filled without spilling too much, you are welcome to join us. I don't totally approve of this scheme that you and Scala have hatched but at least this way I can keep my eye on you."

With scorn in his voice, Donato added, "The ambassador wants to impress the bankers so he even asked me to import silver belt buckles from Paris that he can give as gifts to his guests. There is no jewelry finer than Italian silver, but di Pontremoli insists that the belt buckles come from Paris, as if bankers don't already have enough silver."

Donato always tried to accommodate his clients but he didn't always share their views.

Donato was right, attending the reception as one of his workers certainly let me eavesdrop on the ambassador and the guests. It might help me learn the intention of the Milanese as well as hints of which notables were mounting struggles for power within our Republic. As a newly anointed doctor of jurisprudence, I knew this ruse was not illegal but it did raise troubling ethical questions. Do those attending the reception expect that their conversations are private, or do they realize that their words might be overheard by servants who would repeat them? Have they ever even considered the possibility? If Scala uses my information to prevent bloodshed or war, does that outweigh any personal privacy of these bankers? The answers to these questions could only come from someone wiser than me. If only I could pose them to Aristotle, he would have the answers. He seems to have had answers to everything.

Donato had just finished describing the evening's arrangements to me when a worker called from the kitchen. "Nico, there is someone here to see you. He said his name is Orsino."

I said aloud, but to myself, "I didn't think he would come," then I swiveled to face the kitchen worker and responded, "Send him in."

Orsino entered wearing the same pair of roughly cut trousers he wore the day before, but his tunic, although similar to the one he wore yesterday, and also bearing a pattern of indelible dye stains, was freshly laundered. His hands were clean and his hair brushed. Orsino either valued cleanliness, or this meeting was important to him, or both.

He walked in slowly, his eyes downcast toward the floor and his shoulders hunched. It was good that he was not standing tall for at his full height he could not have fit through the doorway. As he approached I pushed back a chair for him, but he decided to remain standing. I looked up and said, "I was not sure whether you would come today. I thought you might be at work."

"I work in the dye shop in Piazza dei Mozzi. The ship from England, the one that brings us wool, is missing. It should have been here five days ago. The shop no longer has any wool so there is no work for us."

"Ah, I see. So that is why you had time to try a different kind of work when we met yesterday."

He replied softly, "Yes. I am sorry. The shop does not pay us when there is no work. I have a wife ... and a young son." His voice trailed off.

Simone and I had told Donato of our encounter with highwaymen including my invitation to Orsino. Directing my words to Donato I said, "As Orsino explained, he needs work, and as you can see he is a big man who looks like he can do a full day's work."

Donato stood and extended his hand to Orsino. "I am Donato. Welcome to my club. Nico is right, you are big and look to be as strong as a bear too. The name Orsino fits you well. Just a few moments ago I was telling Nico that I can always use good help. In fact, a wagon just arrived from one of the vineyards in Fiesole. It is carrying wine casks that need to be unloaded and stored in a shed. Do you think you can you do that?"

Orsino nodded.

"Good, then you can start working right now. Go outside and beyond the storage building you will see the wagons. Find Giulio, tell him I sent you and he will tell you what to do. If Giulio is happy with your work today, then come back tomorrow and there will be more work for you."

In a voice filled with emotion Orsino said, "We ... my family ... will never forget this chance you give to me."

As Orsino turned to leave, Donato called after him, "Orsino, ask Chola, the light-haired girl in the kitchen, what food remains from dinner last night. The pappardelle will not be good any longer but the bread and some of the vegetables should still be fine. When you leave, take some home to your family. And milk. We always have enough milk. Take a jug for your son."

In mid-afternoon the first members of Donato's staff set out for the Milanese embassy. They were known as the cleaners because their first duty was to make the dining salon at the embassy spotless. When they finished, the dining table would shine and there would not be a fingerprint on any surface in the room. They dusted bookshelves and any sculptures, and they straightened any paintings hanging in the room. It was this attention to detail that earned Donato his reputation as il Festatore. Attendees at his events might not consciously notice whether paintings were all hanging perfectly straight, but details such as these added up to an overall impression. When all the incidentals are perfect, then the total event seems perfect.

Next, the cleaners set out decorations. The choice of decorations depended on the type of event. Usually, these items are selected by Donato's people, although if the host or hostess makes special requests Donato does his best to accommodate them. For this reception the only decorations would be flowers.

Because Florence is the City of the Lily, lilies are the most popular floral decorations, but since this reception was being held at the Milanese embassy, Donato felt red roses would be more fitting. Ambassador di Pontremoli specified neither flowers nor any other details; he left all the decisions to il Festatore. No entertainers would be provided for this reception other than a cellist who would provide soft background music while the guests sipped their after dinner digestivo in the garden.

The one service that Donato never provides is female companions or 'escorts' as they are sometimes called. All attendees at this reception would be men, so it is possible that the ambassador would want to have escorts to relax his guests after dinner, but di Pontremoli knew he had to arrange for escorts elsewhere.

Chapter 8

Donato and I were discussing my role at the reception when the wide main door of the club opened, letting light and a wave of afternoon heat flood into the room from the street-facing entry. Simone and Alessa floated in through the doorway wrapped in laughter. To anyone else their rapid banter might have sounded like a foreign dialect, but they had no trouble understanding each other, and they delighted in their quick exchanges.

As soon as Simone saw me he fell silent while Alessa aimed an unbroken stream of words at me. "First we went to the Cathedral - did you know it has paintings by Venetian artists – two paintings I think - Simone says the Cathedral is very different from Saint Mark's - that's the Basilica in Venice - then we went to the Palazzo de Podestà - I never knew that it is the oldest official government building in the city – Simone told me that - he knows things about Florence that I did not know - we are now on our way to the Ponte Vecchio - Simone says they have a bridge in Venice called Sighs, but it's small - it doesn't have shops on it."

Finally, Alessa paused to take a breath so I interjected quickly before the opportunity would be lost, "Are you telling me you spent the whole morning together and only saw the cathedral and the Podestà? Are you sure you didn't spend all your time strolling in a quiet garden somewhere?"

Alessa was well used to my baiting her, responded in kind without hesitation. "Oh, you mean like the garden near Santissima Annunziata? The one with the hidden grottos where you used to go with Lucia? No, we haven't been there yet but that's a good idea, maybe we'll go there after we visit the Ponte Vecchio."

With her exuberance finally dissipated, Alessa's speech slowed to a more orderly pace. "This morning after you left someone came to our house with a message for Simone. It was an official messenger of The Most Serene Republic of Venice." She used the full name of the Venetian state to emphasize the importance of the visit.

Both Alessa and I looked toward Simone who explained, "Bernardo Bembo is in Florence. He is traveling as a special envoy of the Council of Ten on a mission to Rome, and he stopped here for a few days to meet with our ambassador, I mean with the Venetian ambassador. They would like me to join them this evening for dinner at our embassy, I mean the Venetian embassy."

"I take it then that you know Messer Bembo?"

"Our families are close, but he travels so frequently on missions for the Republic that I rarely get to see him. It is my father who really knows him. As a member of the Council of Ten father is always meeting with statesmen and officials of the Republic."

Alessa asked, "Who is Messer Bembo and if you don't know him well why are he and the ambassador inviting you to dinner?"

Simone explained that Messer Bembo was a statesman held in high regard in the Venetian Republic. "His family is wealthy and is listed in the book of Venetian aristocrats, the so-called Book of First Families of the Republic."

Alessa interjected, "I remember hearing about Venice having a Grand Council but I never heard of the Book of First Families. I always believed that in Venice the government is controlled by the Doge."

Simone nodded as an acknowledgment that he understood Alessa's confusion about the workings of the Venetian government. To remedy that he gave her a brief explanation. "It's a common misconception that the Doge is all powerful in Venice, but that's not so. The Doge administers the laws, but he doesn't make the laws. Laws are enacted by the Grand Council. The Grand Council is a large body, an unwieldy group to actually draft laws, so they appoint a subset of their members to a small body called the Council of Ten that does the real work of creating new laws."

"I understand the Council," Alessa stated. "Now tell me about the Book of First Families."

Simone explained that the First Families were those who could trace their ancestry to the earliest settlers of Venice more than 700 years ago. Their descendants are the aristocrats of present-day Venice. His explanation revealed that both his father's family and his mother's family were listed in the Book.

While I was registering this new information Simone said jokingly, "Messer Bembo probably invited me as a favor to my father. Father is happy that I have this opportunity to visit Florence as long as he can keep track of me."

Simone's lips curled up in a slight smile then he said to me, "Don't worry, I won't tell him that we were assaulted yesterday by Florentine bandits."

My original plan of spending the day showing Simone the cultural sights of my city was thwarted by the meeting with Chancellor Scala, although my absence hardly mattered to Simone. He was more than happy having Alessa as his guide.

"I wonder," Simone said thinking out loud, "if it would be proper for me to bring a guest to dinner."

I had not yet had a chance to tell Simone or Alessa that I would be spending the evening at the Milanese embassy allegedly helping Donato so he didn't know that I could not join him for dinner. However, my concern evaporated when Simone shared the reason for his thinking. "Messer Bembo has a daughter about our age so I think he might enjoy meeting Alessa."

Looking toward Alessa he continued, "It can be exciting to visit an embassy and meet the ambassador, especially this ambassador. Messer Cappello is not a stuffy old diplomat. Well, he is old, but definitely not stuffy. He was in the military and loves regaling people with his war stories, some of the most entertaining stories I've ever heard, especially those from his time in Crete. I should warn you though, his language can be a bit crusty."

With a twinkle in her eye, Alessa said, "Sounds like fun."

Not wanting to crush their enthusiasm, but knowing they were not considering the possible downside to Simone's idea, I injected, "That might not be such a good idea. Messer Bembo may have a personal message to deliver from your father, and it could be uncomfortable for him to do that with a stranger present."

Both Alessa and Simone registered disappointment at hearing my words, but they agreed it might be awkward for Simone to bring an uninvited guest to the embassy dinner. To lessen the impact I suggested, "You could invite Messer Bembo, and perhaps the ambassador too, to come here, to the Uccello, tomorrow night for dinner. Donato could arrange for us to use one of the private rooms so Alessa can join you. Women are not permitted in the main dining room except on special occasions, but they are welcome in the private dining rooms at any time."

Simone enthusiastically accepted my proposal. Alessa nodded to show that she agreed as well, although her demeanor showed she was disheartened at missing the opportunity to visit the Venetian embassy.

Chapter 9

In late afternoon I joined the servers who were preparing to leave for the Milanese embassy atop wagons loaded with foodstuffs and casks filled with wine. These workers are called 'servers,' but they might just as well be called ‘food artists’ because their culinary creations show as much skill as Masaccio's frescoes. Donato provided me with clothing like theirs, black pants and a white tunic embroidered with a single red lily so I could blend in with the other servers. I lacked completely any skill to help the ‘artists’ with their cuisine, but I felt confident in fulfilling the task Donato had assigned to me, keeping the guests’ wine glasses filled. It was an ideal task because it gave me a reason to roam among the guests within earshot.

Embassy receptions often consist of a formal dinner where guests all arrive at a specified time, then are escorted by members of the embassy staff to a dining salon and seated for a meal. But this reception was different. Di Pontremoli's goal in hosting the event was similar to mine. He wanted to ply information from his guests and he felt that having drinks before dinner would free their tongues. Per his instructions, arriving guests were guided to a large gallery for drinks and antipasto. Drinks for this occasion were vinoro. Vinoro is a delicious golden liquid that Donato created from a fortified white wine, a hint of wildflower honey, almond, and one or two other ingredients. The exact recipe is one of Donato's secret formulations. Vinoro is the perfect choice to make guests become talkative because its delicate flavor leads them to consume far more than they realize, and consume they did. I was barely able to keep all their glasses refilled.

Guests at this reception were from two distinct groups. One group was the wealthy members of the large banking families, the ones who own the banks and could be courted to help finance the Duchy of Milan with generous loans. The other group consisted of bank agents. They are the managers who actually conduct the various aspects of the banking business. The bankers are members of Banker and Money Changers Guild. The agents are not guild members, but they are often invited to bank related activities and social events such as this reception. They also regularly interact with their counterparts in other banks when conducting financial transactions.

The fellowship of the agents was evident. They assembled in a single large group near the center of the room. Their lively conversations ranged from boasting about imposing excessive fees on clients, to exaggerated claims of sexual exploits with their mistresses. They clearly enjoyed exchanging tales, but their words were of no interest to the ambassador nor to me.

In contrast, the bank owners spaced themselves around the edges of the room in small groups. One could almost feel the heat of competitive hostility radiating from the groups. If there were to be talk of usurping power in the Republic, it would come from these men.

Two of the oldest, and at one time largest, Florentine banks now suffered from failed loans that brought them to near bankruptcy. It was well known that they hoped a collaboration between the two could revive their former success - that two weak hens could give birth to a strong rooster.

Three brothers, owners of another family-owned bank, clustered alone near one corner of the room as if broadcasting to all others that their bank could prosper on its own and needed no alliances. Near the same corner, the principals of a recently formed bank stood together carefully studying the others in the room. They were looking for partnerships, trying to gauge which of those present would make for the best alliance, and which might be willing to join with them. Their bank was small; a well-endowed partner would be needed to boost their hope of opening branches outside the Republic.

Only one of the many Florentine banks had no one at the reception, the Medici bank. Piero de Medici, head of the family and the Medici bank now that Cosimo was deceased, was too ill to attend so his absence was no surprise. Piero's eldest son, Lorenzo, was only fifteen years old. He was an able youth well trained in the family business by his grandfather Cosimo. Even at his young age, Lorenzo had been called upon by the family to represent the bank in essential business transactions; in fact, on the evening of the reception, Lorenzo was in France meeting with agents of the Medici bank in Paris. The shrewd Milanese ambassador doubtless scheduled the reception intentionally to coincide with Lorenzo's absence. If questioned, the ambassador could merely claim that all the invitees were men, not boys. That claim would not discount the fact that no other representative of Medici bank had been invited. This told me that Chancellor Scala's assumption was correct: the Duke of Milan was rethinking his relationship with the Medici bank and considering other options.

My initial assessment that all attendees were associated with Florentine banks proved incorrect. Also in attendance were a small number of guests who were not of the banking profession. Two guests who stood together at the rear of the room were neither bankers nor Florentines. One was dressed in fine silks topped by a cloak embellished in the red and yellow colors of the Kingdom of Naples. He had long thin fingers, chalky white skin, and the same prominent hooked nose as his monarch, King Ferdinand of Naples, suggesting he might indeed be a relative of the ruler. The other was a small, squirrelly figure who wore a purple mantelleta and the jeweled pectoral cross favored by bishops in the Papal States. Although the two stood close to each other they spoke little, but both swept the room constantly with their eyes absorbing the scene.

Ambassador di Pontremoli waited until everyone held a glass of vinoro before entering the gallery almost unnoticed through a plain door at the rear of the room. His entrance needed no announcement as the fur trimmed crimson giornea wrapping his ample body immediately captured everyone's attention. The knee-length silk cloak was custom-made for the ambassador at Milan's finest silk bottega. During the course of the evening, the ambassador let everyone know that per his instructions a single copy of his giornea, made in royal blue silk and trimmed with white Russian ermine, was on its way to Vienna as a gift from the Duke of Milan to the Archduke of Austria. The guests were all free to ponder what future relationship might develop between Milan and Austria.

Although the heat of the day still lingered into the evening, the light silk fabric and narrow fur trim on his open-sided giornea would keep the ambassador cooler than the staid garments worn by many of his guests. His stunning clothing showed a penchant for the latest fashions and it diverted everyone's attention away from his intense eyes as they repeatedly surveyed the room studying his guests.

The ambassador was a loyal adviser and confidant of the Duke, and the Duke's father before him. Ambassador di Pontremoli had faithfully reported every nuance in the Florentine Republic power structure to his benefactor for more than a decade, ensuring that the Duke of Milan learned the thoughts of Florence's elite even before many members of the Florentine Signoria.

Chapter 10

The groupings of bank owners spaced around the room's perimeter gave the ambassador his first indication of the friendships and alliances among these most wealthy Florentines. Ever the cordial host, he moved from one group to another bidding each a warm welcome. Then waving his arm in a gesture meant to encompass them all, he proclaimed in a voice loud enough for all to hear, “As you can see, the quality of our silk,” here he reached down and flared his garment, “is outstanding, and in such great demand that the Duchy is being pressed to expand our silk offerings. Silk is a profitable trade. Perhaps it is an area of interest to some of you.”

His approach was blunt and direct. He wasted no time on inconsequential matters, clearly wanting to learn which of them were serious in wanting to do business with the Duchy. They would learn soon enough, if they had not already surmised, that a willingness to extend credit to the Duchy was the price for gaining a stake in the lucrative silk trade.

The first banker that the ambassador approached agreed that Milanese silk is of high quality, but he showed little interest in pursuing a financial arrangement. His tepid response led di Pontremoli to move on quickly to another group.

To those who expressed interest the ambassador made his purpose crystal clear: "The Duchy has resources and skilled craftsmen. To be successful we will need funds for new shops and merchant ships."

The timid showed their lack of confidence by only nodding while their more eager colleagues asked for an opportunity to discuss the possibility at length in private. Those eager bankers were the ones the Duchy would target if arrangements with the Medici bank were to falter. The eager ones were also of most interest to Bartolomeo Scala as they were the ones that might actively work to dissolve the Medici empire.

My conversation with the Chancellor had focused on possible military actions, but the discussions of these bankers brought forth another possibility as well. Trust in the Medici bank was crucial to the financial stability of the Republic. If confidence in the Medici bank eroded, that could also lead to turmoil.

I could not position myself close enough to hear the ambassador's conversations with each group, but I got a sense of the outcomes by observing their expressions. One encounter was particularly unusual. After the ambassador finished talking with the owner of the Borromei bank, the banker beckoned for his agent who left his colleagues at the center of the room and joined signor Borromei. The agent listened to Borromei's instructions, nodding frequently to confirm that he understood his leader's edict. The agent then returned to the center of the room where he spoke briefly with an agent of a different bank. That agent, in turn, walked from the cluster of agents, sought his principal and whispered a few words to the banker who looked across the room to Borromei and nodded. The episode ended with the two bankers moving as inconspicuously as possible across the room to join each other. The two men engaged in a lengthy conversation that I was unable to hear, but their expressions suggested they ultimately reached an agreement that was satisfactory to both.

The two foreign guests, the Neopolitan and the bishop, were as intent as I in noticing how easily an agreement had been reached between the two bankers. I wondered whether the foreign guests were serving as extra eyes for the Milanese ambassador or whether they had their own agendas.

In keeping with his direct approach, di Pontremoli posed an identical question to each group, "Do you think the Medici bank will be hurt badly by the death of Cosimo?"

All but one guest gave non-committal answers. Di Pontremoli's eyes brightened and he struggled to suppress a smile as he listened to the response from the one exception, a portly man with greasy hair and an ill-fitting tunic. He responded in a voice loud enough to be heard by everyone in the room. "The Medici empire is already weakening and now it is going to fall even faster because

Piero lacks the ability and experience of his father. His incompetence will be felt by everyone who does business with the Medici bank. Patriotic Florentines must not allow his incompetence to infect our Republic."

One flaw in my plan was that I did not know the names of all the bankers, and I certainly did not know the agents. I had to remember the descriptions of anyone who made significant comments so I could learn his name later.

I intended to spend most of my time listening to the bankers as I refreshed their drinks. The plan suffered because when I drew near to refill their wine glasses, they tended to suspend their conversations. Did that mean they were discussing a sinister scheme or were they merely guarding their privacy?

Most of my time was consumed serving vinoro to the banking agents who were constantly waving empty glasses to attract my attention. Satisfying their thirst had me scurrying up and down to the kitchen with a bottle in each hand. As the pre-dinner hour neared its end, both their meaningless babbling and the pace of their drinking accelerated. I vowed to tell Donato he should try to find workers who have four hands the next time he arranges an event that will be attended by banking agents.

The agents' banter ceased suddenly when a short, rotund man, whose feet struggled to support his wine-filled belly, drew everyone's attention by announcing loudly, "Don't trust that bastard, he's plotting something. I know it."

A slurred voice added, "They say he killed his wife, and I

believe them. He's a bad one. And that son of his is even worse, like the devil himself."

Several others nodded in agreement and then, without additional comment, the banter resumed around a different topic.

The rotund man I recognized as one of the money changers. I was unable to see the owner of the slurred voice. Unfortunately, I did not hear the name of the person who was the subject of the outburst. Without a name could knowledge of the episode be of value to the Chancellor? It would be for him to discern which of all the fragments I brought him were truthful and which were just the vinoro speaking.

At dinner the ambassador introduced the two foreign guests. I was correct that the hooked-nose man was from Naples and the bishop was from Rome. No reason was given for their presence in Florence nor for their attendance at the reception. The Neopolitan was seated at the opposite end of the long table from the ambassador. Throughout the meal, he spoke to no one and seemed bored the entire time. The bishop said he was not feeling well, excused himself, and exited the dining salon.

After dinner many of the bankers prepared to depart, while other bankers and most of the agents moved to an outdoor garden where glasses were set filled with a digestivo made from pressed grape skins. The ambassador touched my arm to get my attention and instructed, "It is time to distribute the gifts. You will find them on a tray in my study. Go fetch them and bring them to me."

I had seen the silver belt buckles as they were being wrapped earlier. Large buckles with carefully engraved designs were wrapped in gilded red paper as gifts for the bank owners. Smaller buckles with simpler designs wrapped in blue paper were intended for the bank agents. Donato was correct in saying that had the items been made by Italian silversmiths they would have been at least as fine as those made in Paris.

I found the tray, piled high with the gifts, on a side table in the ambassador's spacious study. As I turned to leave carrying the tray, my eye was struck by light reflecting from a small red object on the floor under a desk on the opposite side of the room. I set the tray down, walked across the room, and stooped to pick up and examine the object. I have little knowledge of gemstones but its deep red color led me to believe it might be a ruby, possibly dislodged from a piece of jewelry the ambassador was wearing while he was seated at the desk.

As I placed the stone on the desk, so the ambassador would be sure to see it, my eyes fell onto a letter being drafted by the ambassador to the Duke of Milan. I re-read the incomplete draft several times to be sure I could accurately convey its damning accusation.

Chapter 11 Monday, August 6, 1464

Bartolomeo Scala requested that our second meeting be at San Miniato al Monte where a church and Olivetan monastery stand on one of the highest hills outside the city. The enclave began with a simple church more than 300 years ago and has grown as the monastery and more recently a beautiful cloister were built. In addition to being the location of the splendid church, the hilltop affords an excellent view of Florence and the ancient town of Fiesole to the North. Because they are all sites that Simone would appreciate, I invited him to join me.

The meeting with Scala was not until mid-morning, which allowed ample time for showing Simone some other sights of the city as we headed to the meeting place. From the cathedral in the center of the city, we wended our way through a maze of small streets to Via dei Pandolfini. Halfway down that street was a modest building with a simple stone front and above its entrance an emblem with four blue stars on a blue background. I pointed to the building, "This is the Judges and Notaries Guild Hall. It is where I will come to apply for membership in the guild. All notaries and lawyers must join the guild before they can practice law in Florence."

Simone shook his head, "I know that the lawyers and notaries here in Florence belong to a guild, but still it seems strange to me because in Venice only our artisans belong to guilds. We have no guild for lawyers. Why are Florentine lawyers required to join a guild?"

"One purpose of the guild is to ensure that anyone practicing law is qualified to do so."

Simone asked somewhat incredulously, "Does the guild even have to approve someone who has a degree from Bologna? Why is the university degree not sufficient proof of competence?"

"Certainly the guild consuls would not doubt the ability of anyone with a degree from Bologna, but they can prevent other unqualified persons from receiving magisterial appointments. There was a time in the past when a deceitful member of the Signoria tried to get his cohorts appointed as magistrates. The guild protects against that happening again.

"How does Venice protect itself against unqualified lawyers," I asked.

"Venice does not prevent anyone from establishing a law practice, but the Council deals swiftly with any instance of malpractice."

I scanned the building, my eyes settling on its blue and gold insignia, my thoughts anticipating my future.

"Within the next few days, I'll come back here and file a membership application."

"How long before you will know their ruling?"

Laughingly I said, "If I were a Medici or a Pitti they would probably announce their ruling before the ink dries on my application. Seriously though, how quickly they act depends on what other business they have at the time. If they are involved in an important matter, that will take precedence over routine items, so membership approvals might be delayed. Generally though, the consuls act swiftly so it takes no more than one week to learn their ruling."

"One week isn't enough time to investigate an applicant's qualifications," Simone stated. "Do they decide just by looking at the information on the applications?"

"The applications themselves do not give them much information. Mine will say that I have a degree from the University of Bologna. In addition to having a law degree, there are a few qualifications that every applicant must meet: he and his family must have paid all their taxes, there must be no scandals in the family, and there must be no criminals in the family."

Simone's jaw dropped in disbelief. "That seems totally unreasonable... having the membership and your career depend on the actions of family members."

"I agree with you, but the rules were set by the guild a long time ago, and none of the existing members are inclined to change them."

"Who is considered part of a family?" Simone asked, "If I have a cousin who was jailed for a crime would his crime have me disqualified?"

"No. Only close relatives are considered. Although since my parents are deceased and I have no siblings, the consuls will view Donato and his wife Joanna as my family. Fortunately for me, not only do they satisfy the guild's criteria, they are very well regarded by everyone."

"What happens after your membership in the guild is approved?"

"One option would be for me to enter private practice. My roommate at Bologna intends to do that by working at his father's law firm. Private practice doesn't interest me. The other option, which appeals more to me, is public service. Florence is blessed, or cursed, with a large number of tribunals and commissions. We have four supreme level tribunals. In addition, there are local tribunals with jurisdiction over minor criminal and civil matters... and there must be a few others I can't recall. But by far the largest opportunities lie in the many commissions created by the Signoria."

Simone was awed as I voiced the list. Jokingly he said, "Florence must be a crime-ridden city to need so many tribunals. We certainly have far fewer in Venice." Then he asked, "Does the guild also appoint people to the various positions?"

"Generally, the chief magistrate of the tribunal selects his own deputies and the head of each commission selects members to serve on his commission. Some commissions have dozens of members so in total there are hundreds of magisterial positions."

I smiled and added, "There are always positions open for new laureates with law degrees. Maybe next year when you graduate you'll consider moving here."

As we talked, we turned onto Via dei Calzaiuoli, one of the oldest streets in the city and also one of the noisiest with apprentices loudly hawking products to all passersby. We approached a cheese shop that announced its presence with a mix of odors wafting into the street, and as we passed the entrance a lanky youngster with a pimply face urged us to sample the shop's soft goat cheese specialty.

Finally we reached the heart of the city, Piazza della Signoria, which Simone recognized from the previous day. "Yesterday Alessa brought me here to show me the Palazzo Vecchio. She told me the Palazzo is built on top of an ancient Roman theater."

"Yes, it is. The building next to the Palazzo is where the Tribunale della Mercanzia meets. It is the tribunal that rules on disputes between merchants and on all claims by foreigners against Florentine merchants. Do you recall the reluctant highwayman we encountered coming from Bologna, the one called Orsino?"

"Yes, the big one. The one who didn't stink."

"He said the wool mill where he had worked could not operate because the ship bringing wool from England was missing.

I heard that the incident is becoming a legal spectacle and the case is being presented here at the Mercanzia. I am curious to see for myself how the case is proceeding."

Several isolated groups of people were standing near the entrance to the assembly hall as we approached the building. I pointed out to Simone two magistrates talking together near one corner of the building. "Their long red gowns and red sashes mean they are senior magistrates. This tribunal has six senior magistrates so either the others are already in the assembly hall or they haven't arrived yet."

Proceedings in the Mercanzia usually involved two parties, yet there were four separate groups present this morning each consisting of several well-dressed gentlemen with their cadre of notaries. I approached a young clerk who was holding an armful of documents and standing behind one of the notaries. Clerks care little about privacy. It makes them feel important to talk about any cases they are associated with.

"Can you tell us about the claim that is being deliberated this morning?" I asked.

Simone and I leaned in close to hear the clerk who answered me in a low voice so as not to disturb the notaries, or to not let them know he was speaking to strangers about the case. "A ship carrying wool to Pisa from England has gone missing."

Seeing our keen interest, he continued, "The wool merchant is seeking compensation for his lost business from the French shipowner, but the shipowner says that the Florentine bank insuring the wool merchant is liable for the loss. The Florentine bank says that a French bank, the one that insures the ship, should be the one to pay."

I could not help but ask, "And what does the French bank say?"

"They claim it is too soon to declare that the ship is lost ... but if it is lost then the loss is an act of God, so they are absolved of any responsibility."

I thanked the clerk for sharing the information, turned to Simone and said, "Ah, such complexity, it is a magistrate's dream. Orsino should be thankful that he is now working for Donato. The wool company that was his employer will not be calling him back to work for a long time."

After scanning the crowd of magistrates, lawyers, and notaries, Simone stated a truism of the legal profession, "The only ones who are sure to benefit here are the lawyers and notaries. The longer it takes to reach a resolution the richer they will become."

I grinned, rested a hand on Simone's shoulder, and said sarcastically, "After six grueling years of study, are we not deserving of princely rewards?"

"This is a public service tribunal with intriguing cases. Is it your first choice for an appointment?" Simone asked.

"Maybe someday, but all of its members are senior magistrates who have long experience on lesser boards. I have tried not to favor any particular tribunal for my first appointment. That way I won't be disappointed."

From Piazza della Signoria we headed south and crossed the Arno River on Florence's oldest bridge, the Ponte Vecchio. We exited the city through one of the city gates and began the long steep climb to the hilltop church.

In deference to the August heat, we wore what are sometimes called peasant clothes, simple lightweight tunics, and no hose to cover our bare legs. No magistrate would consider wearing peasant clothes, but as yet I had no social standing to protect so I could take the liberty of dressing for comfort. Simone enjoyed the convenience of peasant clothes even though his family's stature in Venice would prevent him from wearing such simple garments there. Despite our thin fabrics, the growing heat of the day tired us quickly and caused us to set a slow pace. The trek was arduous for Simone, who was used to living in a city with cooling sea breezes and without hills.

Several paths climb the hill to the church at the summit. We chose a short but steep trail. Wagons were unable to negotiate this path so the only travelers we passed were monks and farmers leading their produce-laden donkeys down to the markets of the city. Even though the bell tower of San Miniato al Monte is visible from the center of the city, we found ourselves climbing for more than an hour before sighting the wall surrounding the church, cloister, and hospital.

Finally having reached the top of the hill we stood before a steep cascade of steps that still needed to be mounted to reach the church, a staircase that brought to mind Dante's ascendance from

Purgatorio to Paradiso. The imposing green and white facade of the church high above seemed to be looking down challenging us to make the ascent. We were about to start the climb when we glimpsed Chancellor Scala talking with a monk at the edge of a garden off to our left. A large chestnut tree provided shade allowing them to enjoy the refreshing breezes always skimming the hilltop.

When they finished their conversation, Scala noticed Simone and me and motioned for us to join him. Following a round of introductions, he said to Simone, "I had the pleasure of hosting your father when he passed through Florence during a journey to Rome. We still correspond, and one day I hope to visit him in Venice. He will be pleased when I tell him that I met his son."

The monk offered to escort Simone on a tour of the church allowing Scala and me to meet privately. The monk's wrinkled face, white hair, and stooped posture were evidence of his age, but he climbed the steps to the church without difficulty leaving Simone trailing behind. Scala led me to a stone bench in the shade of a magnificent cypress tree where we could sit and discuss my findings of the previous evening.

Chapter 12

In our first meeting the Chancellor's demeanor had been intense as he focused on recruiting my service. Today he was like a different person. He held a casually relaxed posture, and rather than press me with questions about the previous evening, he began by asking if the city seemed different to me after being away at the university in Bologna for several years. He asked what sights I planned to show Simone and whether he would still be in Florence to view the horse races on Ferragosto. I agreed that Simone would find the races interesting because they didn't have any similar events in Venice, and also because Simone was an experienced rider who learned to ride at one of his family's villas in the Venetian countryside.

Scala's friendly chatting was unexpected. I was eager to tell him what I had learned. Eventually, impatience got the best of me and I started to recount my experience of the previous evening, but before I could give him any real information he interrupted, "I hope you felt comfortable in your role last night. You were performing a valuable service for the Republic."

Prior to the reception, the ethics of eavesdropping on conversations had troubled me. Last night I not only listened to conversations, but I also read the private correspondence of a foreign diplomat; yet this morning I had not even thought about the ethics of my actions.

"I hope the information I gathered can benefit the Republic, but I am not certain how to feel about it. This is a time when I envy Aristotle. He would not have trouble deciding the ethics."

Scala laughed. "Aristotle was certainly an insightful thinker, but I doubt that even he had answers to all of life's questions."

At the time I thought, 'Thank goodness I am to be a magistrate and not a philosopher. Magistrates have only to make decisions in accordance with well-defined laws.' I have since learned that magistrates too must sometimes contend with vague issues.

We walked in silence for several minutes while Scala considered my answers. Whether he found them satisfactory, or whether they were as he expected, I do not know. After a time, he asked me to describe the reception the previous evening.

"One of the bankers, a short man with a hooked nose, spoke openly of his disdain for Piero de Medici calling him weak and cowardly. He said Piero is incapable of leading the bank, that he is already making mistakes that will cause pain to those who support the Medici bank. He maintained that Piero should not be allowed to have a leadership position in the Republic.

"Luca Pitti and the several members of the Sporcone family were standing with him when the hooked nose man made the outburst. Luca seemed almost embarrassed by the threat. He moved away slightly and looked toward the floor suggesting he did not share the sentiment. The Sporcones on the other hand, especially Salvatore Sporcone, became animated by the vehemence. I know nothing of the Sporcone family but the few words said about them were not favorable."

The Chancellor said, "Although bankers and money changers are members of the same guild, the money changers are regarded with disdain by their more senior colleagues. The Sporcones are money changers who are regarded with contempt even by other money changers. They have been denounced many times for violating guild rules and usury laws but for various reasons they have never been found guilty of a crime. Salvatore Sporcone would sell his soul to be elected as an officer of the guild, which he sees as a step toward becoming a banker and eventually a public official. His ambition makes him a dangerous person who bears watching."

When I told Scala about the outburst made by one of the banking agents, Scala replied, "That characterization fits the Sporcones, Salvatore and his son Alphonso. The accusation of Salvatore killing his wife is believed by many but has never been proven. As you learned at Bologna, a man should not be convicted by rumor."

"There were two foreigners at the reception: one an envoy

from Naples and the other a bishop from Rome. They stood near each other while appertivi were being served, but they said little to each other and neither one spoke to any of the guests. The ambassador didn't say why either of them was at the reception, nor did he say their reasons for being in Florence."

Scala's tone became frosty, "If they are diplomats, they should have informed the Chancery of their arrival in the Republic. They have not done so."

Of all the information I gave to Scala, he found the content of the letter I had seen from the ambassador to the Duke of Milan to be most significant. "The letter claims that the chief accountant of the Medici bank was Cosimo's greatest and most ambitious enemy."

The Chancellor's brow furrowed upon hearing the news. "If the accusation is true then it must be dealt with because the same man is now the principal advisor to Piero."

"Unfortunately, the letter was not yet finished. The portion I was able to see did not explain the reason for its claim."

Scala's lip quivered and he clenched his teeth as though he had not already known what I told him but was not totally surprised by it. "Whether the accusation is true or not," Scala announced, "if that claim becomes widely known, the accountant will become a target of everyone seeking to undermine the Medici bank."

I continued my report telling him about the ruby I found in the study. "It was on the floor under the desk. I might not have seen it except for its bright reflection. I thought it might have been dislodged from a piece of the ambassador's jewelry, so I placed it on the desk. Later in the garden, I noticed the Roman bishop was wearing a jeweled pectoral cross with one missing stone. The ruby I found on the floor in the ambassador's study was an exact match to the other stones in the bishop's cross. The bishop did not have dinner, he claimed to be feeling poorly, but the true reason for taking leave may have been to prowl the embassy."

"Can you describe the bishop?"

"He was small, with a slight, almost frail, build and a face that looked pinched together like a small animal, a squirrel or a ferret."

"Ah yes, his name is Contino. He was born on Sardinia and entered the priesthood there, but he was too ambitious to stay on that island and soon transferred to Rome where he often undertakes missions that are outside the canons of the church. It is not clear whether he is doing the bidding of the Papacy or some other entity. Some say he wears church clothing to hide a wicked soul. I did not know that he is in Florence. I will make inquiries about him ... and the Neapolitan too."

Realizing that I had finished telling what I had learned, Scala turned the focus of the conversation to me. "I suppose you will be applying for membership in the guild within a few days. You are fortunate that there are several vacancies available for new laureates at this time. Do you have a preference regarding your appointment?"

"I haven't had a chance to speak with anyone about which

vacancies might exist. I have not picked a favorite for fear that my choice might not have an open position, or worse yet. if they do have an opening, they might not consider me a worthy candidate."

"Any tribunal would be foolish to think you unqualified, but at the risk of influencing your decision," the Chancellor smiled broadly as he continued, "recently our ambassadors have demonstrated to the Signoria that our means for securing the Republic are inadequate. The Signoria is eager to remove those deficiencies. I believe that their solution will create a new commission. It could be a challenging opportunity for a talented lawyer and I am confident they would be delighted to consider graduates of the University of Bologna." With a wink he added, "Of course none of this is public knowledge yet, but my information comes from an impeccable source."

I listened carefully as he spoke but said nothing.

To further influence my thinking he added, "To safeguard the security of the Republic from outside threats the Chancery is granted broad powers by our constitution. Chancery members are sometimes dispatched to negotiate with other states, both friends and enemies. For this reason, I believe the new commission will work in close association with the Chancery.

"Whatever your intention concerning future appointments, as you observed last night the death of Cosimo de Medici is emboldening forces that are willing to disrupt order in the Republic. I may seem to be exaggerating when I say it, but your continued efforts could help preserve the stability of the Republic.

I hope you are willing to continue our arrangement."

After stating his case Scala did not ask for my decision, and I did not give him one. Perhaps he was giving me time to consider his plea, or perhaps he had no immediate need for my assistance. We parted company with Scala heading down a dirt path toward the city gate and me climbing the marble steps to find Simone somewhere in the church.

Chapter 13

Our descent to the city was an easy walk in contrast to our earlier climb. Simone carried the conversation telling me of the treasures he was shown in the basilica. San Miniato al Monte is not as elegant as the cathedral in Florence or Saint Mark's in Venice, but it has a beauty and charm all its own, and a history dating back over five hundred years. Simone proposed that we return one day to search for the grave site of its patron saint who, according to legend, was buried somewhere on the hillside in the third century. I listened to Simone, but my thoughts dwelt on the prospect Scala held out to me, an opportunity that would stretch the dreams of any new law school graduate. It was the challenge his offer held that gave me pause.

Before we left the monastery, the monks had shared with us a refreshing drink they make from edible flowers. Their concoction helped to fend off the heat, but I decided that something more substantial was needed to clarify my thinking. "Simone," I said interrupting him, "it's time for you to see the seedier side of Florence. I know a tavern where we can round out your view of my fair city."

We passed through the city gate, crossed the Arno river, and entered a maze of small streets so narrow that building overhangs from each side of the road almost touched each other. Sunlight never reached the cobblestones nor the storefronts leaving everything, and everyone, in shadowy gray light. A faint sour smell of dried urine was evident. Walking required careful attention because the cobblestones underfoot were uneven, and some were missing, leaving deep holes to trap the unwary. This section of the city was quieter than the others. Few people ventured here aside from those seeking prostitutes - women, girls, and young boys - who plied their trade in the taverns and inns under the guidance and control of the innkeepers. The streets, safe enough during the day, were frequented at night by men interested in whoring and gambling. Anyone interested only in drinking would do so elsewhere in more reputable establishments. At night thugs lurking in the tiny alleys between buildings were ready to prey on any strangers, with unsuspecting foreigners being their favorite targets. Rarely did I venture into this part of the city, home to the brothels and dingy taverns that are not welcome in other quarters. Simone found the surroundings to be both exhilarating and scary. Truth be told, so did I.

Even those of us who don't frequent these establishments know, by reputation, that each is home to a distinct clientele.

Members of the militia are found regularly in the Panico, a dingy tavern owned by a former mercenary, and each of the various guilds has its own favorite abyss. I picked il Pennello, the brush, as our destination. It is the choice of the city's artists so I assumed it would put us in the company of a less rowdy crowd. Artists favor il Pennello for its cheap Austrian beer and its comely prostitutes whom the artists hire to pose for paintings, as well as to satisfy their physical needs.

A short corridor led from the street to a large open room with wooden tables of various sizes spaced throughout and a bar centered along one wall. Candles placed on a few of the tables provided the only light in the dimly lit space. Gradually our eyes adjusted revealing a barista slumped in a chair behind the bar, a group of six men playing cards at a far table, and four women seated on couches at the rear of the room.

The barista grudgingly raised himself from the chair when we reached the bar, then he stood looking at us but saying nothing, waiting for us to speak.

"Ale?" I proffered.

In response to my request/question, the barista pulled two mugs from a shelf and held them up to examine in the feeble light. He brushed a speck from one mug, then concluded they met his questionable standard of cleanliness and filled them with a foamy brown liquid poured from a pitcher.

"Something to eat?" Simone asked hopefully.

"Dried meat" the barista growled, and from below the bar he

withdrew a blood sausage. I had my doubts, but Simone will eat almost anything.

Still hopeful, Simone tried, "Cheese?"

From the same shelf, the barista produced a yellow block that he placed into Simone's outstretched hand.

Before Simone could utter another word, the barista barked, "This's not a restaurant."

We carried our purchases to a small table. I took a giant swig of the dark brown liquid, downing nearly half the mug, before even sitting at the table. Despite being warmer than I would have wished, it was a welcome refreshment after our hike under the hot sun. Simone set his mug on the table and brushed a beetle from the chair in front of him. The unkempt barista and the bar covered with pools of a sticky substance gave Simone pause to consider whether drinking here was safe. Finally, he decided to take the risk, lowered himself into a chair, then shifted slightly to keep the chair from wobbling. Before he could touch his mug to his lips, a dark-haired beauty approached him. She sat on the edge of the table directly in front of Simone, ran a hand through his thick brown hair, then leaned down until her breasts pressed against his cheeks. She wore a low-cut shirt that exposed her ample cleavage. Her shirt extended to mid-thigh and it appeared that she wore nothing else.

"I am Sisi, and this is your first time in il Pennello," she said. A statement, not a question. Looking to me, while her bosom continued to fill Simone's entire field of vision, she said, "Come to my room, both of you, and I guarantee you will come back again. You will become cherished frequent visitors."

"I am married." Obviously not true, but it was the first excuse that came to my mind.

"Half of the men who visit me are married," she laughed.

"My friend is a priest."

Her eyes brightened and she laughed again. "And the other half of my visitors are priests."

My excuses were no match for her wit. "We will look for you next time, Sisi, but today we are here only for a drink."

She gave a shrug, lifted herself away from Simone, said in parting, "Too bad. You are cute.... both of you," and rejoined the other women on the couch at the back of the room.

When Sisi peeled her breasts from Simone's cheeks, I couldn't tell whether he was relieved or disappointed until he said, "Damn, she smells nice."

Across the room, the paint splatters on the clothes of the card players marked them as artists. My eyes locked on one red-haired young man who must have sensed my stare because he looked up from his cards in my direction. Our mutual recognition was immediate. He dropped his cards onto the table, said to his companions "tardi," later. Getting up from his table he carried his mug to the table where Simone and I were seated and dropped into an empty chair. "Nico Argenti, what brings you to a hole like this? I thought you were studying law. Did they find out about the time that you stole the priest's horse and kicked you out of the university?"

"No, nothing like that. I am no longer a student, I just graduated."

"Congratulations, Nico. It's about time. It seems like you've been studying your whole life."

Sandro, the artist, looked directly at Simone. "Did Nico ever tell you that he stole the horse belonging to his parish priest? The poor old priest had a bad leg and even using a cane he could hardly walk at all. He needed that horse to get anywhere, even though she was an old nag herself. Your friend, Nico, had no compassion for either of them."

I raised a hand, waved it, and shook my head in protest. "Sandro, you have the gift for stretching truth into fantasy. I didn't exactly steal the horse, I only borrowed it to take one of the neighborhood girls to see the grotto at Santissima Annunziata." Exaggerating with false humility I added, "She wanted to see the grotto and I couldn't very well refuse to take her. Anyway, I returned the horse to the parish stable the same afternoon. Father Giupo was probably enjoying his regular afternoon nap the whole time and never even noticed that his horse was missing."

With heavy sarcasm, Sandro said, "Nico believed he could charm all the young ladies, that every girl's dream was to have Nico Argenti take her to the hidden grotto. At least that's what Nico always told us."

Turning to me Sandro added, "Boccaccio could have written your story into his Decameron with all the other fantasies, but now look at you, you've moved on from pursuing young maidens to becoming a wealthy magistrate, wealthy enough to buy a drink for a starving artist... and for his friends too."

Sandro waved to the barkeeper indicating he should bring a round of drinks to us and to his card playing friends.

"Wait, Sandro, I'm not sure I have..."

Before I finished my protest, Simone interrupted to explain the situation to Sandro. "For reasons he has never explained, Nico never carries more than a few coins with him, but it will be my pleasure to see that your glass and those of your friends are refilled."

"It is good to see that Nico has at least one friend who is truly a gentleman." Sandro waved his arm broadly and bowed. "I shall be in your debt forever."

"Simone, forgive me neglecting the introductions. This eloquent gentleman" -- with sarcasm dripping from the word gentleman-- "is Sandro. As you can surely tell he is one of my dear childhood friends and he is now on a path to become a great artist ... or so he tells everyone."

Sandro bowed his head and with all the false modesty he could muster responded, "It is a pleasure to meet you, kind sir. Nico exaggerates my artistic reputation, I am but a humble apprentice who still has much to learn."

"Don't listen to him, Simone. Modesty is not one of Sandro's usual traits. Yes, he is an apprentice, but his apprenticeship is with Fra Filippo Lippi, one of the finest artistic masters of our age.

Lippi has patrons clamoring for his services in Florence, Spoleto, Prato, he even receives commissions from as far away as Naples. Lippi would not accept Sandro as an apprentice if the master did not witness Sandro's exceptional talent."

To Sandro I said, "Simone is a fellow student at the University of Bologna. He will earn his degree next year. This is Simone's first visit to Florence; his home is in Venice."

"This is his first visit to our wonderful city, and you bring him to this rat hole?" Sandro gestured toward the women seated on the couch at the rear of the room and said, "Although, as you can see, the owner of this establishment is very discriminating in selecting his women. You won't find any who are more beautiful... or more satisfying. Nico, you should be treating Simone to a roll with Sisi instead of making him pay for our refreshments. Sisi can teach him some things he hasn't learned at the university."

I needed to change the topic before Simone started to think seriously about Sandro's suggestion. "I heard that maestro Lippi recently returned to Prato to continue his work on the frescoes in Santo Stefano. Will you be joining him there?"

Sandro set his mug of ale on the table and leaned back in his chair. "No, the maestro likes to paint the frescoes by himself. He did take two young apprentices with him to mix the paints and prepare the plaster. Frescoes are a challenge because they are painted while the plaster is still wet, so they must be painted in small sections, one section at a time. Oils are enough of a challenge for me."

"So, while the maestro is away you have nothing better to do than hang out here in il Pennello with your friends drinking and gambling."

Instead of answering my quip with one of his own, Sandro moved our conversation in a more serious direction. "Actually, before the maestro left for Prato, he was commissioned to do several portraits. He painted the figures and has asked me to paint the backgrounds."

"Sandro, how wonderful for you that Lippi has such confidence in your work he invites you to collaborate with him."

Simone asked, "Isn't it difficult for two artists to work together on the same painting?"

Laughing heartily, Sandro said, "It is not difficult for the maestro. He simply paints in his usual exquisite style. All the difficulty falls on the apprentice, me, who must try to match the maestro's style."

He continued with a more detailed reply. "The maestro is in great demand, yet he feels that he cannot turn down any request from the Church, so he finds himself unable to satisfy all the demands made on him. Tomorrow I will be working on the background of a portrait he created for Luca Pitti of his daughter Francesca. I don't want to sound immodest, but I am developing a style for my own painting. Now the challenge when I do the backgrounds is remembering to emulate the maestro's style. I prefer light colors and delicate lines while the maestro likes to use bolder colors. He anchors his figures in the landscapes but I want my figures to float within the scenes."

A bout of loud howling sounded from Sandro's card-playing friends. I leaned closer so Sandro could hear me and asked, "Would it be possible to see your work sometime? Maybe when I become a magistrate, I'll commission you to do a painting for my office."

"Tomorrow. Tomorrow I'll be working on the portrait of Francesca in the garden at Palazzo Pitti. I always do the backgrounds in the same location where the portrait was done to be sure they are authentic. You should come... both of you. I'll bring a sample of my own work so you can see the difference between my style and the maestro's style. It is also possible that Francesca will be there. She likes to watch me work and she always asks questions about my choices of paints and brushes and such. She is very perceptive. Her questions actually help me better understand my choices. It's not clear though whether she is truly interested in painting, or whether she has nothing else to do other than play cards with other lonely women."

We finished one more round of drinks before Simone and I took our leave and Sandro rejoined the other artists.

Chapter 14

That evening Simone, Alessa, Bernardo Bembo, and I gathered in a small private room at the Uccello. Donato had chosen the name Uccello, bird, for his establishment because his chef specializes in dinners featuring game birds. The dinner he prepared for us of goose breast with apricot and chestnut stuffing and glazed with a honey wine sauce was one of his most memorable creations. Due to a prior commitment, the Venetian ambassador was not able to join us, which removed any need for formality in dress and behavior. Even though Messer Bembo is an envoy representing the Venetian council, he set a relaxed and comfortable mood for the evening.

He was delighted to meet Alessa, whose inquisitive nature reminded him of his own daughter who was always in his thoughts when he was away from Venice on his many missions for the Republic. We were all mesmerized by Alessa's account of growing up in Morocco, of being kidnapped and sold in a slave market, and of her life on the ship. She rarely feels comfortable enough with strangers to talk about her childhood.

"I lived with my mother, grandfather, brother and a few goats on a small plot of land that had been in our family for generations.

We made our living by growing fruit, mostly apricots. Our land was outside of the village so every few days my brother and I would bring ripe fruit to the village market where a neighbor would sell them for us. On these trips I enjoyed wandering through the village to look at the shops with fancy clothes and delicious food, but mother always warned us to come straight home after we finished our business at the market.

"One day my brother was sick, so I went to the village alone. After delivering the fruit I walked around the market, past the goat pens to a wadi where boys were playing in pools of muddy water collected there during the Spring rains. They were splashing and having such fun that I followed the dirt path toward the pool hoping to join them. Before I reached the wadi two men grabbed me from behind. I could not see their faces. They stuffed a cloth into my mouth to keep me from screaming, pulled a sack over my head, and bound my hands and feet with strips of cloth. I learned later that they use cloth strips rather than rope because ropes can leave marks if their captives struggle to get free, and children sold at the slave market do not fetch good prices if they are damaged."

Simone and Messer Bembo sat motionless, spellbound by Alessa's words.

"Until the day of the auction, I was kept in a tiny dark room with a boy from my village and four other children. How we were moved to the town with the auction I do not remember. I do remember being pushed out onto the platform where the bidding was done. It was frightening, they taunted us, they said I was dirty and too skinny. Only two men bid for me. The one who bought me, who would be my master, was captain of a ship that carried tropical fruit and grains from Morocco to Naples. During my first week at sea the relentless rocking of the ship kept me constantly sick, but gradually I became accustomed to the motion.

"The captain was not a bad man. He made me work hard, he never beat me ... or anything, but some of the sailors terrified me. When I cleaned the captain's cabin, and when I did his laundry, I would lock myself into his cabin to keep the sailors away. A few times some drunken sailors tried to break into the cabin to get me. The captain had them beaten, but that didn't change their behavior, they would still come to the cabin hoping to find the door unlocked. It was a miracle that Donato found me and took me here. The captain realized it was not safe for me on the ship, so he was willing to trade me to Donato. I never asked about the details of the exchange."

"Did you ever see your family again?" Messer Bembo asked.

"No," she replied softly. "I dream that one day I will visit my village again to see my family. But I know it is just a dream."

By the time Alessa had finished her story, we all had watery eyes. Messer Bembo insisted that she come to Venice to see the city and meet his daughter. "I will pass through Florence again in about two weeks when I return from Rome, then you can accompany me to Venice. I promise you will love our city, everyone who sees it loves it. You can stay as long as you like and when you are ready to return Nico can come to Venice to escort you home."

Messer Bembo turned to me and asked, "Is that agreeable to you, Nico? It will give you an opportunity to meet colleagues of mine in the government of the Venetian Republic, perhaps even the Doge himself. Soon you will be a Florentine magistrate, and the people in my government are always eager to meet magistrates and other officials of the Florentine Republic."

"I will look forward to it. I have been to Venice only once before. That visit was a short one which did not let me see all the wonderful things Simone keeps talking about."

After dinner, Simone escorted Alessa back to casa Argenti. Messer Bembo and I moved to a comfortable couch in the main dining salon to relax with an after-dinner digestivi. It was late and most members had already departed so we were able to have a private discussion. I wanted to learn as much as possible about this trusted envoy of the Venetian council and to learn about his mission to Rome, but I didn't want to probe too aggressively, and I didn't know whether he was free to share information. I began with an innocuous question, "Do you travel to Rome often?"

"I travel everywhere often, much more often than I would like because it takes me away from my lovely wife, Helena, and my wonderful daughter Diana, but travel is an important part of my job, so I accept it," he answered.

Messer Bembo had no reservations about sharing the purpose of his mission, "As you know, the Holy Father has pledges from all the Christian states to mount a crusade against the Turks. All have made pledges, but there is little, if any, progress toward building an army and an armada. The Venetian Republic has already lost many of our overseas territories to the Turks, and we struggle to keep from losing more, so you can easily surmise that we press the others relentlessly to fulfill their promises of supporting the crusade. I go to Rome not to meet with the Holy Father because he is already eager to establish his place in history. He needs no convincing. My purpose is to keep pressure on the emissaries of other states. Rome is a place where every Christian state has an ambassador."

"What means do you have to pressure them; surely not the threat of war?"

"No, certainly not. I use the only course open to a statesman. Diplomacy. Every state is always seeking concessions from others. They want something and Venice wants something, so we try to find a trade, a compromise, that satisfies both of our needs. And I'll tell you a secret to achieving a winning trade, because it might soon be a useful technique for you. Always try to get the other party to give you something now in exchange for a promise of something you will give in the future."

Bembo shared his wisdom and information freely. His insights reminded me of Chancellor Scala, but Bembo seemed more open, not guarded. I felt shamed at not sharing with him the one piece of information I had that might affect his mission, the Holy Father's illness.

Chapter 15 Tuesday, August 7, 1464

A note arrived at casa Argenti from Bartolomeo Scala inviting Simone for a personal tour of the Chancery offices in the morning followed by a visit to the Palazzo della Signoria where Simone, as the Chancellor's guest, would be permitted to attend a meeting of Florence's ruling body. Foreigners were normally excluded from sessions of the Signoria, but high ranking officials like Bartolomeo Scala were able to bend the rules. After Cosimo's passing, debates in the Signoria became heated as opposing forces tried to wrest power from the Medici and from each other. The most influential members of the body sought to draw others into their power base. Weaker members tried to predict which of the power brokers would be successful. None wanted to join with a loser. We expected that Simone would be witness to an exciting show.

After leaving Simone with Scala at the Chancery, I walked to Via dei Pandolfini and followed that narrow road to the office of the Magistrates and Notaries Guild. I paused in front of the building briefly looking up at the blue and gold emblem above the door and thinking that I was only beginning my career, yet I had already devoted much of my life to getting here. My father had not been extraordinarily wealthy, but he managed his spending carefully which let him save enough for my inheritance to provide me with capable tutors and an excellent university education. I wished he could have been by my side at graduation. He would have been proud of the choices I made, and of my success at the university that his legacy made possible.

A large meeting area filled the entire ground floor of the guild building. The walls of the room were lined with portraits of former guild consuls, very few of whom I recognized. All administrative and consular offices were on the upper floor, reachable by a broad open staircase. At the top of the stairs a short corridor led to several rooms. One of them was a reception area where a lone scribe sat behind a desk piled with a stack of folders and sheaves of papers. Other than the single desk, the room was bare. The austerity made even the warm August day feel cold. Skinny and with facial blemishes common on young boys, this clerk did not fit the image of a competent administrator that I expected to find at the headquarters of the prestigious guild. Upon hearing my approach, the scribe looked up briefly, saw that I was neither a magistrate nor a notary, and returned his attention to the papers on his desk.

I waited a proper interval before announcing, “Good morning, I am here to apply for membership in the guild.”

Without looking up he responded in a disinterested voice, “I am busy. Come back later."

"How much later?"

His voice gained an edge of annoyance. "Later, just later. I told you I am busy now. This afternoon. Come back this afternoon."

I turned to leave but just as I reached the stairway a man with thick white hair and wearing the red sash of s senior magistrate passed by the entrance to the room heading for the stairs. When he saw me standing there he stopped, studied me a moment, then with a flash of recognition he said, "You are Gustavo Argenti's son, isn't that so?"

"Yes, sir."

He puzzled a few more seconds. "Nico... Nico Argenti. I knew your father when he was the representative of the military to the Tribunale Esecutore. He was a valued emissary of our Republic during the foreign assignments early in his career. Later when he served at the Tribunale Esecutore he was a good friend of this guild. What a shame that God took him so early in his life. You were just a small boy when I saw you last, and now I am told that you have a Docturus Juris degree. Congratulations; the program at Bologna is a rigorous one. Many who start do not even finish, but I understand that you graduated with distinction. Last week when I had dinner with your contract law professor, Carlucci, he spoke very highly of you."

Seeing my surprise he said, "Forgive me for not introducing myself. I am Enzio Carlucci, and your law professor is my cousin. I am one of the Guild Consuls.

"I travel to Bologna frequently to visit my cousin and to meet with other members of the university faculty. It is a way for me to follow the progress of our Florentine law students, as well as fine students from elsewhere. Siena and Venice always send capable students to Bologna, and we are always eager to have talented graduates join us here in Florence. Bartolomeo told me that you just arrived from Bologna and that you have been showing our beloved city to another student from the university."

"Yes, sir. Simone Pisani is from Venice. He has one additional year of study before earning his degree. This is his first visit to Florence."

"Yes, Pisani. I know his father as well. He is a competent and influential member of the Venetian government. Do you know him?"

"No, sir. I have not had the pleasure of meeting him yet."

"I am sure that young Pisani is finding much to enjoy in our city." With a wink, he added, " Be sure he attends a mass at the Duomo. The Duomo choir gets its voice from heaven, and no one ever says that about the choir at Saint Mark's."

As he turned to leave, he flashed me a smile and said in parting, "I look forward to getting your application for membership in the guild."

I turned to follow him down the stairs when the clerk called after me. "I have a free moment. I will be able to prepare your application now."

The clerk asked for very little information to complete the

application. He asked neither my name, the nature of my degree, nor the university I attended, which confirmed that he had overheard my exchange with the consul. His only questions concerned my place of residence and the names of my family members. I had previously arranged for a banker to pay the application fee. The clerk must have already had a record of the payment because he did not ask about that. I understand why the consuls communicate with faculty members because the perfunctory information in the membership application is hardly sufficient for judging the suitability of a candidate.

Kind words to me from a guild consul transformed the once surly clerk into an efficient, helpful worker. It took him only moments to finish processing my application.

Chapter 16

It was barely mid-morning when I left the consul office. The day was pleasant, much cooler than the previous two days due to puffy white clouds holding the sun's rays at bay, so I decided to accept Sandro's invitation and meet him at Palazzo Pitti. The Palazzo, large even by Florentine standards, sits on a low hill in the area known as Oltarno, signifying the other side, the Southside, of the Arno river.

Upon arrival, I was greeted by a servant who directed me through the side gardens that framed the building to the terrace overlooking the meadow at the rear where Sandro was working. The well-manicured field extended more than four hundred steps toward the hill behind the palazzo. Carefully placed throughout were statuary set among flowering plants. It is a beautiful backdrop; no wonder Lippi chose this location as the setting for his portrait of Francesca Pitti.

Sandro stood with a brush in hand in the shade of a fruit tree off to the side of the main area of the open central expanse. He saw me approaching as I crossed the raised marble terrace behind the palazzo. "Nico, I hadn't seen you in two years and now I am graced by your presence two days in succession. My luck must be changing."

"For better or worse?" I teased.

"Only time will tell my friend, but I am glad that you did come. I wasn't sure that you would take my invitation seriously. Aren't these gardens lovely?"

"Stunning, just as you said. Signor Pitti had this estate built just a few years ago, so there must be an army of gardeners working here to have created all this in such a short time. What an inspiring place for you to work."

"Much has been done but the gardens are not finished yet. Francesca told me that her father wants flower gardens to surround the house and to be the border for that open meadow. Architects from the Guild of Stonemasons designed the gardens to Luca's liking, and they are supervising the work. They are constantly bringing him new ideas for sculptures and fountains."

Sandro pointed to a marble statue standing in a field of pink flowers. "That statue was installed just yesterday, replacing a similar, but shorter, one. Signor Pitti gives them direction every day commenting on even small details of the design. With both the architects and Signor Pitti giving them direction, the workers feel overwhelmed with constant changes. I consider myself lucky that he is fully occupied with the landscaping, that keeps me free from his attention."

"Here, come look at this, it is a painting that I have been working on. This one is in my style."

He held up a canvas of a young girl who appeared to be gliding, almost floating, through a green field. Her pink dress of thinnest gauze-like fabric drifted behind her as if caught by a breeze. Behind her, in the unfinished work, were light pencil or chalk lines outlining a Greek temple waiting to be painted. "It is beautiful Sandro, almost mystical, a Spring day captured on canvas, and your colors do emulate those of rose petals. Your choice of subject is unusual; is she a Greek goddess? Should I recognize who she is?"

"I enjoy painting from the myths because they free me to use my imagination. The girl in this painting is not meant to be anyone special, just a girl, but I'll tell you a secret, the model who posed for me was one of the women from il Pennello. Maybe that changes your opinion of the painting, but if you still like it knowing that secret, you may have it to hang in your office when it is finished. Then I can boast to my friends that one of my paintings hangs in the office of a Florentine magistrate."

"It would be an honor to display your painting in my office, but you must be sure to sign it so someday when you become famous, I will be able to boast that I have a painting by Sandro Botticelli hanging in my office."

Sandro held his painting next to the one on the easel by maestro Lippi so I could compare the two and see the difference in styles between the two artists.

"Today I have been working on flowers in the background of master Lippi's painting. I have learned to mimic his style well enough. My biggest challenge is getting the paint colors to match the delicate hues of the flowers. We artists are fools to think we can recreate the beauty that God gives to every petal. We will always fail, but we cannot stop trying."

It was important for Sandro to use the paint he had mixed before it set. To let him proceed without interruption, I wandered off down one of the many stone paths to examine the statue of a nymph set into one of the garden fountains. Many years past, someone - could it have been my mother - told me stories about nymphs at bedtime. I can almost recall one story about a sprite who was turned into a fountain. Might this statue be depicting her?

When I returned to where Sandro was working, a young woman was standing behind Sandro looking at the portrait, her portrait. She stood with her shoulders slumped forward and her brow furrowed. Her stance and movements indicated that something was troubling her. At first, I thought she might be unhappy with the painting, but when Sandro looked up at her, he too noticed that she was disturbed. He set down his brushes, took her quivering hand, and led her to a low stone wall. By all social standards, Sandro's manner was highly improper. Artisans should never initiate physical contact with the daughters of their aristocratic patrons. Yet his action came out of sincere concern, and she accepted it as such without offense.

"Sit, Francesca, tell me what is wrong?"

Her gaze moved from Sandro to me, signaling that she wanted to share her burden but was unsure whether to reveal her problem in my presence. "You can speak, Francesca. This is my friend, Nico Argenti. I have known Nico since forever, you can trust him."

"Last night Salvatore Sporcone came here to speak with my father. His son was with him, the one they call Bruttono, big ugly one.'"

Sandro acknowledged to Francesca, "Yes, I know of Bruttono."

Then to me he explained, "He got the name from the scar that extends from above his ear to under his chin. He boasts that he got it in a brawl over a tavern girl. Others have said that he killed his adversary, but he was not punished for the crime because all the tavern patrons claimed they did not see what had happened."

Francesca spit out the words, "Bruttono is unpleasant in every respect, he looks slimy and slithers like a snake when he walks. He tried to take my hand, but I wouldn't let him come anywhere near me. I still shudder at the thought of him touching me."

She clasped her hands tightly together to dispel her stress before continuing. "The men exchanged only a few words before their voices became loud and angered. My father is a peaceful man who can broach any subject with calm deliberation. He never has outbursts like that. Whatever they were telling him upset him greatly. Although I have little insight into his business affairs, I know he is unhappy with the government and wants to press for changes. I am confident that he wants to do so by persuasion, it is the gift he has always relied upon. The Sporcone are despicable creatures who will do anything to have their way. I fear they are trying to entangle my father in one of their treacherous schemes. I barely slept last night thinking about that confrontation. It is not something I can ask father about. Whenever I broach difficult subjects with him, all he ever says is not to worry."

Sandro asked, "Could you hear what they were saying?"

"No, all I heard clearly was one of the Sporcones bellowing 'we must get rid of him.' He repeated it over and over, louder each time."

When it became clear that she had nothing further to add I spoke, "Will the Sporcone be attending the meeting that your father is hosting next week?"

Francesca's head swung around to face me and her eyes bored in with a penetrating glare. She said nothing but her action and expression were clearly asking 'what do you know of my father's business affairs?'

To answer her unspoken question I explained, "My cousin, Donato Argenti, il Festatore, mentioned to me that he has been engaged by your father to arrange dinner for the meeting."

Her stare softened, but only slightly so Sandro explained further hoping to put her at ease. "As I said before, I've known Nico since we were both young boys. He recently graduated from the University of Bologna and has been appointed as a magistrate of a tribunale superiore."

Sandro exaggerated my status while cleverly avoiding the name of any specific tribunal by saying only that it is one of superior importance.

"I swear, Nico is a person of the highest integrity with no political ambitions. He will not betray your confidence."

If Sandro weren't destined to be a great artist he might enjoy a successful career as a politician. He can fabricate 'truth' effortlessly. His eloquent delivery had the desired effect of releasing the tension that gripped Francesca. She dispatched a servant to summon Luca's secretary. The secretary was unavailable, as he and Luca were in a business meeting elsewhere, but one of the assistants joined us to answer Francesca's questions. She asked if the Sporcone would be attending the forthcoming event.

At first, the assistant was reluctant to disclose details of Luca's affairs, but Francesca's rigid pose and penetrating stare reminded him that she is the mistress of the house.

"The Sporcones had been on the list of invitees. Then, just this morning, your father told us to remove their names, but it was too late, the invitations have already been issued."

After the assistant departed, I decided to share some of my information with Francesca. "On the night before last, the Milanese ambassador held a reception for Florentine bankers. You may already know this as your father was one of the guests.

At that reception there was vehement criticism of Piero de Medici with words that sounded like threats. Signor Sporcone was among the most vocal. If a threat is being concocted against the Medici there is a strong possibility that your father may come under additional pressures."

"My father has not told me of this. As I said, he always tries to shield me from business matters."

I had taken Francesca's earlier distress as a sign of weak character, but I was mistaken. She threw off all signs of emotional stress, stood erect with square shoulders and faced me with a severe and intense expression. She did not ask how I knew what had transpired at the Milanese embassy reception. She merely watched me keenly as if hoping that I might offer a way to keep her father from becoming involved in something he would regret - an unreasonable expectation of someone who is just a recent university graduate. Her hope stemmed from Sandro having overinflated my reputation.

The meeting arranged by Luca was an opportunity to learn more about the Sporcones. I could not masquerade as one of Donato's workers as I had done at the Milanese embassy. News travels quickly among the Florentine aristocrats, even minor items such as the names of applicants for guild membership. Sharp eyes would become suspicious if a guild candidate were refilling wine glasses and lurking within earshot of conversations intended to be private. Being recognized might jeopardize my career. I could not take such a significant risk. A possible alternative would be for

Francesca to observe their conversations, but how could I convince her to do so?

While I was still mulling ideas Francesca asked, "Sandro said you have influential contacts. How can that be, someone as young as you? Who are these contacts of yours?"

Her questions voiced a degree of skepticism, but they were actually a positive sign, an indication that under the right circumstances she might look to me as an ally.

I gave the best answer I could. "When my father was a magistrate on the Tribunale Esecutore I met many of his colleagues in the judiciary and the militia."

I would like to blame Sandro for being the bad influence that had me stretching the truth, but doing so would be unfair to him. At least my response was not distorted to total falsehood. My statement was true, although misleading as I had no contact with any of those men in the past decade. I decided not to reveal my one influential connection, Chancellor Scala.

To encourage her trust, I spoke as if we were already working together for a common purpose. "We need facts before we can enlist the help of my contacts. At the meeting your father is hosting, the guests may reveal information that can help us."

Either she found my words convincing, or she reached the same conclusion on her own: that she eavesdrop on the upcoming meeting, and we then decide together what action, if any, would be appropriate based on her findings. At that moment I felt sorry for her. She is a woman of high social standing, living in a vast palazzo with countless servants; yet in some respects, she is as isolated as if she were in prison. She is willing to rely on me only because she has no one else to trust.

"I will not be allowed to attend the meeting, but I can find reason to be in an adjacent room where it will be possible to hear their discussions. If the Sporcones are as loud as they were yesterday it will be easy for me to hear their every word."

"May I call upon you the morning after the meeting so we can decide how to proceed depending on what you learn?" I asked.

She nodded affirmatively.

"You must be careful, Francesca," I cautioned. "These are powerful men who could be dangerous if they feel threatened. Do nothing that might let them see you as a threat."

I left the palazzo when Sandro and Francesca resumed their discussion of his work on the Lippi painting. Francesca's mention of Salvatore Sporcone and his son had aroused my curiosity. I knew only that they are money changers, not bankers, but if they were conspiring to use violence then I should learn more about them.

Chapter 17 Wednesday, August 8, 1464

Money changers conduct their business along with other vendors at the Mercato Vecchio. Tables scattered throughout the piazza display a rich assortment of products, some made in Florentine shops, some carted daily to the city from local farms, and some items brought from exotic foreign lands. Money changers gather in one area under a covered arcade where each is granted space for a table or stall.

Every known coinage is auctioned by money changers who establish prices by shouting requests for bids from other dealers. At the busiest times, the sound can be deafening as they try to outshout each other with near-simultaneous requests. As I listened, one mousey person's high-pitched voice punched through the roar of all others as he repeatedly screeched appeals to buy gold doblas minted by the Kingdom of Castile. A column at the side of the arcade was an ideal vantage for observing transactions being done at the Sporcone table. From his scar I surmised that the big one was the son of Salvatore Sporcone, the one whom Francesca called Bruttono. Watching him as he moved about gave credence to her characterization of him as a snake. The father, Salvatore Sporcone, was not present and I did not recognize the other man at the Sporcone table, a younger man of small stature, possibly another of Salvatore's sons.

The transaction was telling because a customer who had just made his way to the Sporcone table had no money to exchange. After a brief conversation, a quiet one in contrast with the boisterous activities at other tables, the customer signed a document and then walked away with a bag of coins. Money changers are permitted to exchange currencies and to issue letters of credit, but guild regulations forbid them from making loans which are the exclusive province of the bankers. Although bankers and money changers belong to the same guild, the activities of money changers are restricted.

Unscrupulous money changers, including the Sporcones, have been known to flaunt guild rules by making loans to desperate clients who, for lack of creditworthiness, are not able to get loans from the banks. Often their loans have interest rates so high that they violate the usury laws of the Republic and the dictates of the Church. Money changers judged guilty of violating usury laws have been sent to prison, and flagrant violators have even been banished from the Republic, but high profitability leads then to continue the illegal practice.

As I watched I observed that every transaction finished with the Sporcones retaining the signed contract. No papers were given to the borrowers that might implicate the Sporcone in any wrongdoing. If the Sporcones are making illegal loans, the evidence would be a written document. The difficulties would be in obtaining a contract and then using it as leverage to learn what the Sporcones are planning.

Another customer approached their stall and was also greeted by Bruttono. The other Sporcone, the small one, stood unobtrusively in the background and said nothing. Bruttono became upset by whatever this customer was telling him. I was too far away to hear their exchange, but suddenly Bruttono grabbed the man's tunic and pulled him close. Bruttono's hand closed into a fist ready to strike the man until he noticed his action had attracted the attention of everyone in the arcade.

Onlookers fell silent and stared at him. He released the man who slumped backward, struck a chair, and then fell to the floor. Bruttono's face reddened as he stormed off muttering to himself. His tightly clenched fists waved through the air as his arms swung rapidly up and down. Those around him took the display in stride as though they had seen similar behavior before, while others moved aside to avoid becoming a target of his anger. With all eyes on Bruttono, the customer slipped away unnoticed.

The other Sporcone, a frail figure, reacted as though the outburst had not happened. He moved to the table, picked up one of the documents, and began copying information into a ledger. Later, Bruttono returned to the stall and immediately started criticizing the smaller man as a brutish older brother might belittle a younger sibling. This time he combined a mixture of gestures, arms waving, table pounding, and verbal abuse to emphasize his dissatisfaction with his companion, but Bruttono's antics had little effect on his victim, who had become immune to such frequent harsh treatment.

I watched for nearly an hour, then at the end of the business day, Bruttono suddenly left the stall and the Mercato and disappeared without a word to his haggard stall-mate. Later when all other money changers closed their positions the younger Sporcone closed his as well and, clutching the ledger and loose papers to his chest with both hands, he ambled, with his head hung down, to Via delle Cipolle and followed it in the same direction that Bruttono had gone earlier. I needed to learn more about this young Sporcone.

Chapter 18

Bartolomeo Scala had invited Simone and me to be his guests for dinner at a small tavern in San Lorenzo Parish. Many years ago Bartolomeo had spent a year as an envoy to the royal court in Vienna where he developed a taste for Austrian sausages and ales, so he was delighted when a Florentine tavern owner married the widow of a Bavarian brewmaster because the woman knew her late husband's methods for making beer and ale. To honor his new wife and her brewing skill, the tavern owner changed the name of his establishment to Halbmond, a German word meaning 'crescent moon.' The owner claims the crescent shape resembles his wife's birthmark that he had the pleasure of discovering on his wedding night.

The owner's wife supervised the kitchen where beer battered bread, German sausages, and other featured offerings were prepared. She also oversaw the small brewery that was housed in a separate building behind the tavern. It took time for native

Florentines to accept the new German fare, but it became instantly popular among the small community of immigrants from the Germanic kingdoms to the North.

Many of us Florentines love strolling the streets of our city at dusk after the August heat has released its grip on the city. Sounds fill every vicolo as people flow from their homes to share greetings in the fresh evening air. The sun had already sunk below the western city wall when I turned onto a lightly traveled road and headed toward the two lanterns hung alongside the entrance to the Halbmond. It is one of the few establishments in that quarter of the city that is open at that hour. The other shops along the small street, two cobblers, a bakery, and a butcher, were already shuttered for the evening.

As I pulled open the Halbmond's heavy door, I was struck immediately by the smoky essence of grilled sausage and the sweet aroma of yeasty ale. The latest trend among Florentine taverns is toward dim interiors lit only by a thin scattering of candles, but Halbmond did not follow this trend. It was brightly lit by lanterns hanging from wooden ceiling beams. Above each lantern was a polished metal disk that reflected light downward toward the patrons seated below. It made for a pleasant environment where patrons can see their food and don't feel that they are hiding from others.

More than half of the tables were filled and judging from their animated behavior all the patrons were enjoying the food, their dining experiences, and each other. Their conversation was lively, but not boisterous, and much of it was in German. A motherly waitress, her hair tied in a bun, smiled and called 'Willkommen' to me as she passed by carrying four tankards of ale to a nearby table.

Scala was seated alone at an isolated table in a rear corner of the room. In front of him stood a tall pewter tankard overflowing with foamy ale. Behind him the wall held an image of a snow-capped mountain, a generic painting made in the Alps, but whether it was Bavaria, Austria, or the Italian Alps was impossible to know. Simone's absence was not surprising because Scala wanted to have a private discussion with me before Simone joined us. Since Simone is not familiar with the city, I was concerned about how he would be able to find Halbmond. Scala allayed my worry by explaining, "Simone became intrigued by an unusual case that the Signoria has been deliberating. He was so fascinated by it that I arranged for him to remain at the Palazzo della Signoria today so he could have more time to study all the evidence. As you told me, he is a brilliant student; maybe he will even have an insight into something that we overlooked. One of the Chancery clerks will escort Simone here shortly. In the meantime, we can talk."

I pulled a chair out from the table and was about to be seated when the waitress crossed to our table. She appraised me quickly then said something in German to Scala who nodded in agreement and replied, "Ja, sehr gut. Danke."

Turning to me she asked in Italian with a strong German

accent, "What would you like?" The corners of her mouth were slightly upturned giving her face an unforgettable smile, and as she spoke a small mole on her chin danced up and down.

While at the university I had occasionally joined Viennese students who frequented the sole tavern in Bologna that offered German fare. On every visit, the students chose a different style of beer or ale from among the tavern's broad menu and then regaled me with tales how much of that particular kind they had consumed as undergraduates in Vienna. Those Viennese are among the happiest and most fun-loving characters I have known, and I thoroughly enjoyed their company, but they failed to turn me into a beer aficionado. Although ale is refreshing on a hot summer day, it is too bold and brash for my taste, like a crude loud-mouthed relative. I prefer instead the sweetness of cool fresh fruit juice in the morning and a fine cultured Italian wine in the evening. But to be hospitable I acceded to the spirit of the establishment, gestured toward Scala's drink, and said, "I'll have the same."

Upon hearing my reply her mouth curled more into a genuine smile, she winked at Scala and set down in front of me the tankard of ale she had carried to our table. Scala smiled too. "She makes a game of trying to guess what people will ask for. You made it easy for her."

We had much to discuss before Simone joined us, so keeping in character the Chancellor spent no more time on pleasantries after the waitress left us. He began with the most straightforward matter. "I had a brief encounter today with a consul of the Magistrates guild who told me it will take longer than usual for your membership application to be processed. The delay is no reflection on you and nothing to be concerned about. Two of the consuls are on holiday, one in Savoy and the other in Castile."

Shaking his head to emphasize his disbelief he added, "Why anyone would visit Castile in August is beyond my understanding. The Kingdom is pleasant in the cooler months, but in August it is like an oven. Both men are due to return in eight days. Guild rules would permit the remaining consuls to act on membership applications but as a courtesy, they will not act until their colleagues return. Whenever possible they prefer for all selected candidates to have the unanimous approval of the consuls."

"Is it possible that they will have pressing matters waiting that must be addressed when they return causing my application to be delayed even further?" I asked.

"There is little doubt that matters needing immediate attention will be waiting when they return, but those should not add to the delay. Your application has been reviewed already making acceptance by the full suite of consuls a mere formality. In all likelihood, the two absent consuls will never even see your application.

"Your next step is to select from among the appointments that may be offered to you. One of my clerks is searching out all the vacancies. You know that First Chancellor Accolti and I would be delighted if your choice of magisterial appointment is closely associated with Chancery, but in many ways your first appointment will shape your entire career. This will be one of the most important decisions of your life so you must consider every opportunity," he said.

"When I have the full accounting of vacancies I will forward them to you. I am confident that every tribunal and commission having a vacancy will view your application favorably, so the final selection will largely fall to you. The delay in approving your application is fortunate because it gives you more time to consider all the possibilities."

Chapter 19

With that topic completed, Scala quickly moved the discussion in a different direction. "This morning I paid a visit to an old friend of mine, Gentile Becchi. Do you know him?"

"As I recall he is the tutor of young Lorenzo de Medici."

"That is but one of his many endeavors. He is also a canon of the church administering the Florentine diocese for the archbishop. I called upon him to see if he could tell me about bishop Contino, one of the foreigners you encountered at the Milanese embassy reception.

"Signor Becchi told me that Contino's claims of being an envoy of the Papal Curia are untrue. He said that Contino is a minor official in the government of the Papal States, but he is not assigned to foreign missions on their behalf. He is, instead, acting on behalf of a sect that calls itself the Priors of Constantine."

I closed my eyes and tried to recall a discussion from one of my classes. When the memory returned, I said, "The Priors of

Constantine were mentioned briefly in a class on religious practices. If I remember correctly, the group was started in the 1200s when the Moors were expelled from Sicily."

Scala looked doubtful and gave a non-committal shrug.

"That is one belief. My belief is that the origin of the Priors remains a mystery as is their membership, but their mission is clear, to inflict pain and punishment on sinners, and they are prepared to go to any length to achieve their goal."

"The Holy Father must know of their existence. Do they operate with his blessing?" I asked.

"Yes and no. The Holy Father certainly does not condone their methods, but the consequences of their actions are usually favorable to the Papal States, so they are tolerated."

"Signor Becchi did not know why Contino is in Florence meeting with a representative of Milan. He is as concerned about Contino's presence in Florence as am I. He did give me one bit of information that may prove useful: the Priors all wear similar rings so they can identify each other. The rings are made from braided strands of silver and gold. On the top is a silver oval and set into the oval is a gold Constantine Cross. Becchi is certain that no priests in the churches of his diocese wear the ring, but there are many monasteries in the diocese and a ring is easily hidden under a monk's robe."

"Last year one of the Roman students at the university told us of an official in Rome who was killed, found in his office hanging from a ceiling beam. Embossed in his forehead was an oval containing an image of the Constantine cross.

"Many such stories circulate among the students and there is no way to tell which of them are true. I did not give much credence to that story at the time."

Scala paused then said, "That sounds like the work of the Priors. They must have believed the Roman official to be guilty of a serious offense against God."

Scala said nothing of the other foreigner, the Neapolitan, whom I had seen at the reception. I felt it could be impertinent of me to question him, but my curiosity overcame discretion and I asked if he had identified the man. He took no offense at my questioning.

"As you suspected, he is an envoy of the Kingdom of Naples. Lately, Neapolitan and Genovese ships have been squabbling over fishing rights. Neither side wants to break the peace, but the conflicts are becoming more frequent. Naples hopes to use its influence with Ambassador di Pontremoli to gain Milan as an ally. The envoy is in Florence specifically to meet with the ambassador. It would have been an affront not to invite him to the reception."

In a crisper tone Scala added, "However, the envoy should have reported his presence in Florence to the Chancery. We will be filing an official protest with the Kingdom. Nothing serious, just a slap on the hand to let them know we are aware of their actions."

Scala changed the direction of our conversation. "Simone told me that you were invited to visit the Pitti estate. It is a magnificent structure. Did you accept the invitation?"

"I did visit the estate. The gardens are certainly beautiful; however, I did not have the opportunity to see the inside of the palace. The invitation was not from a member of the Pitti family, but from an artist friend of mine, Sandro Botticelli; do you know him?"

"I have heard the name, that is all."

I described Sandro's relationship with maestro Fra Filippo Lippi and Sandro's purpose in being at the Pitti estate. "As Sandro was showing me the gardens and the work he was doing on the portrait of Francesca Pitti, she joined us in the garden. I was surprised by her strong convictions and her willingness to share her beliefs candidly. She worries that her father will be drawn into the current political turmoil."

"Your assessment of Francesca is correct. She is an impressive woman with a broad knowledge including matters that are usually kept hidden from unmarried young women. I have known her since birth and watched her grow into a remarkable woman whose candor is always refreshing. She has many talents. She accomplishes much and does it in a straightforwardly manner. Others, both men and women, who underestimated her abilities have regretted their poor judgment."

"She told me that Salvatore Sporcone and his son paid a visit to her father, and she didn't mask her feelings when speaking of them. I believe her word for Salvatore was 'despicable,' and her words for the son were even stronger. She never mentioned the son's name. She only referred to him as Bruttono."

Scala startled at my mention of the name Bruttono. "I am surprised that a proper woman like Francesca would use that derogatory name," he laughed. "No, I am not surprised. For any other woman it would be surprising, but with Francesca nothing can be unexpected,"

"The one known as Bruttono is the oldest of Salvatore's three sons. His family and business associates call him by his given name, Alphonso, but to everyone else he is Bruttono."

I told Scala of signor Sporcone's anger, and his implied threat "we must get rid of him," and of Francesca's fear that her father would become trapped in an insidious plot. "The Sporcones will be among those attending a gathering tomorrow evening at the Pitti estate. Francesca believes she may be able to overhear information about any scheme if indeed there is one. She has agreed to meet with me the following morning to share whatever information she discovers."

Scala's expression stiffened, "I would never have asked for your help in observing guests at the Milanese embassy reception if I thought it could put you in danger. The information that you obtained will be of great value when combined with material from other sources. From what you are telling me, I fear that your collaboration with Francesca could put you both at risk. The men meeting with Luca Pitti are dangerous. The Chancery and the Guardia have agents who are trained to deal with danger. You and Francesca are not. I urge you to step away."

I nodded, to show that I heard his plea, but Scala probably interpreted the nod as an indication that I would do as he suggested.

I had intended to tell Scala of my surveillance of the Sporcones at the Mercato, and my belief that their violation of guild regulations, and possibly of usury laws, might give leverage to uncovering a more sinister plot. Scala's warning gave me reason to withhold that thinking from him.

At that moment the tavern door swung open and an ebullient Simone Pisani flowed in like a Spring breeze. He came directly to our table, grasped the Chancellors hand, and thanked him profusely for the opportunity to observe the Signoria in closed session. It is a privilege rarely afforded to a foreigner.

Taking hold of the Chancellor's hand was a breach of social etiquette that would have offended many of Scala's stature, but Scala welcomed it as a sign of friendship. His position doesn't let him make many friends.

Simone dropped into a chair and immediately began recounting his experience. "Listening to the proceedings it struck me that Florence and Venice have similar laws, but our governments are very different."

Scala smiled, pleased that Simone found the day's activities so stimulating. "What differences do you see as significant?" Scala asked.

"The biggest difference, it seems to me, is that members of our Council of Ten are only allowed to serve a single term in office.

That keeps them from selling favors to gain re-election. I don't see what prevents members of your Signoria from using corrupt means to remain in power."

Scala responded, "A very astute observation. You found no mechanism, Simone, because there is none. Ideally, all elected to the Signoria are committed to the prosperity of the Republic, but there are those, and I am one, who believe it is naive to think that none of the members are self-serving. Long tenures in office can turn men into tyrants. Perhaps one day we will amend our constitution to eliminate that possibility."

Chapter 20 Thursday, August 9,1464

All members of the Argenti household awoke in cheerful spirits despite the gray morning sky and steady drizzle. A cold wind-driven November rain might have upset our plans, but the light August drizzle did not dampen our enthusiasm. Every Thursday morning Donato dispatched a wagon to fetch casks of wine from his father's vineyard near Fiesole. This week we each had our own reasons for wanting to make the trip to the vineyard. By the time we finished breakfast the rain had lessened to hardly more than a mist. We were confident that our hooded oilskin cloaks would keep us dry during the journey.

Giorgio was always eager to make the trip and would do so whenever he had no schoolwork nor household chores to finish. The big attraction for him was that the wagon master let him handle the reins once they reached the open road outside the city. It was a new accomplishment for the young boy this year, one he boasted about to his friends. On this morning he was denied the privilege because rain had fallen steadily throughout the night making the road muddy, demanding a skill beyond Giorgio's ability to keep the wagon from bogging in deep ruts.

My motivation was to visit with uncle Nunzio whom I had not seen in more than a year. For a short time after he transferred ownership of the Uccello to his son, Nunzio returned to Florence frequently following his fatherly instinct of offering help and advice even when they weren't needed. Gradually Nunzio admitted to himself that Donato ran the club better he had, and his absences from the city grew longer.

Two years ago he decided to try growing a tasty variety of Greek olive in a small orchard adjacent to his vineyard. He learned of a widow living in Florence who had worked in an olive orchard on the Greek island of Samos. Nunzio hired the woman, Lexia, and every day she traveled from the city to his estate to instruct the field hands. Eventually Lexia ended her daily commutes by moving into the villa with uncle Nunzio. Since then he rarely traveled to Florence.

Alessa and Simone, the other members of our entourage, planned to visit the farm briefly then continue on to the nearby hilltop town of Fiesole. At breakfast, Alessa enthusiastically described the historic town to Simone, who listened intently to her narration.

"In my village in Morocco," she recounted, "we knew nothing of our history. There are ruins in the hills near my village, but no one knows anything of the people who lived in the ruins or when they lived there. Italians know everything about their history. They know the Etruscans built a walled city at Fiesole long before Rome was founded."

Alessa punctuated the statement by raising her arms in an emphatic gesture. She must have learned the gesture from the Neopolitan sea captain because Moroccans were not given to such displays.

"Italians have written history, and that seems wonderful to me because in my village our beliefs came only from legends told by the old ones. As a child listening to the old ones tell their stories, I wondered how much of what the legends say is true."

"Does anything remain of the Etruscans at Fiesole?" Simone asked.

"Yes, we will see both Etruscan and Roman ruins. I am bringing a lunch so we can spend the entire day exploring the sites," Alessa answered, packing bread and cheese into her basket.

Uncle Nunzio's villa sits on a bluff almost halfway up the long road leading to Fiesole. Dozens of villas and vineyards like his dot the hillside. Some are estates owned by the wealthy men of Florence, men like Cosimo de Medici. His villa hangs at the edge of a cliff near Fiesole where it commands an unrivaled view of Florence and the Arno valley below. Before he was exiled, Dante Alighieri owned a villa in that valley.

The appearance of Uncle Nunzio's villa is like many others, with white stucco facades and a red tile roof. One difference is that he had his house constructed in the style of the ancient Romans with two wings separated by an enclosed peristyle.

By the time we reached his villa, the rain had stopped entirely, and the dark clouds were thinning revealing patches of blue above. From the farm road we noticed that a table and chairs had been set out on the terrace. As we drew closer, we saw the assortment of fruits and tasty pastries on the table awaiting our arrival.

Giorgio jumped from the wagon and darted to the terrace. He paused for an instant to give his grandfather a quick hug before turning his attention to the delicious treats. The rest of us followed Giorgio's lead, but at a slower pace. When everyone was sufficiently refreshed, uncle Nunzio gave us a tour of the farm, first leading us along a pathway to the highest point of the estate. Even though walking was difficult for him, he struggled until he reached the very end of the path driven by pride and a desire to show us the entire expanse of crops that stretched into the distance. Below us were countless rows of gray-green leaves in delicate hues that delight artists like Sandro. Uncle Nunzio reached into a vine-covered trellis and freed a bunch of pale green grapes that he passed to us.

"Here on these upper slopes are Trebbiano grapes for our white wines. Trebbiano is not native to this area. These plants were brought here from the island of Cyprus. Although they are not native, they are a hearty plant that grows well in this soil."

He pointed down the slope. "Those are Sangiovese grapes for our red wines. Sangiovese is native to this area. Some folks believe the name is from the Etruscan words 'San Jove' meaning blood of their god Jove. If you look carefully, you can see a difference in color between the leaves of the Trebbiano and the Sangiovese vines."

Directing his attention to Simone he pointed toward a distant vineyard and explained, "When I bought this land it was just open farmland. My brother, Nico's father, and I bought adjoining parcels. My brother bought the land on the far side of the pond, that land now belongs to Nico. It is his father's legacy. My people work the vineyards and the income goes into a trust that Nico's father set up for him. The trust paid for Nico's tutors and for the university."

After the tour, Simone and Alessa borrowed two horses so they could ride to Fiesole, and Giorgio went off to investigate a newborn lamb, giving me an opportunity to talk with Nunzio, the uncle who is like a father to me.

Nunzio listened attentively as I described my recent discussions with Bartolomeo Scala. "If I did not know you better, Nico, I would think that you are asking my advice to help you decide, but I do know you. Whether you realize it or not, you have already made a decision. So, are you telling me this only to make conversation with an old man, or are you looking for my approval?"

"I suppose you are right, I have made a decision and I am hoping that you approve."

"My approval is of no consequence. Any doubts you hold cannot be eased by my words. There are two kinds of knowledge: the kind taught at the university, and practical knowledge that is only taught by experience. All you can do is choose a path. In time you will know if it is the right path for you. If it is not the right one, you will find another path to follow."

I said nothing for a few minutes, recalling words that Bartolomeo Scala had used: "We can read what the great philosophers have written, but in the end, each of us must formulate our own philosophy, and creating a philosophy to guide us through life is not easily done."

I then described my session with Francesca Pitti and my observation of the Sporcone business dealings at the Mercato Vecchio. When I mentioned Salvatore Sporcone, Nunzio interrupted me, "Signorina Pitti speaks the truth. Salvatore Sporcone is a vicious person, and his son Alphonso is worse. Be very careful in dealing with them.

"The young person with Alphonso Sporcone was his younger brother Jacopo," Nunzio explained. "Jacopo is the only smart one in that family, and there is a reason why he is not like the others. When Jacopo was about five years old, a servant in the Sprocone house won a large sum of money on a horse race during the San Giovanni festival. To celebrate his winnings the servant went from one wine bar to another telling all of his good fortune and sampling the finest wines at each tavern. The wine made him talk, and one thing he talked about was the affair between Salvatore's wife and Alphonso's tutor. He said the affair started before Jacopo was born and went on for years. He told everyone Salvatore was blind to it the whole time."

Uncle Nunzio took a raspberry pastry from the tray, brushed it with honey, and took a bite. As he chewed, I could tell he was replaying the story in his mind to be sure his recounting to me would be accurate.

"When Salvatore learned what the servant had said he was furious. His anger became uncontrollable when he learned further that the young boy, Jacopo, was not his son but a product of the illicit affair. Later, the gardener who had witnessed Salvatore's outrage said that Salvatore reached for the nearest object, a sculpted bust of Hercules, lofted it above his head, and hurled it in the direction of the servant. It barely missed the cowering man, crashed against a wall, and shattered to pieces. The statue, fashioned by a famous Greek sculptor, had been a favorite piece in Salvatore's collection.

"The servant ran from the room fearing for his life. That night his beaten and bloodied body was discovered in an alley. That same night both the tutor and Salvatore's wife disappeared. Salvatore claimed the adulterers fled to the South, he did not know where and he did not care as long as they never returned.

"A short time later the parish priest who was Salvatore's confessor was sent away from Florence. Word spread throughout his parish that the priest refused to give absolution because Salvatore would not confess his actions. Salvatore pressured the archbishop into replacing the priest. Salvatore claimed he had nothing to confess, that he was not guilty - 'to God and the Holy Mother, I swear it.' Of course, this is just hearsay, and the truth may never be known."

I sprang up from my chair, propelled by my uncle's account, and paced across the terrace. I threw my arms into the air, exasperated to think that any person could behave as Salvatore had. Gradually my composure returned. I turned back toward uncle Nunzio and said, "Surely there must have been an investigation by the Guardia."

"There was an investigation, but it wasn't worth sheep dip. The investigator said the servant was killed by a foreigner who stole the gambling winnings and then fled the city. The Guardia never questioned Sporcone about the disappearance of his wife or the tutor. At the time they had no reason to suspect that the sudden absence of the wife and the tutor was a crime."

He continued the story, "The investigation ended quickly, and a short time later the officer in charge of the investigation moved out of the dingy rooms he had been renting and into a large house. He is now a captain in the Guardia with a farm in Prato as well as a house in the city. Many in the Guardia were surprised by his sudden success."

From the edge of the terrace I walked back to my chair and sank into it.

"What about the boy, Jacopo?" I asked. "What happened to him? Why didn't his mother take him with her if she truly went to Rome? No mother would leave her child behind."

"It is a mystery. Many believe the woman and her lover did not travel south as Salvatore claims, but instead that they met the same fate as the servant only their bodies were never found. We may never know the truth."

Uncle Nunzio rose and motioned for me to follow. We strolled from the terrace and crossed the grassy field adjacent to the villa. When we reached a row of vines he continued.

"Salvatore could not let it be known that the child was not his, so he kept Jacopo as his own, but the boy was not treated like the other sons. He was made to work hard with no rewards for his efforts. In time the boy displayed skill with numbers, which Salvatore uses to advantage. Jacopo was never tutored nor did he attend school; yet he is the one who does all the accounting for the family businesses."

After uncle Nunzio had finished speaking, I began telling him what I had seen of the Sporcones at the Mercato, and of my belief that they were making loans illegally. Based on what uncle knew of the Sporcones, he said my conclusion seemed plausible.

My mind raced to combine what I already knew with the information uncle Nunzio had just given me. "Do you believe Jacopo knows the story you told me about the fate of his mother and his real father?"

"I am sure he does not," Nunzio answered. "Salvatore certainly would not tell him, and Salvatore would punish anyone who did."

The epithet Francesca overheard, 'we must get rid of him,' kept running through my thoughts. If Salvatore and Alphonso do intend violence against someone, Jacopo may have overheard their planning. They would have no reason to hide their plans from him. There is no one he could tell. He has no friends. And if he knew the truth about his parents, vengeance might make him willing to reveal their plan. But I cannot be the one to tell him about his parents. Jacopo would not believe the story if he heard it from a stranger.

"Is there anyone who could tell Jacopo the truth? Anyone he would believe?" I asked.

"There is one person, Sister Teresa at the convent of San Giuseppe. Jacopo's mother had a difficult birth and needed asistance caring for her newborn. She asked for help, and the church agreed to let Sister Teresa stay at the Sporcone compound after Jacopo was born. She loved the infant and returned to the Sporcone house to care for Jacopo again after his mother disappeared. In that house she was the only person who ever cared for the poor boy.

"I say again, Nico, Salvatore is a vicious person. The first time his secret was disclosed a man was brutally killed. Two others may have been killed as well. If that secret is dredged up again, Salvatore's hatred may boil once more. You must not do anything foolish."

My mouth spoke the words "I understand, uncle," while my thoughts said, "If I can learn the target of Salvatore's plot then Chancellor Scala should be able to arrange protection for the intended victim."

Chapter 21

Lexia approached the terrace on a path leading from the newly planted olive orchard where she was consulting with the master gardener about irrigation of the young olive trees. As she reached the terrace, I noticed that she was much younger than uncle Nunzio. Her tan face, almost chestnut brown, was smooth and radiant with no hint of age, not even a wrinkle around her hazel eyes. She walked with firm even steps and the erect bearing of a farmer proud to be raising bounty from the land. Her long brown hair bounced against her shoulders in cadence with her pace. Her snow-white apron remained spotless, untainted by her morning spent laboring in the orchard. Under the apron was a tunic like those worn by others working in the orchard, but hers, unlike theirs, was neither ill-fitting nor soiled.

Climbing to the terrace, she crossed behind the serving table. She paused briefly, considered a tray filled with peaches and plums, but opted instead for a glass of lemon water. When Lexia reached for a chair, intending to pull it closer so she could sit with us, uncle Nunzio tapped the edge of his reclining couch. She took his cue and sat on the couch near him. He bent and kissed her on the forehead.

Uncle Nunzio took her hand and said, “Cara mia, Nico wants to learn about the Sporcone. Tell him what your son heard about them.”

With Lexia there are no short stories. Her tales are always embellished with details. Is that her own unique style, or is it a trait shared by all Greeks?

Lexia's face showed a flash of disgust upon hearing the Sporcone name. “At the age of ten my son Demetrios was apprenticed to a master goldsmith, a wonderful man who taught my son well. My son learned his craft so well that when we came to Florence from Greece it was easy for him to find work at one of the jewelry shops on the Ponte Vecchio. He went to work at Mondo d’Oro, World of Gold. The shop owner was happy to have him. He is their best designer, the only one who does the miniatures.

“My son works long hours toiling over tiny gold ornaments, so at the end of the day he stops at a local tavern to relax and share drinks with other working men. Last week two men he had never seen before came to the tavern. They were loud, they complained about everything, and they argued with each other. They annoyed everyone so my son and the others didn't stay long. Before Demetrios finished his drink, he heard one of the men mocking his companion saying he was the number one because he had been chosen by the boss to fetch Lo Spruzzatore from Pisa. After the two men left the bar, the bartender told Demetrios that the two work for Alphonso Sporcone."

I looked from Lexia to uncle Nunzio as I puzzled, "Lo Spruzzatore, would mean someone who dusts or sprinkles. That doesn't make any sense."

"No, it doesn't unless Lo Spruzzatore has a slang meaning," Uncle Nunzio suggested. "Your friend Signor Scala has a friend who teaches linguistics at the university here in Florence. He might know if Lo Spruzzatore has other meanings. People in the South often use words in different ways from us."

"I can't ask the Chancellor about a name. He has gone to Genoa and I don't know when he will return."

"One of Scala's friends, Carlo Marsuppini, still teaches at the university," Nunzio continued. "Marsuppini was one of Scala's teachers when Scala was a student there. Scala once called him a world champion puzzle master, and that is high praise coming from Scala. You could go visit Marsuppini yourself. If he can't help you, perhaps he can refer you to someone who can."

"Have you ever met him, this professor?" I asked.

"I met him once at a lecture given by Scala. Scala was invited by Cosimo de Medici to lecture on the poet Virgil. Marsuppini was in the audience. He cast himself in the role of an examiner by putting his former student, Scala, to the test with an endless stream of questions. He beamed every time Scala answered his question correctly. Later Marsuppini told someone 'as it should be, the student has surpassed the teacher.'"

Lexia, who had gone into the house earlier, rejoined us carrying a freshly baked apricot tort. The inviting aroma of the pastry ended our conversation. As she cut a generous slice for each of us, uncle Nunzio declared, "In addition to her other talents Lexia is a great cook. Her secret is the Greek tradition of adding ouzo to everything."

"The secret of this recipe," she corrected, "is a honey butter glaze spread as soon as the tort comes from the oven." Then she laughed and added, "and a touch of ouzo in the filling."

After downing two slices of the tort and licking the last crumbs from my fingers, I turned to uncle Nunzio. "Did you know Scala well? What made him move from the academic world to government?"

"Actually, I only met Scala a few times. If you want to know about Scala, ask Marsuppini. He loves to talk so I'm sure he will be happy to tell you stories about Scala."

Donato's wagon master waved to me and called out that the wine and produce had been loaded aboard the wagon for transport to the Uccello. It was time for us to return to Florence. Giorgio was already seated alongside the wagon master, reins in hand, eager to drive the wagon now that rain had stopped and the muddy road had become firmer. I took another slice of apricot tort to enjoy on the journey, thanked Lexia and uncle Nunzio for their hospitality, and promised to visit them frequently now that I was back from Bologna.

Simone and Alessa had not returned from Fiesole. They might ride back to uncle Nunzio's later in the day and either return to Florence on another wagon headed to the city or spend the night at his villa. It would not be surprising, though, for them to watch the sunset from the hilltop vantage and then spend the night at one of the inns at Fiesole.

At the city gate, Giorgio stopped the wagon for the Guardia inspectors who examine all incoming cargo looking for taxable merchandise. Import duties are a major source of revenue for the city treasury. I took advantage of the lull, climbed down from the wagon, and congratulated Giorgio on his handling of the wagon on our return to the city. His desire to prove himself comes more from seeking his father's praise and the admiration of his friends than from any interest in becoming an able wagon master. After thanking Giorgio and the wagon master for the ride, I set off on foot for the Ponte Vecchio to speak with Lexia's son Demetrios.

Chapter 22

Mondo d'Oro is not the most productive gold brokerage on Ponte Vecchio. Rather than striving to sell a great many items, it built a reputation as the purveyor of the most exquisite quality jewelry, expertly crafted in gold of the highest purity. Initially, the owner relied on his own skill, which he gained as a teenager from a master goldsmith in Athens. After learning all that Athenian craftsman could offer, he journeyed to Egypt to acquire additional techniques from masters in Cairo and Alexandria.

Now, with an old man's eyesight, even his powerful magnifying lens cannot compensate for the wispy veils in his eyes that grow cloudier every year. Worse than the veils are the tremors of his hands that no device can suppress. So now he must rely on the skills of others.

His prayers were answered when Demetrios, a young Greek, entered his shop seeking work. "The young people of Florence expect instant success," the old man had said. "They are not willing to work hard to achieve a goal. It takes practice, many years of practice, to craft pieces that are truly art. Pieces their owners will treasure forever. I hope you will be different from them."

Demetrios proved that he was different. He was satisfied only when his newest creation was more perfect than the last. "He reminds me of myself when I was young," the owner told himself.

The old man was showing a selection of bracelets to a young couple when I entered his shop. Each one he set on the girl's wrist was beautiful with exquisite details. She was thoroughly enjoying the experience. No doubt she would find it a challenge to choose just a single piece. The sparkle in her eyes captivated her companion. If the price of the bangles were an issue for him, he did not show it.

At a bench toward the rear of the shop, a young man sat working on a gold medallion. He had the broad face of a Greek, bushy eyebrows, and the dark curly hair I had last seen on crew members of an Athenian merchant ship. Not wanting to interrupt his delicate engraving I watched silently. A minute later he held the medallion up so I could admire it. "I will make this into a brooch, a birthday gift for the wife of a customer. The image is of a farm near Lucca where she lived as a child."

He offered me a looking glass so I could examine the piece closely and motioned toward an easel behind the workbench that held the painting he was copying onto the gold medallion.

"I am not able to capture all the detail of the original in such a small scale," he said modestly.

"It looks perfect to me. Amazing. I am certain it will be a

treasure to the woman who receives it."

My words made him beam with satisfaction. Seeing that the old man was still occupied with the young couple, he asked, "How may I help you?"

"Are you Demetrios?"

He nodded. "I am."

"I am Nico Argenti. I just returned from my uncle Nunzio's vineyard where I met your mother. She sends her greeting. I am seeking information and she said you might be able to help me. Is there a time when we can talk? Perhaps after the close of business I can meet you."

"We can talk now. With intricate designs such as this piece, my hands must rest frequently, or they cannot hold the stylus steady. Let us go outside. We can walk along the river while you tell me what information you seek."

We joined the parade of others who were enjoying a relaxing stroll on the path that tracks the course of the Arno. There are rumors, I told Demetrios, that the Sporcone might use illegal means to advance their standing - there was no reason to share the entire complexity of the situation with him. "Your mother told me of a conversation you overheard among two of Sporcone's people. She thought you might remember their words. Can you tell me what was said?"

"I sometimes go to a nearby tavern after work to relax. The owner is a Greek, so they have Tsipouro, the Greek brandy. No other tavern in Florence serves it. That is only one attraction of that tavern. Another is the daughter of the barista, mmmmm.

"Two men were standing at the far end of the bar when I arrived. I had never seen them at that tavern before, and they are not easily forgotten. They were loud and obnoxious and did not care that they were disturbing everyone else. One kept bragging to his companion that he was chosen to bring Lo Spruzzatore to meet with Alphonso."

"Your mother told me that, but we do not understand what is meant by Lo Spruzzatore. Did they say anything to indicate its meaning?"

"They both seemed to know the word, so they gave no explanation. It means nothing to me," Demetrios replied.

"Did they say when Lo Spruzzatore will arrive, or where from?"

"They did not say when, but the one doing the talking said he was going to bring Lo Spruzzatore to meet with Alphonso at il melo gallegiante."

Seeing my confusion he said, "That makes no sense to me either. I know of no place called the floating apple."

Speaking slowly as I formed the thought in my own mind, I pondered, "Is it possible he meant il molo gallegiante, the floating dock, instead of il melo gallegiante."

"Yes, that's possible. They spoke with thick accents from somewhere in the South so they might have said molo rather that melo, and I misunderstood them. Does that have meaning to you?"

I brightened. "I know an inn by that name on the Arno river not far from the town of Empoli. I stayed there once to meet a friend who was traveling from La Spezia to Rome. The inn takes its name from a unique dock built for them by a young engineer from Siena. The dock not only floats higher when the river floods from the Spring rains, but it also moves to stay in position alongside the bank as the river widens. In late Summer when the river dries, the dock descends and also moves outward from the bank to stay at the edge of the narrow river current. The clever design makes it possible for barges to load and unload at the dock at any time of year."

I paused when I noticed Demetrios looking at me with a bemused expression. He laughed, "You seem to find that dock very intriguing."

"Forgive me for getting distracted, Demetrios, but I was so impressed when I learned about the mechanism that moves the dock that I actually sought out the engineer who designed it on one of my visits to Siena."

Returning to the subject at hand I said, "If Alphonso Sporcone is going to receive Lo Spruzzatore at il molo gallegiante, then it must certainly be at this inn because there is nothing else like it."

Demetrios wondered aloud, "But why would Signor Sporcone go to an inn at a small town for the meeting rather than bringing Lo Spruzzatore to Florence?"

"That is an excellent question," I replied. "Perhaps the final destination is not Florence. The inn is located where several roads meet and cross the river. Anyone arriving from Pisa either by river barge or by the Via Pisana road could continue to Florence, or head north toward Lucca and from there across the Alps to Paris, or he could go south to Siena and then to Rome."

My answer to Demetrios' query listed a number of possible destinations, but it did not answer the fundamental question. The Sporcones want to advance their stature in Florence, so what purpose can be served by bringing something, or someone, to a different destination?

Demetrios reversed direction and returned to Mondo d'Oro. I sat on a stone bench and gazed out at the river watching ripples in the slowly flowing water and thinking about my conversation with Demetrios. He provided me with another bit of information, but I parted from him even more confused than when I had arrived. I still did not know the implication of Lo Spruzzatore, and now I had another mystery to add: What was Alphonso's destination if not Florence?

Chapter 23 Friday, August 10, 1464

Even though classes were not in session during the summer holiday, I believed that professor Marsuppini might be at the university. Younger faculty members generally left the city during their holiday to escape the summer heat, but the old ones, those of Marsuppini's generation, tended to remain at the school. They found it more difficult to endure travel than heat.

The University of Florence was not a prosperous school. It had no large campus like the University of Bologna. It consisted of only a few modest buildings surrounding a small central piazza. The Signoria had been so miserly with funding that the university was forced to close for extended periods. That was unfortunate because the school had an excellent, although small, faculty and had graduated accomplished scholars in a wide range of disciplines.

My assumption that there would not be students at the university proved to be wrong. When I arrived there were students everywhere, sitting by themselves and in groups, studying, talking, and merely relaxing under trees and in the shade of buildings. My belief that students abandon schools in summer had been formed by my experience at Bologna. As the world's premier law school, Bologna attracted students from everywhere: Greece, Turkey, France, and even from as far away as England. All the foreign students looked forward to returning home during the summer holiday. At the University of Florence the students were mostly Florentines. They had no reason to travel because they were already at home.

Near the central piazza of the small campus, a large chestnut tree gathered students in its welcoming shade. I passed the musicians, the orators, and those enjoying afternoon naps until I spotted one student carrying a folio of Seneca's essays. If anyone knew where to find professor Marsuppini it would be this student of the great Roman philosopher. Uncle Nunzio had told me that Marsuppini's specialty was philosophy.

Following the student's directions, I entered an arched passageway into one of the oldest buildings. The dim light of the narrow archway revealed only that its gray stucco walls needed repair and its floor needed sweeping. The passage led to the rear of the structure where it angled sharply to the right and opened into a large and unexpectedly well-lit reading room.

I paused at the room's entrance to orient myself and to let my eyes adjust to the sudden brightness. Maps covered one wall. Shelves covering the other walls held a collection of books, and in each corner a pedestal held the bust of an intellectual giant: Dante, Virgil, Cicero, and Petrarch. A writer, a poet, an orator, and a scholar. Two Florentines and two ancient Romans. A suitably diverse choice.

Several well-worn tables were positioned haphazardly throughout the room. Young people, obviously students, conversed quietly in small groups at several of the tables. At one table sat a lone gray-haired figure wearing the black robe and yellow sash of a professor. His appearance matched perfectly with the description that uncle Nunzio had given me. Even during summer holiday, Marsuppini did not abandon the formal trappings of his position. Spread before him were an assortment of open books. I watched for several minutes as he read a short passage from one book, moved to read from a second book, and then another. After consulting all the tomes, he scribbled notes on a paper, and then repeated the process. Either he was collecting information from the array of sources or he was comparing them, seeking contradictions or errors.

"Excuse me, professor."

He looked up startled to hear himself being addressed. His face was the gaunt one of an old man who spends his days in reading rooms away from the sun, and his eyes were reddened from hours of straining over barely legible text, but his mind did not suffer from age. He looked at me for only a moment before announcing. "You are not one of my students." A statement, not a question.

"You are a student but not one of our students. I would say you are a law student, and since you are not one of our students you must be at Bologna. Am I correct?"

"I was a student. I recently graduated. And you are correct that I was a law student at the university in Bologna. How do you know that?"

"Deduction based on observation. Law students are so practiced in courtroom behavior that it becomes part of them. You stand away from me with the respectful distance of a student standing before a professor while your stance has the confidence, some might say arrogance, of a magistrate."

Uncle Nunzio had said that Marsuppini was a puzzle master. Now I had an example of his talent. He waited a few moments with a serious face and then burst forth with a hearty laugh. "Young man, I am having fun at your expense. I am able to deduce many things, but in this case, it is the shiny new ring on your finger that tells your story. Only law students from Bologna wear that insignia. What I cannot tell for certain is why you have come to see me, other than that you seek knowledge which I am justifiably known to have in abundance."

His lips curled upward into a smile. "Are you seeking advice about women? I was very popular with the women in my younger days, a regular Marc Antony, although no one believes that now. No, that cannot be your purpose. Surely a handsome lad like you must not need any help with young women. That leaves only one possibility: you have a puzzle that you cannot solve, and you would like my help."

"You are correct again."

"Of course I am correct. As one of those old Greek philosophers, Plato as I recall, once said 'when there is no other possibility then there is only one possibility,' or something to that effect. I could have expressed his sentiment more eloquently, but his meaning is clear, and no, I am not old enough to have known Plato personally... although on some days I feel that old."

Shifting slightly in his chair caused Marsuppini to wince. Even that slight movement brought discomfort to his aging body. I waited for him to settle before speaking again.

"It is said that your ability to solve puzzles is unsurpassed."

"Ah, then you were sent here by Bartolomeo Scala or one of his acquaintances. He is the one who spreads these rumors about my being a puzzle master. He exaggerates the truth," the professor smiled, "... but only a little.

"Because I have a reputation for solving puzzles, people bring me puzzles to solve. I am not a dolt, so of course I am able to solve them, nearly all of them, and since people bring me so many puzzles the number that I have solved grows and that feeds my reputation. Do you know that Scala was once a student of mine?"

Before giving me time to answer Marsuppini continued. "You are a law graduate from Bologna and you are involved with Scala. It doesn't take a genius to guess that he has already entangled you in the intrigues of government. Always he is going here and going there, meeting with this person and that person, regarding secret affairs affecting our Republic. He must be away on a mission at this time or he would have accompanied you on this visit. He does come to visit me occasionally when he is in the city."

"You are right again. The Chancellor is in Genoa."

Marsuppini pushed his books and papers aside clearing the space immediately in front of him, a welcoming gesture suggesting that we could share the table. Pointing to the chair opposite he said, "I need a rest from reading and your appearance here arouses my interest so tell me your puzzle."

"A person is being dispatched to Pisa to fetch Lo Spruzzatore and bring it to somewhere, possibly in the Republic of Florence but not to the city of Florence itself. I am trying to understand what is meant by Lo Spruzzatore."

After a lengthy silence Marsuppini said, "Yes, go on. Tell me more."

I raised my hands from the table and opened my palms outward in a gesture signifying that I had nothing else to tell.

"The secret to solving puzzles is in assembling a sufficient number of clues. Each clue becomes a piece of the puzzle. Only when there are enough pieces can a puzzle be solved. I am sorry but no solution can be deduced from your one scant clue. The best I can do is to give you a hint that might help you solve the puzzle yourself.

"I once visited an unfortunate student of ours who was detained in a cell at the Bargello prison on charges of fighting in public and striking a member of the Guardia. In a nearby cell two grizzly, foul-smelling characters were barking epithets at each other. One of them used the words Lo Spruzzatore. I remember thinking at the time how unusual it was that criminals in a prison cell would be talking about a duster. I did not hear the context... nothing they said had any context so I could not discern their meaning. I suspect that to solve your puzzle you will need to find someone who knows about the underbelly of our society. I assume it is a term that has a special meaning to criminals and low lifes."

Marsuppini folded his hands and leaned back in his chair indicating he had nothing more to offer.

"Professor, may I ask you about something else. You taught here at the university when Bartolomeo Scala was a student. Can you tell me about him?"

Marsuppini's eyes brightened as my question brought to his mind pleasant memories of a longtime friend.

"Bartolomeo was my student, one of my best. We became friends when he attended the university and we have remained close friends."

"But he did not finish his studies here in Florence, did he?" I asked.

"While he was a student a lack of funds compelled the university to shut its doors. It is disgraceful that the greatest republic in the world cannot sustain its university. As much as he loves Florence, Scala was forced to continue his studies in Milan. When Scala finished his studies, he returned to Florence and was hired by the Medici bank. Cosimo came to appreciate Scala's talent. He elevated Scala to a senior position where he wielded enormous power and influence.

"Later, Bartolomeo was offered a position at the Chancery. It was an opportunity he could not resist. Scala is one of the few who understands that the Chancery holds the ultimate power in our Republic. Part of the Chancery's responsibility is the security of the Republic. It can, and does, carry out clandestine activities with impunity. It answers to no one. In principle the Signoria could challenge it, but no member of the Signoria dares to do so. Thanks to God that the ones who lead the Chancery are men of high integrity like Accolti and Scala."

I began to feel guilty for calling upon the professor without an appointment, interrupting his work, and taking much of his time. I thanked him for his help and rose to leave. As I did so he said, "I wish I could have been of more assistance. When you do solve your puzzle perhaps you will return and share the solution with me."

Chapter 24

The most direct route from the university back to the center of the city put me on a small vicolo that angled across between two larger streets. On this obscure vicolo the paving stones are not leveled carefully as they are on the main roads, demanding that I focus on my footing to avoid stumbling. Ahead in the shadows, sitting on an upturned basket against the front of a vacant shop, sat an old woman. Her head was bent down so her face was not visible, and her arms were folded across her lap. I might not have paid any attention to her except that despite the summer heat she had a heavy wool wrap around her shoulders and a thick black scarf on her head.

When only one step separated us, she extended her hand, palm open and facing upward. Our city has an ample number of poor citizens and I cannot help them all, so I often leave the beggars unrewarded, albeit with a pang of guilt. For some reason though, I could not ignore this one. From my coin sack I pulled a token and bent to place it in her palm. My hand did not touch hers, but as our two hands drew near my fingers chilled as though immersed in icy water.

She raised her head and looked up at me. Strands of scraggly hair escaping from under her scarf showed as black as coal, and her eyes were blacker still. In a soft raspy voice, she uttered a cryptic phrase, “the dust of death.”

Her accent was thick and unfamiliar, but her words were clear. The words, or her mere presence, chilled the air. She radiated the cold of winter. “What are you saying,” I asked. “What is the dust of death?”

“I see nothing more,” and she lowered her head.

I stood motionless for only an instant before moving on with quickened steps. As I neared the far end of the vicolo, one more word reached me from far behind: "ovatos." [Hungarian: careful]

Chapter 25 Saturday, August 11, 1464

My eagerness to learn what had transpired at Luca Pitti's gathering made me one of the first to awaken in the entire city. The eastern sky barely hinted at the promise of sunrise as I climbed from my bed. Descending from my bedchamber to the dining salon my footfalls on the tiled staircase echoed through the otherwise silent house.

How long before Donato will arise? I asked myself. I knew he would not awaken for hours because the poor man might have settled into bed only minutes ago. Il festatore worked alongside his staff during the entire event to ensure that Pitti's guests received impeccable service. Then, after the last guest had departed, he supervised and helped with the cleanup: removal of service items, removal of trash and litter, sweeping, and whatever other cleaning was needed.

Their chores did not end when they left the palazzo. Donato and his staff then returned to the Uccello to clean all the service items. Donato maintains the discipline that cleanup is part of a job and should not be postponed to the following day. It is a noble practice but one that keeps him from his bed.

I was gaining confidence that the Sporcones were plotting something, but, as professor Marsuppini had said, their plan remained a puzzle because I lacked enough pieces to solve it. I hoped Donato might have learned something that would give me another piece of that puzzle.

Rather than pace inside the house I cut a thick slice of crusty Tuscan bread, layered it with honey, and stepped out into the still dimly lit street in the hope that a long walk would ease my anticipation. There were no people to be seen, just a small brown dog trotting in the opposite direction on the far side of the street. His gait suggested that he had a destination in mind until I passed him, whereupon he reversed direction, sniffed my shoes, and then followed along behind me. Are you seeking a friend, or are you merely hoping for a taste of honeyed bread?

The walk served its purpose because my mind didn't snap from its reverie until the bells at the convent of Sant' Agata began calling the nuns to early mass. I do not recall what thoughts were in my head during the walk. The only thing I do remember was handing the last chunk of bread to the little canine who trotted off with the prize in his mouth. Loyalty must have a higher price than a single crust of bread. Time had moved during my walk so I hoped Donato might have awakened. I reversed direction and quickened my pace back to the house.

The eastern sky brightened with clouds showing a blood red glow. A bad omen? Our ancient Roman ancestors believed blood dripping from the sword of Mars, the god of war, colored the morning sky as Mars battled beasts from the underworld who had escaped onto the Earth. We are all at risk, they believed, of encountering one of the evil creatures until Mars finally dispatches the last of them. We know now that was just a myth, clouds do not drip with blood, and Mars is not really a god, yet the superstition remains.

Before I even reached out to open the door of casa Argenti the aroma of freshly baked delicacies set my stomach rumbling. Inside I passed through the loggia to the open courtyard where Donato, Joanna, and Giorgio were seated around a table laid with a bowl of fresh fruit and a platter of assorted cheeses. In cooler months they took their first meal of the day in the dining salon, comfortably warmed by heat from the fireplace. In summer months the interior courtyard, open to the sky and crisp morning air, was their preferred venue. I greeted them with three quick gestures, touching Donato on the shoulder, kissing Joanna on the cheek, and tousling Giorgio's hair, before turning my attention to the cheese platter. Mozzerella di Bufala is prized for its creaminess but my choice, as always, was a generous chunk of pecorino, the soft sheep milk cheese with a tangy, almost nutty, flavor.

As Joanna passed the pitcher of lemon water to me, Alessa came out of the kitchen carrying a serving platter covered with the biggest frittata I had ever seen. The golden combination of egg and prosciutto extended past the edges of the platter on all sides. Trailing behind her Simone bore a basket of pastries, the ones whose aroma had called to me earlier.

At breakfast Simone and Alessa gave us the details of their adventure at Fiesole. “It was inspirational to see the Roman and Etruscan structures,” Simone explained. “Their civilizations are part of my heritage too, but we have no evidence of them in Venice. We have legends that say the Etruscans were the first ones to excavate our canals, but no evidence has survived to support that contention. There are also stories that say an ancient Roman city stood less than a day’s journey from Venice, but again there is no proof. If it did exist in the past it was totally destroyed because nothing remains of it today.”

Addressing them both, Joanna said, with her sly Neopolitan smile, “I didn't hear you return to the house last night.”

Alessa pulled clips to free her pinned-up hair and shook her head to let the silky black tresses fall loosely on her shoulders. “We found a delightful inn in Fiesole run by a charming old couple. All the rooms have windows that look out from the hilltop toward Florence. The view is spectacular. It is even possible to watch the sunrise without getting out of bed. The morning air smelled so fresh and clean after the rain that we walked back to uncle Nunzio's estate from Fiesole. We spent the whole day with him and Lexia. Lexia showed us the proper way to press olives without bruising the oil. Early this morning we rode back from Fiesole on the wagon of a farmer making his morning milk delivery... while all the old folks in Florence were still sleeping.”

Donato reached out and took a hand of each. “Well, thank

you both for making such a delicious breakfast. I am one old folk who appreciates it."

Saturday is a day of rest for many, but not for Donato. It is the most hectic day at the Uccello, the one day when women are allowed in the main dining salon for the noontime meal. There is rarely an empty seat in the dining room. Usually Donato leaves for the Uccello after breakfast to get an early start on preparations for the day's activities, but on this day he delayed his departure to tell me about the meeting at Palazzo Pitti the previous evening.

"I have information for you, although probably less than you had hoped for. The gathering was not a dinner or a reception, so we did not serve food or drinks while the guests were engaged in discussions. Luca Pitti had us set food and beverages on side tables in an anteroom so guests could prepare their own plates and carry them into the meeting room. Luca is a member of the Uccello, and we have arranged private events for him, but this is the first time I have been inside his mansion. Every aspect of the structure is done on a grand scale, and no detail escaped the meticulous attention of Luca and his architects. Approximately thirty guests attended the meeting, but the room could have held twice that number. And that meeting room was not the main dining salon, it was just one of the drawing rooms. The Palazzo is huge."

"Were you able to hear any of their discussions?" I asked.

"No, unfortunately not. As soon as the guests were all seated in the meeting room one of Pitti's servants closed the door. My workers and I had nothing to do but wait until it was time to clean up after the meeting ended. I sent half of my workers away, better for them to be home with their families than just standing around with nothing to do."

My spirit sank. If Donato was unable to hear the conversations how could he have any information that would be helpful to me?

Donato continued, "You said that Pitti wanted the Sporcone removed from his list of invitees, but they did attend, at least a portion of it. Both Salvatore and Alphonso were there.

"However, the Sporcones did not remain throughout the entire meeting. Less than an hour after it started I heard loud voices emanating from the meeting room. Two or more people were shouting at each other. They were loud angry shouts, but I could not identify the voices nor could I tell what they were saying.

"When the shouting began I was outside on a terrace at the rear of the palazzo, but I could look through an open doorway into the hallway where the meeting room was located. Suddenly, the door opened, and Alphonso Sporcone stormed from the room with his father following close behind. Alphonso was fuming and blasting forth a stream of curses in several different dialects and languages. Salvatore too had a face red with anger and clenched fists that looked ready to strike something. One of Pitti's servants who had been standing in the hallway pressed himself flat against a wall to avoid being struck by accident.

"Both of the Sporcone rushed outside, climbed onto a carriage, and drove off. Clearly, the carriage was not theirs, but that was of no concern to them. Several of the guests drove themselves to the meeting and left their carriages tied outside. Salvatore simply took the first one in the line."

Simone commented, "It takes two sides to have an argument. It sounds like the meeting attendees are split into two camps."

I leaned back in my chair and ran my forefinger slowly along the rim of my lemon water glass pondering Donato's finding and Simone's comment. "Possibly," I said, "but it could also be that there are three camps: Pitti and the moderates who hope to wrest power from the Medicis by peaceful means allowed by law; the Sporcones and their followers, if they have any, who are bent on a violent course for their own personal gain; and there may be a third group who are willing to try a lawful solution first but if that fails then they would have no compunctions about resorting to violence."

"If you are right," Donato said, "the Sporcones represent the most immediate threat. They have no moral principles and are already acting on some devious plan."

As I nodded my agreement the thought returned that somehow Jacopo Sporcone might be the key to learning what his family was planning.

Donato continued, "I recognized almost all of the meeting attendees as influential members of the guilds. Some are clients of mine, and several are members of the Uccello. Three of them are also members of the Signoria."

"Were they all Florentines?" I asked.

"Yes, with one possible exception and that was my second significant observation. The exception was a monk. The cord cincture at his waist marked him as a Franciscan, and the black color of his robe said he is of the Third Order."

"Inviting a monk to a discussion about the future of government is strange," I said. "On the other hand, nefarious people hope that a mere blessing can protect them from the consequences of their evil."

"But the real surprise," Donato asserted, "was that the monk wore one of the rings that Messer Scala described to you. It had intertwined strands of silver and gold and the Constantine Cross."

"The Priors of Constantine," I said reminding myself of Scala's words. Then to Donato I asked, "Did you recognize the monk?"

"No, I did not, but with so many monasteries in this city, and throughout the Republic, that is not surprising. I doubt that even the Archbishop recognizes all the monks."

"According to the Chancellor, the Priors of Constantine oppose evil. If that is so, why would one of their members consort with people who plot to usurp power through violence?" I wondered.

"He may have secured his invitation with subterfuge. His goal and yours might be the same: gathering information about the conspiracy."

I recounted to Donato what Lexia's son overheard regarding the Sporcones, and then my encounter with the old woman. I had not yet finished speaking when the words "Lo Spruzzatore" erupted from Alessa's lips with the force and in the dialect of a Southerner from Calabria or Sicily.

Startled, we all stared at her.

She looked at me with an intensity rooted in an old memory, a deeply unpleasant old memory. "You live in a wholesome world, Nico. During my time on the ship, I met men who live in a very different world. Lo Spruzzatore," again she pronounced it with a Southern dialect, "is not a thing, it is a person. Lo Spruzzatore, the duster, is an assassin skilled in using arsenic. In the South white arsenic is known as the dust of death."

Simone interjected, "Arsenic is a soft white metal found in the mountains of Sicily. Because it is soft, it is easily ground into a powder. And since arsenic powder is tasteless and odorless, it has been used as a poison for over a thousand years. I read in a history of ancient Rome that emperor Nero used arsenic powder to poison his brother."

Alessa continued, "It has been a favorite means of killing in Sicily for hundreds of years. On the ship I saw arsenic powder being smuggled by crew members from Palermo to Naples and Genoa. Of all the items smuggled, arsenic is a favorite because it is easy to hide and very profitable."

I voiced the obvious conclusion: "The Sporcones are recruiting an assassin."

Chapter 26

Alessa and Simone accompanied Donato to the Uccello leaving me alone when Francesca's message came. The brass door knocker was rapped so lightly that I almost didn't hear it, but Carlo, the ever-ready house servant, responded quickly. Standing in the open doorway was an elfish girl of not more than fifteen years. Her distance from the door and her nervous demeanor evidenced her discomfort in calling at the house of strangers. She did not raise her eyes to meet ours but timidly held out her hand that contained a small slip of paper. I expected her to turn and leave after handing me the paper; instead, she stood expectantly.

After a long silence, she summoned the courage to speak, "I was told to wait for your answer."

I nodded to show my understanding, smiled pleasantly, and read the paper.

My house at I. F.

The brief note was the message I had been eagerly awaiting:

Francesca Pitti wanted to meet with me at her hours at one hour after sunset.

"Please tell Signorina Pitti I will join her as she wishes." Without another word, the girl turned and departed to inform her mistress that the invitation was accepted. Re-reading Francesca's message made me laugh. The brief note was composed as an order, not a question or request. It had neither salutation nor closure nor even a signature, only her initial. We have no royalty in the Republic of Florence, but aristocrats like Francesca are raised from birth to issue commands and to treat everyone as a servant. Yet did she did show a certain humility by referring to the magnificent Pitti residence not as a palazzo nor an estate but modestly as a house.

I am by nature an impatient person. Waiting until the first hour was a torment worthy of Dante's Purgatorio.

Chapter 27

Via Guicciardini is the street that leads from the Ponte Vecchio to an expansive piazza that directly fronts Palazzo Pitti. As soon as I stepped from the Via into the piazza and became visible from the house, a door swung open. I arrived at the exact time Francesca had specified and I was evidently expected. The opened door was not one of the ornately carved double doors of the main entrance at the center of the mansion's facade through which Luca Pitti's celebrated guests pass. It was, instead, a rather unadorned opening near one corner of the building. The young girl who had delivered Francesca's message stood in the doorway watching me approach. She did not call or signal to me, expecting that her appearance alone would draw me to that entrance. It did.

When I reached the house, I realized that the door was not as dull as it appeared from a distance. It was decorated with delicate carvings and wood inlays and framed on each side by a large peony plant. Stepping inside the small sparsely furnished entry space I was greeted by a painting of a woodland scene of dogs burrowing for truffles. It did not have the depth of color that Sandro achieves in his paintings, but it was a pleasant rendering, and large enough to cover the wall facing me. In this instance a decorator opted for size rather than the quality of the art.

To the left was a small padded bench and two interior doorways; to the right a staircase. My guide uttered a soft "this way," and then we ascended the winding stairway to the mansion's second level, the residence level. The staircase was not the exquisite one used by Luca's important callers at the main entrance, but it was, nonetheless, genuine Carrara marble covered with a handsome runner patterned in blue and black and accented with gold streaks. In this environment, the Pitti Palazzo, the carpet was unremarkable, but it would be a memorable feature in any other house. I wondered whose eye the design choices reflected. Was an architect given a free license, or did the colors evidence another of Francesca's talents? Perhaps Luca himself had a hidden artistic skill.

We passed through a long corridor before my guide opened the door to a room where two figures stood silhouetted by bright light streaming in from a large window. I entered the room and moved toward a side wall out of the glare. From there I recognized Francesca, who was facing me. The second woman I did not know. She stood facing Francesca and with her back to me. I saw only her honey golden hair shining in the window light.

To me, Francesca said, “Nico, we have much to discuss. I'll be free shortly."

Then to the young servant, "Take Nico to the Grecian room. Set out a pitcher of lemon water for him."

The young girl held the door open waiting for me to exit. As I did so Francesca called, "Forgive my lapse of civility. Nico, this is Bianca."

The woman turned toward me and smiled, revealing bright azure eyes and fair skin, not traits of Italian heritage.

Francesca continued, "Bianca designs all of my clothes. She is the most creative fashion stylist in.... in the world. She made this gown I am wearing. It is called a kleid. The design is largely unknown here in Florence, but it is the latest fashion in the Archduchy of Austria. Bianca knows everything that is happening in fashion."

Francesca may have said more about the dress. I don't recall, and any further description was wasted on me as I know nothing of women's fashions - anyway, my attention was held by Bianca.

Chapter 28

The Grecian room earned its name from the collection of marble busts of ancient Greek notables that lined the room's periphery. I made two circuits around the room reading the name plaques of men who must have been the giants of their age but were mostly unknown to me. Aristotle's image was easy to recognize, but I always had trouble distinguishing between Plato and Socrates.

While circling the room, I wondered why Francesca had introduced Bianca to me, but not introduced me to Bianca? Had she already told Bianca about me? If so, what did she say?

Before I could imagine answers to my questions, Francesca entered. With no preamble she got to the issue at hand. "Even though my father did not wish to invite him, that bastard Salvatore Sporcone came to the meeting and he brought his horrid son Bruttono with him."

Most women of Francesca's social standing avoided vulgarities.

Francesca is not most women.

"My cousin Donato told me that Sporcone did not remain for the entire meeting, that he left when a disagreement occurred."

"Disagreement is too kind a word." -- the same phrase used by Scala -- "There was some support for his position until his uncontrollable tirade. All of those present abandoned him at that point."

"Were you able to hear their discussions?"

"Some of them. I was in a nearby room. The walls between the rooms are thick, but there are grills in the walls to permit air flow for wintertime heating. I opened one of the grills before the meeting started.

"Salvatore Sporcone believes that Piero de Medici must be dealt with quickly before he establishes a following in the Signoria. My father and many others believe they can convince members of the Signoria that the Medicis grip should end, but they feel it will take time to accomplish the change."

"What about the others? Are they willing to wait?"

"Some are willing to try persuasion first, but all are impatient. The moderates agreed to pressure their colleagues as a way of controlling the outcome of the next election. Then, if the outcome is not favorable, they can take more direct action at that time. That proposal inflamed Sporcone. I heard someone, Sporcone I assume, pounding the table. He shouted that waiting would be senseless, Piero must be removed now and since they all have 'mouse testicles' to use Sporcone's phrase, then he would see to it himself. Then both Sporcones charged out of the room."

"Did Sporcone have many supporters in the meeting?"

"I could not see their faces so I cannot be certain, but none voiced agreement with his position. Several spoke in favor of the proposal to influence the election. Many different ideas were expressed. Unfortunately, often several men were speaking at the same time so I could not understand what was being said."

"Soliciting votes is a perfectly lawful way to influence the election. You must be pleased that your father was not pulled into an illegal conspiracy."

"I am content for now, but the election is only two months away. If they do not prevail in the election, they will not accept the defeat and may drag others, including my father, into a violent alternative."

Recalling the facts of the Holy Father's illness and the First Chancellor's illness I said, "Much can happen in two months."

"Did anyone say what they will do if the election outcome is not favorable to them?"

"No. One person, and I could not tell who, asked that very question. His query was ignored by the others. They also avoided discussing how power would divide among them if they are successful in defeating Piero's supporters."

Following Francesca's reasoning, I postulated, "Florence could suffer prolonged chaos as they battle each other for control."

"Nico, do you believe Sporcone's threat is real, or are his words only the rantings of a madman?"

"He has a violent history. I believe his threat is real."

Since Francesca shared information with me, it was fair for me to share some information with her. I told her that Sporcone's thugs mentioned Lo Spruzzatore implying that Sporcone may have already contacted an assassin, an expert in the use of arsenic poison. "The words you overheard suggest that the assassin's target could be Piero de Medici. The only remaining unknowns are when and where the assassin will strike."

Francesca responded to my premature conclusion with an insight that I did not appreciate at the time. "Salvatore's hatred is clearly aimed at Piero deMedici. Alphonso's anger seemed to encompass other targets as well, although he mentioned no names."

"If the assassin succeeds, the demise of Piero de Medici will benefit not only Sporcone but others as well, including your father," I ventured.

"I know my father. He believes the Medici have become too powerful, and their control over the government must be curtailed, but he does not want that accomplished through violence. Father is a peaceful man who cares about the Republic."

With our discussion concluded, Francesca led me into the corridor toward a stairway at the far end that leads to an exit. As I descended, she called down from above, "Bianca is not Italian. Her father came from one of the low countries. I know only that her mother is not Italian either."

Francesca's statement froze me in mid-step. Why is she telling me this?

"Do not look so surprised, Nico. Even the blind poet Homer could see how you looked at her. I am planning a small gathering of friends two days from now. Bianca will be there. Join us and you can ask her the country of her birth."

Another command from Francesca and this one will be a pleasure to follow. By the time I turned to look up at her, she was gone. I departed the Palazzo with a happy spring in my gait.

Chapter 29

Donato, Francesca, uncle Nunzio, Alessa, and even the old crone in the vicolo had provided bits of information pointing to the Sporcones' assassination plot. Unfortunately, all those bits had gotten me no closer to solving the puzzle. Since Jacopo lived in the same house as Salvatore and Alphonso, there is a good likelihood that he had overheard details of their plans. If so, he could be the key to unlocking the mystery of when and where the assassination would take place. Slowly I was forming the basic idea of how to secure Jacopo's cooperation. To speed my thinking, I sought Donato's help.

When I arrived at the Uccello Donato was examining a cartload of fresh Tunisian apricots. Every day fruits and grains carried by ship from North Africa arrive at the port city of Pisa, where they are transferred from ships to barges that move items up the Arno river to the markets and restaurants of Florence. Donato selected one of the apricots, carefully raised it into the light to view its light pink color, and then inhaled its delicate aroma. Through long experience, Donato had found color and fragrance to be the best telltales of quality and freshness. Fruit that sat too long in the hold of a ship during a slow sea voyage lost sweetness, and a skilled person like Donato could detect that with a sniff.

While Donato negotiated prices with a vendor, Joanna led me to an isolated food storage area where we could chat without disturbing the kitchen workers who were busily preparing items slated for the evening menu. Joanna relished hearing about life at the university, while I enjoyed nibbling the delicious snacks that are always available in the kitchen. On one counter I found a bowl of tasty pistachio candies. Before I had eaten the last candy Donato joined us. "The apricots were disappointing," he said with a shrug, "but the figs and dates are excellent. They will have a place on tonight's menu."

Joanna squeezed closer to me so Donato could join us in the small space. I began outlining my plan. Donato nodded affirmatively. Either he agreed with my idea or he was merely acknowledging that he understood the scheme. I was about to ask which when I glanced over at Joanna. Her eyes were downcast, her expression held concern. She caught my glance and looked up. "Nico, these are dangerous people. Why are you involved with this intrigue? It is the Chancery's problem. They must have people to deal with these things. Becoming a magistrate -- hat is where your attention should be."

Her words echoed those of Chancellor Scala, and she was right, I should step aside. I was tempted to respond by saying 'every citizen has a duty to the Republic,' but that would have sounded naive even to me. Was it possible I was helping Chancellor Scala only because it might improve my chances of securing a desirable magisterial appointment? That would be a self-serving motivation, but would it be a dishonorable one? In the prolonged silence Joanna rose and walked from the room without speaking another word.

I turned my attention back to Donato and continued describing my plan. When I finished, he offered his comments. "Your plan to gather evidence against the Sporcones seems feasible, although Joanna is right, the plan has risk both to you and to Jacopo. If you decide to proceed how will you get Jacopo to collect the evidence? He has no reason to help you."

I told Donato what I had learned from uncle Nunzio, that Salvatore had driven away Jacopo's birth parents, or, even worse, had them killed. "If Jacopo were to learn the truth about his parents that should turn him against Salvatore and might make him willing to seek revenge. He could get at least some measure of justice by exposing Salvatore."

"Sister Teresa must have reasons for keeping Jacopo's past secret from him," Donato pointed out. "If he goes to her now, she may still be unwilling to break her vow of silence, especially if she believes that doing so could put Jacopo in danger."

Donato was right, it would be foolish to assume that Sister Teresa would reveal Jacopo's past if she thought that might bring harm to him. I needed to enlist Sister Teresa's support before confronting Jacopo.

Orsino was working nearby repairing a chair that had been damaged the previous evening by a raucous patron. He overheard me describing the plan to Donato, and I noticed that the discussion was making him uneasy. When I asked what he found upsetting, he initially declined to say. Upon further urging he explained, "My brother owned a small farm. One day his old plow horse went lame, it could no longer pull the plow. A money changer said he would lend money to buy a new horse. The loan paper had words my brother did not understand. Maybe it was foolish for him to sign, but he needed a horse to work his field.

"My brother tried to pay back the loan, but it was never enough. Always they demanded more. At the end they took his farm. It should not happen. Maybe when you are a magistrate you can fix the laws. Now, it is good that you stop this money changer from stealing farms from others like my brother."

He paused for a moment, then added, "I heard you say that you need help. I will help if you let me."

The person needed to execute my plan did not require any special skills so Orsino could fit the role. He was big and strong, a possible advantage if the plan were to go astray, and even though we had just met I believed Orsino to be trustworthy. I explained in detail how the scenario would unfold. He grasped his part quickly, a simple but important role

.

Chapter 30

The short walk from the Uccello to the Sant' Apollonia convent did not give me much time to think of the best way to approach Sister Teresa. A nun who had answered my knock led me to a small garden between the convent and the church where Sister Teresa was teaching a group of girls. She was seated in a chair, reading from a book, while the girls sat on the ground listening to her. The nun who accompanied me took over the teaching duty, allowing Sister Teresa to meet with me. We walked from the garden toward an outdoor oven where we could speak in private.

"My name is Nico Argenti. I would like to speak with you about Jacopo Sporcone. I understand that you cared for him when he was a youngster."

She showed no reaction at hearing Jacopo's name.

"Yes, I did. I have not seen him in all the years since."

"The person who told me of your relationship with Jacopo

also said that Salvatore Sporcone is not Jacopo's father."

I was not sure what to say about the disappearance of Jacopo's true parents. Two widely held beliefs contend that either they fled to Naples or they were killed by Salvatore's henchmen. Sister Teresa may have heard these possibilities, but if not I did not want to be the one to tell her that Jacopo's parents might have been killed. If she knew what actually became of them she might disclose that fact to me, so I decided to avoid mentioning the fate of his parents.

"I believe it is time for Jacopo to know those parts of his life that have been kept from him thus far."

It was a bold statement from a total stranger. I was not certain how Sister Teresa would react.

She answered slowly. "You are not the first one to feel that way. I am aware of the abuses that Jacopo suffers at the hands of Salvatore Sporcone. My silence is a shame I carry with me every day. Do you know why no one has said anything to him until now?"

"They fear that speaking out will make them targets of Salvatore's revenge."

"Some may feel that way, but I, and others, feel that Salvatore's anger would be directed at Jacopo. It is his well-being that we wish to protect. Revealing information about his true father, as you propose, could bring harm to him."

Sister Teresa's compassion reminded me of one mock practice trial we studied at the university. The exercise involved a landowner wanting to prevent the construction of a new road. The landowner believed that building a road would change the slope of the land and that could cause spring rains to flood his vineyard. All the students in the class felt compassion for the landowner similar to the feeling that Sister Teresa held for Jacopo. We sought a solution that would prevent the possibility of the landowner suffering any injury.

We felt right about our handling of the exercise until we were all reprimanded by the professor. "The law does not operate on speculation," the professor admonished. "The landowner did not demonstrate that his property was in immediate danger. His belief is mere conjecture. Unless he can show that a definite threat exists, the law dictates that road should be built."

We learned a valuable lesson that day: laws themselves make no allowances for compassion. Balancing compassion and law to achieve justice is the function of magistrates. That is why magistrates have discretion in interpreting and applying laws. Here, I was called upon to balance thwarting Salvatore Sporcone's threat against concern for Jacopo's safety. Sister Teresa knew nothing of the Sporcones' plan. Jacopo's well-being was her only concern.

To obtain her help, I told her of Salvatore Sporcone's scheme including the possible assassinations. Further, I told her why I believed that Jacopo could be instrumental in finding details of Salvatore's plans. I shared with her the information I had learned, and the gaps that were still unknown to me. From time-to-time, she interrupted to ask questions. Some I could answer. Some I could not.

When I finished, she said, "Salvatore Sporcone is a vicious man. When I was at the Sporcone residence, I saw him mistreat Jacopo's mother and Jacopo himself. From what you have told me I agree that the Sporcones must be stopped. However, if Salvatore were to learn that Jacopo turned against him, the boy would be in mortal danger. Jacopo must be protected."

"I share your fear. You can warn Jacopo of the danger and tell him that he must not let Salvatore know that he has learned about his true parents. I will do the same, although he is sure to find your words more credible than mine."

Sister Teresa asked, "What will happen to Jacopo after Salvatore's plan is exposed?"

"The actions that Salvatore is planning are criminal. Once they are exposed, he should be prosecuted and no longer be in a position to harm Jacopo."

With uncle Nunzio's villa in mind, I added, "Until then, I can arrange a safe place for him."

Sister Teresa closed her eyes and her lips moved in silent prayer. When she reopened her eyes, she agreed that if I were to send Jacopo to her she would tell him the truth.

Chapter 31

Both Jacopo and Alphonso were staffing the Sporcones' money changer table when Orsino and I entered the Piazza del Mercato. We lingered at the far end of the piazza while the Sporcone brothers dealt with another customer. As usual, the Mercato was filled with people standing around engaged in idle conversation. I could never understand what drew these bystanders because most of them had no intention of making purchases from any of the vendors. Through the crowd, we caught glimpses of the Sporcone brothers, Alphonso and Jacopo, whom I identified to Orsino.

When the transaction was completed Alphonso rose, rested a hand on the customer's shoulder, and held a wolfish grin as the customer turned to depart, clutching a bag of coins. Orsino and I took separate paths through the array of vendor stalls filling the piazza. As we had rehearsed, Orsino went directly to the Sporcone table while I positioned myself behind a nearby column to observe and listen without being seen.

In a booming voice Alphonso greeted Orsino. "Welcome good sir. I am Alphonso Sporcone. How may I be of service today? If you have money to change, then you have come to the right station. None will give you a fairer rate than the Sporcone."

"I need a loan," Orsino responded with a quivering tone.

Continuing in his deep resonant voice, Alphonso proclaimed for all around to hear, "We are simple money changers. It is banks that are in the business of making loans." The statement was a fiction meant to avoid prosecution by the banks. Everyone knew that loans with usurious interest gave money changers their biggest profits.

Alphonso rested a hand on Orsino's shoulder, leaned forward, and spoke softly near Orsino's ear. "Please sit and tell me what you require."

Alphonso maneuvered Orsino into a chair and pulled another close so he could speak without being heard by his competitors. I was forced to move nearer to continue listening.

Once he was seated, Orsino repeated, "I need a loan."

Alphonso regained the look of a predator, "As I said, we are not a bank, but we always try to help those in need whenever we can. For what purpose do you require a loan?"

Orsino began reciting the story I had devised, "Uncle Pubo died. He has... had a farm near Panzanino that will be sold. They say some money will come to me, but first I must pay a fee... some kind of tax. I must pay tomorrow. I need a loan to pay the tax."

"How much do you need?"

Orsino was bewildered by the question. He gained a blank look and fidgeted silently as we had not rehearsed an answer to that question. Finally he said, "The message they sent said I must pay a tax. It did not say how much, only that I must pay tomorrow."

Orsino was playing his part perfectly.

"Do you have work ... a job?"

"At the Uccello. I work every day."

Alphonso leaned back, folded his arms across his generous midsection, and broadened his smile. "Good. Very good. The Uccello is a fine establishment. The owner is a friend of mine."

Donato enjoyed hearing that bit of fiction when I told him later.

"How big is the farm? How many men work there?" Alphonso asked.

"It is not big," Orsino responded. "There are no men, only uncle Pubo."

Alphonso looked thoughtful as though he were calculating a sum and then spoke, "I cannot know the exact amount of the tax, but we have helped others in your situation. I am confident that fifty florins will be sufficient."

Orisno remained expressionless indicating he had no idea whether fifty florins was a reasonable sum.

"When will you repay the loan?"

"Tomorrow. I go to Panzanino today. Tomorrow I pay the tax and come back."

"You understand there must be a fee for the loan."

Orsino nodded.

"It is complicated for us to make loans for only one day so the fee must be ten florins. When you repay the loan tomorrow the amount you pay will be sixty florins. If you repay after tomorrow, then the fee must be greater."

I gasped out loud when I heard Alphonso quote the interest charge for the loan. It's a wonder that he didn't hear me. By all civil standards, a twenty percent fee for a single day is outrageous. Now I could understand why the Sporcone had been accused of practicing usury.

Orsino calmly accepted the terms and said only, "I will repay tomorrow."

Alphonso stood and motioned to Jacopo who was diligently writing in a ledger at the other end of the table. To Orsino he said, "My brother will prepare the contract."

I feared that Alphonso might turn and notice me lurking close behind, so I moved away. From my new position, I could not hear the exchange between Jacopo and Orsino. I watched Jacopo ask a series of questions and record Orsino's responses in the large ledger. Later Orsino told me that Jacopo had asked his name and where he worked. He also recorded the amount of the loan, and when the loan was to be repaid.

Alphonso stepped away from the table allowing me to move

again close enough to overhear. Jacopo copied information from the ledger onto a contract form, then he signed the prepared contract and slid it across the table to Orsino.

"This paper is our contract. Read it to see that it has the terms we discussed and then sign it."

Although their discussion was short, the contract was long. It contained long words and phrases that Orsino could not read, but he made his mark and handed the paper back to Jacopo, who slid it into a folder containing other signed contracts. Jacopo reached below the table to retrieve a small metal box from which he counted out fifty gold florins and put them in a coin purse. He handed the purse to Orsino. As we had rehearsed, Orsino asked for a copy of the signed contract, knowing that Jacopo would not give him one.

"The paper is only for us," Jacopo told him. "We each have something. We have the contract paper, you have the florins. That is how business is done."

Orsino said nothing in response. Looking resigned he quietly rose from the table, hooked the purse to his belt, and walked away.

I was delighted with his performance. "You were perfect, Orsino," I told him.

Chapter 32 Sunday, August 12, 1464

It was late afternoon, the end of the business day, as we watched the money changers closing their tables. Orsino and I sat at a small table outside a shop that sold drinks that it claimed were cold and refreshing. The cold came from a tub of water that was replenished frequently from the flowing Arno river but this late in summer even the Arno succumbed to the heat. We both had tumblers of barely cool fruit drinks in front of us. I took occasional swigs from mine, Orsino had yet to taste his.

The second part of my plan required a somewhat different performance by Orsino. Yesterday's actions, getting a loan, seemed natural to him. Today he would need to intimidate young Jacopo, and intimidation wasn't in Orsino's nature. I recalled our first encounter, the day that Simone and I arrived from Bologna when Orsino stayed at the side of the road uncomfortable with confronting the two travelers. The world would be a better place if everyone had Orsino's gentle soul.

In his eagerness to meet my expectations, Orsino had memorized the words that he planned to say. As we sat watching the money changers, he kept repeating the words to himself.

Alphonso had departed early, as was his usual practice, leaving Jacopo to collect the ledger and the folio of contracts that he would carry to the Sporcone residence at the close of business. The boxes containing cash were collected from all the money changers by members of the Medici bank who secured the boxes overnight in a vault within the bank.

Jacopo stuffed the ledger into a pouch that he slung over his shoulder. He tied a cord around the folio to help secure the papers within. Exiting the Mercato he paused briefly to exchange words with another of the money changers, then he crossed the piazza and entered Via del Corso.

Via del Corso is one of the busiest streets in the city flanked on both sides by all manner of shops. Although the business day had ended for the money changers, these shops continued to serve a steady stream of customers, but Jacopo was not among them. He walked with his eyes aimed straight ahead and his gait holding the steady plod of someone who leads a monotonous life.

Orsino and I moved out across the piazza to follow Jacopo. Orsino took a position ten paces behind Jacopo, and I followed an additional five paces back. We followed until Jacopo turned onto a side street devoid of people, then Orsino quickened his step. He passed alongside Jacopo, turned to face him, and presented the coin purse that held the fifty gold florins borrowed the day before plus ten that I added to pay the interest fee.

"Here," Orsino barked, "I want to pay the loan."

The startled boy stammered, "You cannot pay now, the Mercato is closed. You must come back tomorrow when the Mercato is open."

Orsino raised his voice. "Tomorrow the fee will be more. I want to pay now. I said the loan was for one day."

Orsino thrust the purse forward, striking Jacopo's chest, throwing him off balance and against a stone storefront. Instinctively Jacopo reached out and grasped the purse.

"I am paying the loan so now you give me the paper," Orsino commanded.

This was the most critical part of the plan. Retrieving the signed contract would prove that the Sporcone make loans in defiance of guild regulations and that their fees violate usury laws.

"The paper?" a frightened Jacopo stammered.

"Yes, the paper I signed."

"No. No. We keep the contracts for our records."

"You take the money. I take the paper," Orsino insisted.

Orsino pulled at the folio held fast by Jacopo. The tussle sent the folio flying into the air and then arcing downward to the street, scattering signed contracts across the cobblestones. Some landed in muck at the side of the road, others were trampled underfoot by passersby. The reaction propelled Jacopo backward against a storefront. He winced as his elbow struck the stone facade. This was not the outcome Orsino had expected. He had imagined that seizing the papers would be a matter of Jacopo simply releasing his grasp on the portfolio. Orsino's mouth dropped open and he stood paralyzed, uncertain what to do. Jacopo stared at the giant standing before him and trembled like a leaf caught in a breeze, fearing more what Alphonso might do to him for losing the contracts than an assault by Orsino. Panic-stricken, Jacopo turned and ran.

"I am sorry. It was an accident," Orsino said as I approached him.

I put a hand on his shoulder. "Don't worry. There is no problem," I told him as I bent to recover the contracts scattered along the road. After we had recovered all the documents, I extracted the one signed by Orsino and returned the others to the folio.

"It is good," I told Orsino, "in fact, it is better than good. I have more than I need."

"I did not mean to hurt him."

"Don't worry, Orsino, he will be fine. I'll look after him."

I glimpsed Jacopo in the distance still running from us when he veered right onto a road that would not take him to the Sporcone house. He was driven by instinct alone, and I knew exactly where that would take him.

Chapter 33

A short distance beyond the imposing cathedral of Santa Maria di Fiore I reached the small parish church of Santissima Annunziata whose flock includes the Sporcone family. Salvatore, the family patriarch, can be found there on all high holy days, believing that attendance on those few days is sufficient to gain him entrance to the heavenly kingdom when his time comes.

It was there I expected to find Jacopo, whose life had suddenly become more than he could bear without divine support. Upon entering the nave, I paused a moment to look across the darkened interior. I scanned the side chapel as I walked up the center aisle toward the altar. Two of the faithful knelt in the chapel praying to their patron saint but there was no sign of Jacopo.

Eventually, I reached the chancel and stood facing a beautiful altarpiece. I could not tell if it was an original Giotto or an excellent copy. To my right, a doorway led from the transept to a cloister alongside the church. A whimpering sound drifted into the otherwise silent church through the partially open door. The sound could only be from a wounded small animal or Jacopo Sporcone.

I found him sitting alone on a stone bench, his head bent low and his hands clasped in his lap. He was not crying, just whimpering. He took no notice when I sat beside him until I placed the folio in his hands; then he looked up at me. Although my action confused him, he said nothing.

"I cannot imagine what ill might befall you if you return without these," I said.

He still said nothing. His eyes were red and wet. Apparently he had been crying earlier. I handed him a handkerchief, which he took and used to wipe his eyes. He still said nothing.

I introduced myself although my name meant nothing to him. Eventually his whimpering ceased, and he gained enough composure to thank me for returning the folio. He did not ask how I came into possession of it.

When I first handed him the folio, he clutched it tightly to his chest with both hands. Gradually he relaxed and lessened his grip on the folio, letting it drift down to rest in his lap.

At that point I said, "I have something to tell you." And I began telling him about his true parents and their fate, the same story that uncle Nunzio had related to me. Jacopo interrupted me constantly with a string of protests: "That cannot be. I don't believe it. How do you know this? Who told you?"

I continued speaking without being disrupted by his comments. Gradually his expression softened from disbelief to uncertainty, and eventually he fell silent and listened without further objection until I finished. He leaned forward and let his head drop until his chin rested against his chest. He was silent for several minutes. I imagined him assessing whether my story explained why his mother had suddenly disappeared, and why Salvatore never treated him kindly.

Finally, he looked up and said, "No one has ever said these things to me. How do I know you are speaking the truth?"

"There is one whom you trust. Sister Teresa at the convent of Sant' Apollonia. She can confirm what I told you."

At the mention of Sister Teresa's name, Jacopo became alert. "Why are you telling me this? How do you know the Sister?" he asked.

"I need your help with an important matter, but first, go talk with Sister Teresa. Listen to her, then come to see me. One more thing, and this is crucial. You must not confront Salvatore with this information. Sister Teresa and I both believe that doing so would put you in great danger. Salvatore is a violent man. His actions have shown what he is capable of doing."

I helped Jacopo to stand. We left the cloister together. He went in the direction of casa Sporcone where he planned to leave the portfolio of documents and then go to the convent to find Sister Teresa.

Chapter 34 Monday, August 13, 1464

A chestnut mare ran free, stopping only at each especially tasty patch of grass. Gradually she meandered in our direction hoping for a handout. She was here for the upcoming Ferragosto events just as we were, except we would be spectators while she would be a participant in one of the events. Her tall lean build suggested that racing, rather than jousting, was her game, and her spirit indicated that she would give a good account of herself.

Ferragosto is the church holiday also known as the Feast of the Assumption. The lavish annual celebration would not be diminished despite Florence being in mourning for the passing of Cosimo de Medici.

Equestrian events in this campo are just a few of the many holiday activities. Boys today are drawn to this field just as I was years ago. When the field is idle, they charge through its soft grass inhaling the sweet fragrance and imagining themselves as champion racers atop a speedy mount. Alessa, Simone, and I were here to watch Antonio, the brother of Alessa's friend Margherita, prepare for the jousting competition. Antonio is a cavalry officer in the Florentine militia and had achieved victories recently in military tournaments at Lucca and Pistoia.

Antonio's wins attracted the attention of a highly successful trainer at a well-known stable. Antonio demonstrated skill and showed confidence in the practice runs. The real test of his ability would come in a few days against the more experienced jousters.

While waiting for Antonio to make his next practice run, Alessa turned to me. "My friend Margherita is having a gathering tonight so we can all wish Antonio well during the competition tomorrow. We are certain to have a good time because Simone is getting an entire pipa of wine from the stock of the Venetian embassy. Simone certainly has influence there. The ambassador even arranged for embassy staff to deliver the wine."

"Simone is a good friend to have," I said, then have her a wide beaming smile. "Be aware though that he is capable of drinking half of it all by himself."

"Oh," she responded, "I was going to invite you but then you might drink the other half pipa, and there would be none for the rest of us."

"Spare yourself any mental anguish, Alessa, I will be occupied elsewhere. I have already accepted an invitation from Francesca Pitti."

"Mother of God! You and Francesca Pitti! I heard that her bed pillows are imported especially for her from Constantinople.

Tomorrow you can tell me whether there is truth to that rumor, or do you already know it?"

"My interest is not in Francesca, although she certainly is an amazing woman. There is another person I met on my last visit to the Pitti estate..."

Alessa placed her hand over my mouth to interrupt me. "Person?" she mimicked, "Are you not able to determine this person's gender? Is this person soft, perchance with the sweet fragrance of a flower? If so, your person might be a woman."

She swung from me to face Simone who, along with two strangers standing nearby, was gurgling with laughter at the exchanges between Alessa and me. "I did not live in Florence when Nico was young, but I heard that he began chasing girls as soon as he learned to toddle."

Simone reined his laughter enough to add, "I heard similar tales from his friend Sandro."

Alessa continued, "The moon has not yet hidden itself from the sky since Nico returned from Bologna and already he abandons us, his good friends, to be with another 'person'."

Simone freed me from Alessa's teasing. "Nico, the Venetian embassy maintains a generous stock of Valpolicella, the deep red wine from Verona that you enjoyed at the university. If you can join us after you leave signorina Pitti I will save a caraffa for you."

In a serious tone Alessa said, "Please join us. Bring your friend with you." Suddenly she thrust her arm out, pointed, and exclaimed, "There he is! I'm sure that's Antonio!"

Each practice run made by the jousters emphasized a different aspect of their required skills. During practice, they do not don the colors of their stable, so it is difficult to tell one competitor from another. On this run, identification was especially tricky because his trainer had placed a black sack over Antonio's head to deprive him of sight. The purpose of this run was to feel how his armor coupled to his horse and how his lance balanced when held in its proper position. He did not need to guide his horse. She had run that course hundreds of times. She knew when to accelerate and when to expect the impact from an opponent's lance.

We watched as Antonio was helped onto his mount by one of the stable hands. He settled into position, trying to sense the animal and his armor. He leaned forward, positioned his lance, and spurred the steed forward. A gray blur of horse and armor flashed by us.

The competitors took turns on the track so it would be a while before Antonio's next practice run. Simone and Alessa stayed at the practice field waiting for Margherita to arrive while I returned to the house.

Chapter 35

Afternoon shadows played on the walls of the courtyard at Donato's house. My focus jumped between the shadow patterns and thoughts of Bianca. I was about to reach for the glass of peach nectar on the nearby table when Carlo entered from the logia accompanied by Jacopo Sporcone. He behaved like a different man from the one I had encountered at San Giuseppe. His head was erect, his shoulders square, and his back straight. He held no handkerchief and his clothes bore no tear stains. He looked at me with confident eyes.

"I went to see her... to see Sister Teresa. She said that she prayed every night for the truth to come to me. She thanked God for answering her prayer, and then she held me like she did when I was a little boy, and she wept."

"You must be saddened as well."

"No, not saddened, angry. I am angry at those I have been living with, I can no longer call them my family, for making my life a lie. I am angry with the ones who knew the truth and lacked the courage to tell me. And I am angry with myself for accepting the condition.

"After seeing Sister Teresa, I went back to the house and confronted Salvatore. I told him what I had learned. I told him that he and his sons will burn in the ninth circle of the Inferno. Then I left."

"Oh Jacopo, that was not wise. I warned you not to speak with Salvatore."

"What did you expect me to do?"

"I wanted you to come here after Sister Teresa confirmed what I had told you so we could discuss a proper course. I sought you out for a reason, Jacopo. Salvatore and Alphonso are bringing an assassin to Florence. Forgive me, but I wanted your help in learning the details of their scheme so it could be thwarted."

"I am aware of their plan."

"They discussed it with you?"

"No. They tell the statues in their garden more than they tell me. They speak to each other oblivious to my presence."

"Did you hear them mention Piero de Medici?"

"No, I did not hear them name a target, but they curse the de Medicis constantly. Salvatore refers to Piero as a weak little beetle that needs to be crushed."

"Did you hear when the assassination is to take place?"

"Not exactly," he replied.

I was beginning to think that Jacopo had no information

beyond what I already possessed.

"But I did hear where it is to take place, Siena."

"Siena? Are you sure?" I asked excitedly.

"Very sure. Alphonso is going to meet the assassin somewhere and escort him to Siena. Mention of an assassin prompted a heated argument between Alphonso and his father. I only heard fragments of their conversation, but my impression is that Salvatore preferred a different course. Later I heard Alphonso tell one of his bullies, 'I wish I could be there when that son of a whore is sent to meet his father in Hades.'"

The selection of Siena as the location for the assassination was puzzling. Piero de Medici's illness confines him to his villa at Careggi. He rarely makes carriage rides to Florence. What possible reason would cause him to travel all the way to Siena? While I tried to analyze the actions being planned by Alphonoso Sporcone, Jacopo was replaying his encounter with Salvatore.

"I needed to hear him admit the truth. At first he denied it, but when I mentioned Sister Teresa, he became furious. He hurled a wine bottle across the room smashing it against a wall and spraying its contents onto one of his prize tapestries. That enraged him even further.

"He called my mother a tramp who would sleep with anyone, and he said the tutor, my father, was a lazy thief who deserved to be punished for his betrayal. If he had not already smashed the wine bottle, I would have thrown it at him. He said I should be thankful that he had given me a place to live. I stormed out, not wanting to hear another of his lies. I cannot stay another day in his house knowing what he did."

"Where will you go?"

"I don't know. It doesn't matter as long as I get away from him," Jacopo declared, growing more agitated.

"If Salvatore had your mother and father killed, he will not want you making accusations to the Guardia. You will be in danger if you remain in Florence. My uncle has a vineyard near Fiesole. You can stay there until you decide where to go."

Instead of helping Jacopo by letting him know the truth, my plan had put him in danger. Previously he was an abused victim, but at least he had a place to live. Now he is free from further abuse, but he has no place to live, no money, and no friends. I was eager for Chancellor Scala to return. His experience might offer alternatives for Jacopo. Also, I was anxious to tell the Chancellor what I had learned of the plot against Piero de Medici.

Chapter 36

As afternoon light surrendered the sky to the evening star, my worries over Jacopo faded behind the anticipation of once again seeing Bianca. The route to Palazzo Pitti brought me through piazzas dotted with groups of people. Some sat quietly enjoying a respite from the daytime heat. Others talked incessantly of their latest sorrows and joys. The buzz of human conversation faded as I crossed the river to the Oltrarno quarter of the city where Palazzo Pitti stood. There, outside the city walls, it was still countryside with animal sounds more common than human voices.

The moon had not yet risen above the hills to the east, so only a few dim lanterns posted outside shops illuminated the Via Guicciardini. In contrast, the Palazzo ahead shone like a beacon, its facade brightly lit by four lanterns, two on each side of the central entrance. The small door I had used during my last visit was dark. This time I would use the same central access as

Francesca's other guests.

Two guards flanked the entrance; their proximity to the lanterns caused them to cast giant shadows into the piazza. From my position, still a distance away, I could see that they were dressed identically. Both carried lances and wore breastplates decorated with the golden lion and red crown of the Pitti family crest.

In the dark I was almost struck by a carriage as it passed by and came to a stop in front of the palazzo. One of the guards helped the passenger, a well-dressed woman, to step down from the carriage, escorted her to the door, and let her enter the palazzo unannounced. She must be a frequent visitor.

As the carriage rolled away, I stepped aside to give it a wide berth. In doing so I was struck with the thought that my visit to the Palazzo could be a foolish waste of time. Francesca was kind to invite me, but those of us who walk to our engagements do not mesh with those who arrive in carriages driven by servants. There seemed little chance of my being accepted by Francesca's associates. Were it not for the prospect of seeing Bianca, I would have turned around and joined the party being held for Antonio.

Stepping into a shadow at the edge of the road I pulled a handkerchief, my finest silk handkerchief, from a pocket and used it to wipe road grime from my shoes. I may not have a servant or a carriage, but my lack of those assets is not a reason to advertise that I travel through the city by treading in muddy roadways.

It was comforting to learn that my appearance at the Palazzo was anticipated. Both guards offered pleasant greetings and neither made mention of my arrival on foot. To announce my arrival one of the guards pulled on a leather strap extending through an opening on a panel alongside the door. No doubt the strap attached to chimes or bells somewhere inside the building. This method of announcement is superior to a door knocker that cannot be heard throughout a large building, I realized.

Moments later the door opened. I had expected that one of the servants would escort me to the room where Francesca's friends were gathering, but instead, it was Francesca herself who met me. The guards were as surprised as I to see the mistress of the house fetch her guest rather than one of the servants.

She looked elegant wearing the new dress that Bianca had designed for her. I did not think it appropriate for me to comment on her appearance, so I chose instead to compliment the dress. "That is the new gown you are wearing, isn't it? It looks lovely."

"Yes, it is. I've been told it flatters my figure. That the high waist firms my breasts."

When most women mention their breasts it is a prelude to seduction, at least men believe that to be so. Once again though, Francesca is not most women. Her statement implied nothing, so although I was thinking, I agree, they certainly do look firm, I opted for discretion and said nothing.

Francesca's next words made it clear that her purpose in greeting me at the door was not driven by friendship but by her eagerness to know if I had new information about the Sporcones. “Have you learned anything more about that bastard Sporcone?”

“The last time we met I told you that the Sporcones have engaged an assassin skilled in the use of white arsenic poison. I have confirmed your observation that Piero de Medici is the object of Salvatore Sporcone’s hatred. Those two facts point to Piero being the assassin’s target. The latest information I learned is that the assassin will strike when his target is at Siena.”

Francesca frowned as she asked, “Piero is infirm and rarely travels, even the short distance from his villa to Florence. What would prompt him to travel to Siena?”

“That is puzzling to me as well. I have not yet learned why, or when.”

“Many of my friends are here this evening. I will ask if any of them know what might draw Piero to Siena.”

As we talked, we climbed the broad marble staircase and headed toward the wing of the palace with public rooms used for entertaining guests. Mirrors on the wall reflected light from a multitude of lanterns making the corridor nearly as bright as day.

Finally, we reached the salon filled with her guests. It was a spacious room with pale yellow walls that evoke the feeling of an early morning sunrise. Large scenic paintings on all four walls displayed one artist's vision of ancient Rome. He, like most of us, imagine imperial Rome as a pristine city with gleaming white buildings and well-dressed patricians roaming its streets. There was not one filthy peasant or slave to be seen in his paintings.

Throughout the room groups of women were seated around tables playing a game I did not recognize; they used small colorful tiles of various shapes. In the center of the room, a few of the younger women appeared to be rehearsing a scene from a play. One of them stood erect reading from a page held in one hand while reaching skyward with her other hand as though beckoning to a god or goddess. At the far end of the room, another group sat in a circle on low cushions and were reading to each other. One held on her lap a copy of Virgil's Aeneid. As with the other groups, this one was composed entirely of women.

All were fashionably dressed but none as elegantly as Francesca, and none wore a kleid gown similar to hers. I wondered whether others had their clothes fashioned by Bianca.

Upon seeing the gathering of women, I made what I thought was an innocuous comment. "You are fortunate to have so many friends who share similar interests."

Those words caused Francesca to open a window into her soul. "You are a man. You see women passing time playing cards and reading the classics, and you think we do it by choice. My father is a member of the Signoria. You studied law at the university and soon will be taken into a guild. You will become a magistrate charged with passing judgment on others and upholding the laws of the Republic. These women are not allowed to do such things. Society constrains us more than the corsets we wear. It allows us only to engage in polite pastimes and to bear children."

My appearance in the room, the only male, barely registered with the women. Their activities continued without interruption, except for one of the performers who flashed a smile in my direction. If not for her acknowledging my presence, my ego would have been utterly crushed.

One of the readers looked up thoughtfully and quoted,

"He is more than a hero
he is a god in my eyes
the man who is allowed
to sit beside us."

She was gazing generally in my direction, so I foolishly assumed that I might be the inspiration for the passage she selected. Its phrasing reminded me of a Roman poet, whom I knew only because he is one of Alessa's favorites. I ventured a guess and said, "Catullus?"

Her face saddened slightly. To her companions she said, "Obviously this one is not a student of the classics."

Then to me she said, "Not even the same civilization. Greece. Sappho."

I bowed my head slightly to acknowledge my error. Classical literature is another of the gaps in my education. I quickly scanned the room to see if any of the women were engrossed in law journals, a topic I do have knowledge of. Not surprisingly, none were.

Francesca attempted to defend me. "Nico is a magistrate" - yes, she exaggerated - "a recent graduate of Bologna. Sadly, law schools do not emphasize the classics."

To my ears her words sounded more like an excuse than a defense. One reader proclaimed, "Ladies, we should fix that. A good foundation in the classics can make men be more attentive husbands."

"And better lovers," added another.

My ego had been stung by inattention before, now it was learning humility.

Feeling a presence behind us I turned to see that Bianca had entered the room. Francesca noticed her too and, said to me, "Sandro completed the painting that he had shown you in the garden last week."

Then to Bianca she asked, "Would you like to show Nico the finished work?"

So, I thought, it is possible for Francesca to engage people with questions and not only with commands.

Chapter 37

Bianca nodded, then took my arm and rescued me from the room. Behind us, one of the readers said to her companions, "At least he has heard of Catullus. My sister is betrothed to a dolt who has never even read Boccaccio."

The painting was in another part of the mansion. To reach it we first passed through a room with coral colored walls decorated with mosaics depicting the lives of saints. With my attention locked on Bianca, I would not have noticed the walls nor the mosaics had she not commented on one of Saint Peter.

"It was thoughtful of Francesca to suggest that I show you the painting, to free you from the clutches of her friends. They are pleasant when they are alone, but together they can behave as felines."

After a short pause, Bianca confessed, "I am not very comfortable with them either. My education is limited. I know nothing of either Sappho or Catullus."

I leaned forward and kissed her gently on the cheek. She looked up at me, surprised but not offended. To avoid an awkward silence I said, "Now I know two things about you: that you have limited education and your family is not Italian. Francesca told me only that your father came from one of the low countries."

"My father is a doctor who came to Italy from the Kingdom of Denmark to study medicine at the University of Salerno. He met my mother at the university. The medical school has a large garden where plants are grown for use in the medications. My mother tended plants in the garden. She was allowed to do that because her father, my grandfather, was the master in charge of the entire property.

"After my father earned his medical certification, he joined the Santa Maria della Scala hospital in Siena. My brother and I were born in Siena and that's where we live now. So it is true that my ancestors are not Italian, but I am."

"Both of your parents were at the university. Didn't they urge you to continue your education?"

"My father tried to interest me in becoming a physician. He kept saying I could be one of the first women to do so."

"Are there women students at Salerno?" I asked in surprise.

"I don't think so, but I'm not certain. Father never mentioned any. Anyway, I never had a desire to become a physician. My interest is fashion design. When I was about ten years old, I met a man that father was treating at the hospital. Both the patient and his wife are designers from Paris. They went to Milan to meet with a clothier and were traveling through Siena on holiday when the man injured himself in a fall. I became so fascinated by their stories about fashion design that I went back to the hospital every day to learn more until the man recovered. They still write to me with news of the latest fashion trends in Paris."

"And now you have your own clothing design business."

"Yes, it is rare for a woman to operate a business by herself. I can do so because I design clothes for women. Women are willing to buy from me, especially because I create garments in the latest Parisian styles. Men care little about style, so I do not design clothes for men. Anyway, men would never buy clothes from a woman," Francesca explained.

"Is your father disappointed that you did not become a physician?"

"No, he has come to accept my decision. Whenever the opportunity presents, he shows himself to be proud of my success. I did fulfill one of his wishes though. He wanted me to study music, so I learned to play the lute. I will never be a great musician," she began laughing, "but my playing does not drive people away."

We entered the north wing of the palazzo through a room whose light green walls held frescoes of ancient Greek gods. The south wing had paintings of Christian saints that contrasted with the pagan gods in this wing. I wondered whether their presence and separation spoke to Luca's artistic sensibilities or his religious convictions.

Finally, we reached the gallery that contained the Pitti family portraits. Nearly all were unfamiliar to me. Among the few I did recognize were Luca, of course, his father, and also his son who serves as Florentine ambassador to Francia. All the portraits were somber heads with stern expressions on dark indistinct backgrounds. The only obvious difference is that some heads face left and some face right.

Two easels stood at the far end of the room. The one positioned in front of a blank section of white wall held the portrait of Francesca. It was exquisite. Francesca had not told me her impression of the completed work, but she must be delighted with it. The colors were brilliant even in the low light of the oil lamps.

Maestro Lippi had captured Francesca's strong spirit and the intensity of her eyes. Unlike the other portraits, she was not merely a head. Lippi captured her as a real person walking through the lovely meadow behind the palazzo. The image is so lifelike that I almost expected the figure to take a step across the canvas. I wondered if this portrait of Francesca, a vibrant woman, would find a place in this gallery of staid masculine faces.

Sandro had matched the maestro's style perfectly. His background had the same brush stroke lengths, widths, and subtle blending of color as the portrait. It was impossible to tell that the work was created by two different artists.

Fra Filippo Lippi had not yet returned from Prato;

consequently the painting bore no signature. When the maestro returns to Florence, he will examine the complete work and, if he is satisfied with the background that Sandro added, then he will sign the painting.

I said to Bianca, "Lippi is the maestro, and he did create the portrait, so it is fitting that his signature appears, but in my opinion, it is unfair that Sandro receives no credit for his beautiful background."

Bianca laughed. "There is a young girl in Siena who sometimes helps me with the dresses. She can do simple stitching and sew buttons. I wonder if she feels the same. All the completed dresses bear my mark, but she receives no credit for her efforts."

After studying the portrait for several minutes, we moved to view the painting set on the second easel. It was entirely out of place in this portrait gallery. At first glance, it appeared to be a scene from Greek mythology. Set in a springtime garden, it depicts Adonis, the handsome hunter, approaching the beautiful goddess Aphrodite, reclining on a lounge with the cherub Cupid circling above. Adonis displays the physical perfection that could only exist in an artist's imagination. But the reclining Aphrodite was not a fantasy. She was Francesca. Sandro had worked his magic in this painting: Adonis's muscles glisten as though rubbed with oil, and Francesca's hair shows individual strands cascading onto her shoulders. My eyes drifted to the signature in the corner of the canvas, 'S. Botticelli.'

"At least Sandro will get recognition for this one," I said. "I wonder where it will hang. Surely not in this gallery with these staid portraits."

Bianca's eyes twinkled. "Perhaps I should sign it too. I made the gown that Aphrodite is wearing. It is the first one I've made for a goddess."

"I have known Sandro since we were young boys. He has always had a free spirit. I am not surprised that paintings like this one are his passion. Creating portraits like these," I gestured to the wall of faces, "would confine him. Maybe one day he will find a patron who shares his passion."

As we were leaving the gallery Luca's portrait caught my attention. This was my third visit to his estate and I had yet to meet him. What draws him away from his beautiful palazzo and drives him to scheme for political power?

"I have seen Luca at events throughout the city, but I have not yet seen him here at his palazzo. Have you met him?" I asked.

"Yes, once or twice," Bianca answered, "but he spends more time away than he does here at his lovely home. I have seen him come here for only the briefest moment to give instructions to the workmen and then leave to attend another appointment."

Bianca changed the subject abruptly. "I have told you about myself and where my family came from. Now you must tell me about Nico. You have the dark hair and dark eyes of Italians, but you are taller than many Florentines, and your features are softer, less angular. Is it possible that your family too includes a foreign heritage?"

"My uncle Nunzio says his mother once told him that one of her relatives survived the great flood when the original Ponte Vecchio was destroyed. That was more than one hundred years ago. If the story is true, and I have no reason to doubt that it is, then my father's family has been in Florence at least that long. My mother's family, however, is not Italian so your speculation about my foreign heritage is correct. My father met my mother when he was a military envoy to the Kingdom of Aragon. My mother was Aragonese. She was born in a small town in the Principality of Catalonia. Unfortunately, I know nothing of her family."

As we talked, Bianca and I found our way to a terrace overlooking the gardens at the rear of the palazzo. The moon, now risen above the hills, cast a stark white light that siphoned color from the shrubs and flowers turning the garden into a surreal landscape. We sat and talked for hours, and the more she told me of herself the more enchanted I became.

At the university my life was stable and predictable. Now it was filling with uncertainties that competed for my attention. There were career decisions to be made, and the Sporcones needed to be stopped. Yet walking home from Palazzo Pitti my only thoughts were of Bianca. She was returning to Siena in the morning. How long would it be before I would see her again?

Chapter 38 Wednesday, August 15, 1464

Ferragosto, the Feast of the Assumption, is a religious holiday when families attend mass together in honor of Christ's mother Mary. But it is the anticipation of secular events later in the day, not the church services, that drives youngsters like Giorgio to awaken earlier than anyone else in the household. To keep the noise of his scuffling on the stone floors from disturbing everyone else, I decided to take him on an early morning walk away from the house. I cut two thick slices of bread and had Giorgio slather them with olive paste, put a handful of cherries and a water flask into a leather pouch, and headed out with Giorgio at my heels.

We walked to the river and followed it to Piazza dei Priori where a small crowd had gathered awaiting a courier who would bring the latest news. Several times each day couriers on horseback ride to designated locations throughout the city to read announcements of the Signoria and other news. Peasants and students have little interest in news. It is shopkeepers, artisans, and old people who gather in the piazza awaiting the latest happenings.

The gatherings are also social events where neighbors share their latest personal stories. The 'mother' of this group was a gray-haired woman wearing a white apron who passed among her acquaintances offering each a sampling from her basket of biscuits. Today the group's attention was captured by a flabby shoemaker who regaled the group with news of a local happening. Every time a new person joined the group the man repeated his story, and with each retelling he became more animated causing his beefy chins to bounce like the wattle of a gobbling turkey. I moved close enough to hear.

"My wife and I were walking along the river last night. No, late afternoon, not night. She, my wife, has a dog and every afternoon she goes for a walk so she can shit." A bout of laughter from the arose crowd. He tried to correct his statement adding, "The dog shits, not my wife."

An onlooker shouted, "She must be a strange woman. I thought everyone shits." This brought forth another howl from the crowd.

The fleshy one ignored the taunting and continued, "We reached the Rubiconte bridge when the dog started barking and trying to climb down the steep slope to the river. That's when I saw something lying in the river. Well, it was half in the river and half up on a bridge pillar. I've seen all kinds of stuff floating in the river. Sometimes they get caught as this thing did. Once I saw a pig. It was alive and tried to climb onto the stones, but it fell back in.

"This time it wasn't a pig, it was a person. At first I thought some drunk had fallen from the bridge. I've seen that before too. My wife said I should climb down and help him. What a damn fool she can be. I'm not crazy. If I had climbed down the slope, I'd be in the river with that fool. We watched for a long time, but the person did not move, not even a little. I said to my wife 'he could be dead.'

"I sent my wife to the Palazzo dei Priori to fetch the Guardia. 'That's their job. Let them get off their asses,' I told her. Two of them came. They were young and strong, but still they struggled to climb down the bank and pull the man from the river. When they finally dragged him up the slope, we saw he was dead."

"Who was he?" someone asked.

The rotund man raised his short arms and extended his hands. "Never saw him before."

Another person asked, "Where did they take him?"

"One of the Guardia men went to get a wagon so they could take the body to the mortuary at Santa Croce."

When the courier finally arrived, his official news paled in comparison to the shoemaker's tale. Hearing nothing else of interest I gathered Giorgio, who had been playing with a stray dog, and the two of us continued on our way to the church.

My studies at the university kept me from attending Ferragosto mass with my family for the past three years. Today our family, Donato, Joanna, Giorgio, Alessa, uncle Nunzio, and I, along with our friends Simone and Lexia, filled an entire pew at Santa Croce, our parish church. In his homily, Friar Bernardo proffered 'we each must pave our own pathway to heaven.' His words held special significance for me at this pivotal time in my life. I was equally thankful for the stream of greetings from neighbors congratulating me on earning a law degree and welcoming me back home.

After mass I walked from the church with uncle Nunzio. "I hope you don't mind that I sent Jacopo to you without asking permission, but it is not safe for him to remain in Florence."

Uncle Nunzio's squint and wrinkled nose showed his confusion. "What are you saying, Nico. Are you speaking of Jacopo Sporcone? I have not seen the boy."

Jacopo had nowhere else to go. Something must have prevented him from reaching uncle Nunzio's farm. Two thoughts coalesced in my mind: A body was found in the river and Jacopo was missing. I prayed it was just a coincidence. "Excuse me, uncle, I need to see the friar."

I rushed to the sacristy hoping to find Friar Bernardo, but he had already left the church heading for the friary when I fell in beside him. "Father, I found your sermon to be very enlightening."

He took my arm in part as a gesture of appreciation for my compliment and in part to help steady himself. My support let him quicken his step to a more normal pace.

"Thank you, Nico, but I only speak words. It is your

acceptance of the words that makes them special. It pleased my soul to see that the Argenti family is once again reunited. Word has reached my ears that you have earned a Doctorus Juris degree."

"Yes, father, that is true."

"And from Bologna, a fine school. Tell me, what will you do now?"

"I have applied for membership in the magistrates guild here in Florence. If I am granted membership, then I will learn what opportunities open to me."

I tried not to let my impatience show. "Excuse me father, but I must ask a question. Yesterday there was a man found in the river not far from here. I am told he was brought to the mortuary here at Santa Croce."

"Yes, the Guardia brought him. His body is in the mortuary; God rest his soul."

"Has anyone identified him?"

"No one has come forward. Do you know him?"

"Perhaps; may I see him?"

"If you must, but you will find it a distressing sight. He was badly injured."

Chapter 39

When we reached the friary, Friar Bernardo arranged for a worker to guide me to the mortuary located in a building behind the friary. He led me down stone steps to a chamber, no more than a large pit, where the body of Jacopo Sporcone lay on a stone bier.

I barely glimpsed the battered body before the sight and the stench of death raised bile in my stomach and drove me to retreat from the pit. Outside I gulped the pure morning air to dispel my nausea. The worker followed me up the steps, then closed and latched the crypt door.

"That happens to everybody the first time. It's the stink. It will pass. You'll feel better in a few minutes. Do you know him?"

I did not answer. Instead, I replied, "Has anyone come forward to identify him?"

"No. No one."

"Can you tell what happened to him?"

"Drunk I suppose. It is easy for drunks to fall into the river. It has happened before."

"The face has many deep bruises. Do all recovered from the river have injuries such as his?"

The worker paused briefly recalling images of bodies he had seen previously before responding. "Not as much. This one was hurt worse than the others."

"Could he have been beaten before falling into the river?"

The worker answered with only a shrug of his shoulders.

"What did the Guardia say, the ones who brought him here? Did they think he was beaten? Will they do an investigation?"

"They said nothing. The Guardia have many responsibilities. Unless the body is identified..." He left the thought unfinished.

Every day in Florence peasants die, and many from unusual circumstances. The Guardia has neither the resources nor the interest to conduct investigations. Ever since the Black Death claimed hundreds every day, peasants and princes alike, the Guardia and all people of Florence have become immune to death. It is not good to be callous, but the indifference shields them from pain too great to bear and impossible to fathom. Since the time of the great plague, only their loved ones and the servants of God mourn the dead.

The Guardia and the workers at Santa Croce may believe the body in their mortuary is another unfortunate drunk, but I knew that poor Jacopo Sporcone was beaten and probably dead before he was discarded into the river. My stomach recoiled again, but this time it was from anger. The Sporcones were responsible for another killing, the murder of a poor innocent boy. I vowed that they would be held accountable this time.

Rather than returning home directly I followed a route that meandered to the river where I sat on a stone block atop the embankment and stared into the muddy brown water, considering how to fulfill my vow. I remembered sitting on that same block many years ago with neighborhood friends. It was a place we passed every day returning to our homes after school. We sat there and talked about what we might do with the knowledge we were gaining from our tutors. How could we make use of philosophy, Greek, Latin, history, and mathematics? We imagined great futures. Each of us boasted that he would be a future leader of the Republic like Cosimo de Medici or first Chancellor Benedetto Accolti. We pondered the challenges that might face the Republic, and us, when we ascended to those lofty positions.

Maybe Jacopo had rested on this same block and had similar dreams. The muddy water of the Arno gave us no answers then, just as it gave me no answer now.

A young man walked toward me on the Lungo l'Arno, the road alongside the river. He was small and frail like Jacopo Sporcone, and his walk resembled Jacopo's, timid steps as though his mere presence might offend someone. He passed me with his eyes downcast, never glancing in my direction. Was he too a victim of intimidation? How many others are captives like Jacopo in this city of supposedly free men?

When the young man turned out of sight, my thinking returned to the dilemma of getting justice for Jacopo. A person of Bartolomeo Scala's stature could call for an investigation by the Guardia, but a request by me to investigate the death of an unknown person would only be ignored. How would Salvatore Sporcone react if I did identify the remains as his son Jacopo? Would that make me a target? If Jacopo had revealed that I was the one who told him about his parents, then I might already be a target, I realized suddenly.

Chapter 40

Arriving home I found everyone already wearing the bright red of the Santa Croce district. A long-established tradition is for everyone to wear their district colors to the Ferragosto events. Donato and Giorgio wore matching red shirts; Joanna and Alessa wore matching red blouses. My red shirt, a keepsake from my youth, had not grown with me. It would fit Giorgio better than me. Simone had no garment of any kind in the proper Santa Croce red color. Joanna solved the shortcoming by making red armbands for both of us. Simone, ever the fun-loving spirit, eagerly donned the red color of the Santa Croce neighborhood. The excitement of my family members was contagious. It pushed thoughts of Jacopo aside, at least temporarily.

Major city-wide events are arranged well in advance of Ferragosto, but a tradition of the holiday is that smaller events, often stemming from friendly rivalries between neighborhoods, can be initiated at any time. One such involved a challenge from a tavern in the San Giovanni district made to the Uccello. The challenge specified that the Uccello should send 'five of its finest archers' to the San Trinita bridge where they would receive detailed instructions for the competition.

This challenge was typical of the events that made Ferragosto such an enjoyable and memorable holiday. The challengers knew the Uccello could not send 'five of its finest archers,' because it was a restaurant that had no archers. Likewise, Donato knew that the Bull Horn, the tavern that issued the challenge, also had no archers. The event was fashioned strictly for amusement by Laslo, Donato's good friend and proprietor of the Bull Horn. Each establishment would try to find five men who could at least shoot arrows without injuring themselves or anyone else.

Donato discovered that he, Simone, and three other members of his staff had at least some experience with longbows. They would comprise team Uccello. The five designated archers marched to Ponte San Trinita, a bridge spanning the Arno river. The archers, trailed by a flock of cheering well-wishers, waved their bows in the air and shouted to everyone they passed en-route that their victory will bring great honor to Santa Croce. At the river, they were greeted by opponents representing the Bull Horn tavern, clad in identical tunics of San Giovanni green.

Rules of the competition were simple. A 'pig' would be cast into the river from the bridge. Archers lining the riverbank would shoot at the 'pig' as it drifted in the river current. The team that put the most arrows into the target would be declared the winner.

The prize would be bragging rights.

For this tournament, the 'pig' was a log topped with a bundle of straw. It might be possible to drive arrows into the log, but the straw was the easier target. Archers were allowed to shoot as many arrows as possible while the 'pig' floated past their position.

The swift current made it hard for the archers to compensate their aiming. Donato sank two arrows in the straw before the ‘pig’ passed out of range. Giulio, the Uccello’s yard boss, managed one hit, and Simone put two arrows into the straw and landed a third that hung precariously from the log. Their score was easily bested by the archers of the Bull Horn. The outcome surprised no one because advantage in these events always rests with the challengers who have the chance to practice in advance; whereas the contenders do not even learn the rules of the game until they arrive at the venue.

My attention was divided between the archers and a swarthy spectator clad head-to-toe in San Giovanni green. His barrel-chest and narrow hips cloaked in bright green evoked the image of a ripe artichoke, which hampered my ability to recall where I had seen him before. After staring at him for several moments, I remembered him as the carriage driver who had delivered Salvatore Sporcone to the Milanese embassy reception.

At the conclusion of the archery tournament, I moved to the gathering of San Govanni supporters under the guise of congratulating them on their victory. My approach to 'artichoke man' was direct. “It is fortunate for you that Salvatore can do without your service today."

Disarmed by the thrill of San Govanni's victory, he did not suspect a hidden purpose in my comment. "Salvatore isn't going anywhere today," he replied., "I was supposed to drive Alphonso to Pistoia, but he said that today he has private business so he would go by himself. I don't care what he does as long as I get to enjoy Ferrragosto."

'Artichoke man' departed with his San Govanni neighbors for celebratory drinks at the Bull Horn. In the custom of the day, they invited the losers, Donato's archers and supporters, to accompany them as their guests. We walked together from the river to the San Giovanni district, but rather than stopping at the Bull Horn with the others I continued on to the convent of Sant' Apollonia.

Chapter 41

Because Jacopo had mentioned Sister Teresa to Salvatore Sporcone, Jacopo's murder made me fearful for Sister Teresa's safety.

Sant' Apollonia, the largest convent in Florence, occupies a modest stone building fronting on Via Gallo. Sister Cecilia, the abbess of the convent, is the spiritual guide of twenty-two Benedictine nuns, Sister Teresa among them, and five novices who reside at the convent plus six nuns who are placed with families in the parish.

A very distressed novice answered my knock on the door leading to the convent office. She looked at me apprehensively, waiting for me to speak.

"Good afternoon, sister. I would like to see Sister Teresa if she is available."

My simple request brought the young novice to the verge of tears.

"She is not here. She is missing."

"Missing? How long has she been missing?" I demanded.

"She took part in Vesper prayers yesterday afternoon, but she did not attend Compline, her bed was not slept in, and she was not present at the prayers this morning. She did not get permission from the abbess to be away. None of the sisters has ever been absent like that before."

"Surely someone must have seen her leave."

"A boy came to the convent office with a message saying that Sister Teresa was needed at San Marco. The boy said that a monk outside the church asked him to deliver the message. I was the one who passed the message to her." Her voice trailed and tears streamed down her cheeks.

I pressed my handkerchief into her hand. She wiped her tears and sank back into a chair. It was an awkward situation. I have comforted distressed women by wrapping my arms around them and holding them close, but that did not seem appropriate for soothing this young sister of God. I sat beside her and gently held her hand until the sobs faded to whimpers that gradually decreased in frequency and intensity.

"I am dishonoring my vows. I should be praying for Sister Teresa and trusting that God will protect her, not weeping like a child."

"It is possible to have both compassion and faith," I said slowly. Never in my life did I imagine myself giving spiritual advice to a nun. Upon hearing my words, the novice raised her head and looked up at me, surprised to see someone sitting next to her as though I had not been there the whole time. She withdrew her hand from under mine and leaned away.

"May I see the abbess?" I asked.

"Sister Cecilia went to the church, to San Marco, to tell the bishop that Sister Teresa is missing." After a pause, "and to ask that the friars pray for her. If we all pray God will keep her safe."

Prayers are always a good beginning, but in this situation, God might welcome some help. From the convent of Sant' Apollonia I went directly to the church of San Marco where I found Sister Cecilia and Father Matteo in the church office. The priest sat behind a small desk with his hands folded and resting on the desk like a well-behaved student. The nun was seated on one of the chairs that lined the wall of the office. She sat erect but with her head bowed. Her folded hands rested on her lap. Not wanting to interrupt their prayers I paused outside the room.

When Father Matteo finally noticed me standing at the door he beckoned, "You may enter, my son."

Sister Cecilia raised her head revealing the tightened skin and darkened eyes of worry on her normally jovial face. I stepped into the room and moved to the desk where Father Matteo was seated.

"Father. Sister. A novice at the convent told me that Sister Teresa is missing. I believe she may have been taken by the same ones who ... harmed the boy found in the river yesterday."

The two servants of God stared at me, waiting for me to explain my allegation. I told them that Jacopo had asked Sister

Teresa about the disappearance of his parents. I told them my belief that the Sporcones were responsible for Jacopo's death and my fear that they might also be the ones who abducted Sister Teresa. At the mention of the name Sporcone, they both winced, signifying they already knew, or suspected, that the Sporcones are capable of vile acts.

"I hoped that knowledge of his parents would help free Jacopo from his abusive situation. She was his caretaker when he was an infant. She is the one person who could give him the truth and whom he would believe."

I could not say, "I am the one who told Jacopo about his parents, so I share the guilt for his death."

Nor could I say, "I cannot bear it if harm, or worse, comes to another."

Father Matteo heard the words I could not speak. He rose from the desk, placed a hand on my shoulder, and escorted me to the chair next to Sister Cecilia.

"If we tell someone of a horror done by the devil," he said, "that does not make us responsible if the devil commits other horrible acts. Do not burden your soul with a guilt it does not deserve to carry."

His words helped, but only a little. "I cannot let this continue. I must find Sister Teresa. Can you help me? Do you know the monk who took her?"

Father Matteo said, "I spoke with the boy who delivered the message. Although he could give me only a vague description of the monk, from his description I am certain that the monk was not one of us. As you know, at San Marco we are all of the Dominican order and we all wear identical robes. No religious order wears robes that fit the description the boy gave me. Either the boy was mistaken, or the person who left with Sister Teresa was not really a monk."

As he spoke, father Matteo returned to his place behind the desk. He sat and again folded his hands and rested them on the desktop. He no doubt saw the disappointment in my eyes. If we did not know who took the nun, then how could I possibly find her?

Father Matteo spoke again. "The boy watched the monk help Sister Teresa climb into a wagon. The monk told her she was in danger and he was taking her to a house in Pistoia where she would be safe."

How could this be? I thought. Who else would know that Sister Teresa might be in danger? And why take her to Pistoia?

Sister Cecilia expressed the doubts I was thinking, and she did so with conviction. "I do not believe the person who took the sister was a man of God. It is a ruse. No one of legitimate purpose, especially one of the cloth, would remove a sister from a convent without obtaining the permission of the abbess. Sister Teresa can be better safeguarded in our convent than in any dwelling at Pistoia. I will pray for God to lead you to her and for her safe return."

Father Matteo's eyes narrowed in thought, then he stood and

began speaking. "The mention of Salvatore Sporcone and Pistoia reminds me of an incident last year. One of the parishioners, a carpenter, came to mass with his arm bandaged. When I asked him what had happened, he said the arm was injured while he was doing work at Salvatore Sporcone's cabin in Pistoia."

The Sporcones had ordered the killing of at least three people. Would they hesitate to add a nun to the list? Do they know someone in Pistoia willing to stain his soul with the blood of a nun?

Chapter 42

I felt sure that I could travel to Pistoia and find Sporcone's cabin by myself, but I was equally sure that I would need help to rescue the nun from her captors. Although one person masquerading as a monk took her from Florence, there could be more than one person holding her at the cabin. It was also possible that the captors were armed and experienced with weapons. My skill with weapons was limited to a fencing class at the university. I am hardly a match for Salvatore Sporcone's villains.

From the church I went to Campo di Marte. Donato was among the ribbon of spectators lining the jousting track. Upon hearing only the briefest explanation, he was eager to help liberate Sister Teresa. He set out to recruit additional men while I met with the abbess aain to learn whether she had any information that might be useful to us.

I rejoined Donato and the others at a stable called Casa di

Cavalli, the house of horses. Donato arrived at the stable with three rugged looking men whom he introduced as mercenaries. "Nico, you met Giulio at the Uccello. The two men with him are associates of his. They are with a mercenary army here in Florence employed by the Signoria."

Giulio stands a head taller than most men, has heavily muscled arms and broad shoulders. Lifting a pipa of wine can be a struggle for two normal men, but I had seen Giulio hoist a pipa onto his shoulders seemingly without effort. The two men at his side were every bit his equal. They were big, muscled, had nearly identical wavy black hair and were dressed in similar leather jackets, unusually warm garb for mid-August. The most significant distinction between them is that each shows his own unique set of scars.

"These are my cohorts. This is Federico," Giulio said pointing to his left, then to his right, "and this is Roberto. Donato told us that a nun has been abducted."

"Father Matteo and I believe she has been taken to a cabin in Pistoia owned by Salvatore Sporcone. It is my shortsightedness that put her in danger so I must bring her back. As Donato told you, I need help, but I am not able to pay for your services."

Giulio gave a dismissive wave of his hand. "Mercenaries do things for many reasons. Money, of course, is a powerful motivator. I know many who would fight in conflicts for the thrills alone. The three of us, Federico, Roberto, and I, are men of faith. Before coming to Florence, we were commissioned by the Papal

States to keep travelers safe from highwaymen."

Roberto added, "While working for the Papacy we gained a respect for the church."

Donato interjected, "That is why they are willing to help you."

Federico explained further, "My niece is a novice in the same order as Sister Teresa, a Benedictine. I cannot let the capture of a nun go unpunished. There is a place in hell for those who would harm a person of God."

"The seven of us," Donato began, "should be enough to..."

"No," Roberto interrupted, "We three are trained to hunt people. We move quickly and know how to surprise our prey. Seven people are too many. Three is enough."

He looked to Giulio for support.

"Roberto tells the truth. The three of us can enter buildings in silence to recover hostages. We have done it before. We will bring back the sister. I promise."

Giulio looked to Donato then both turned to me.

"I understand what you are saying, but I need to be there. Maybe Joanna was right when she said that I should not have gotten involved in this. Maybe I should have said no to Chancellor Scala when he first asked for my help, but I didn't say no. I let myself become involved. I am the one who put Sister Teresa in danger. I could not bear the guilt if harm comes to her."

Giulio placed an understanding hand on my shoulder. "Very well, four of us will go."

While we finished planning, a stableman prepared four sturdy mounts. It is forbidden for anyone except the military and police to carry swords or other weapons in the city, but despite that prohibition, I expected that the former mercenaries would want to arm themselves for the hostile encounter we anticipated.

When I asked about weapons Gulio replied, “We need no weapons other than these.” He held up one of the gauntlets he carried. “This gauntlet is leather outside and leather inside, but between the layers are metal plates, many small plates that let my hand open and close easily. Fighting is better than with the armor gloves that knights wear. I can move my hand quickly to deflect a sword or to catch it in the air.”

Giulio lifted the weapon held in his other hand, a flanged mace with a wooden shaft and a fluted iron head. “Soldiers carry short swords. The shaft of my mace is longer than their swords. I can reach them before they reach me, and this metal head easily pierces their leather armor.”

He pounded a fist against his chest. “Our leather is stronger than what the soldiers wear. Ours is buffalo hide tanned in a secret way learned from the Goths. Only two members of the Tanners Guild know the secret.”

Roberto pointed to a deep slash on his jacket sleeve. “Look at this cut. A stinking cazzo in Urbino tried to cut me with his long sword.” He raised his arm to his lips and kissed the jacket sleeve. “This jacket saved my arm, grazie a Dio, thanks to God.”

A fiendish grin spread across Roberto's face. “When I finished with that cazzo they buried him with his sword. Maybe he uses it better in hell."

When the horses were readied we rode first to the friary at San Marco where Friar Augustine, whom I have known since we were youngsters, let us borrow hooded monk robes. The robes would mask our identities and, more importantly, they would make the Sporcones believe that Sister Teresa had been rescued by the church. Thinking that the church had dispatched a band of 'warrior monks' to rescue Sister Teresa might prevent the Sporcones from abusing her again.

Finding robes to fit us was a challenge. None were of the proper size for my three strapping companions. The friary has its share of corpulent members making it easy to find robes of ample girth, but none of the friars equaled the height of the three mercenaries. Instead of reaching to men's ankles, as they rightly should, the longest of the coverings scarcely reached below their knees. Although I am taller than average, I found several robes of adequate length. My difficulty was in finding one to fit my slender form. Many of them were broad enough that they could have enveloped both Donato and me simultaneously.

After selecting the most suitable of the ill-fitting garb, we remounted and departed Florence onto the Via Cassia. Via Cassia, originally an Etruscan pathway, was widened and leveled by Roman engineers to accommodate a constant stream of military supply wagons. In Roman times Pistoia was a fortified garrison that shielded the Romans from barbarian tribes in the North.

The mercenaries' demeanor showed they had lost none of the disciplines that had made them victorious warriors. They sat erect with backs straight and eyes attentive to their surroundings. Their horses kept to a single column spaced widely apart, a valued defensive tactic. The men swapped positions in the column frequently to put fresh eyes at the point, although I was always the third in line - a lamb protected by its flock.

By reputation, mercenaries are bands of criminals, thugs who would cut their own as quickly as an opponent for a measure of gold. But the captain of these men sought only men who had distinguished themselves during their military services. He was a strict leader who drilled his charges with rigor, and those methods served him well. They knew loyalty to their sponsor, to their captain, and to each other. They did not know defeat.

Chapter 43

Pistoia lies not far from Florence, a mere twenty miles distant. Between them, the Via Cassia follows the center line of a broad valley. As we approached Pistoia, with the tower of San Zeno cathedral clearly visible, an old woman leading a donkey laden with produce shuffled along the road in our direction. Seeing the oncoming line of monks, she coaxed her reluctant animal to the side of the road, blessed herself, and stood to await us with her head bowed. Roberto blessed the old woman with great sweeping arm movements that formed the sign of the cross in a theatrical display she would not soon forget. Roberto had easily adapted to his clerical role. When Roberto ended his performance, Giulio stepped forward and asked the woman for directions to the Sporcone villa. She did not know of the Sporcone, nor of their villa, but she did point the way to the office of the Guardia.

Pistoia is not a hilltop citadel. Although she was wrapped in defensive walls, Pistoia suffered repeated conquests by her more powerful neighbors, Lucca and Florence. Since then, as a member of the Florentine Republic, Pistoia has enjoyed the peace and prosperity that comes from being a link in the chain of towns stretching between Florence and Lucca.

The directions given to us by the old woman led us to a gate in the city's protective wall that lofted nearly three times the height of a man. From the entry, we headed directly to the central piazza guided by the sight of the San Zeno bell tower. Every road we passed was alive with activity, merchants moving goods, houses and shops being built. We passed a bakery whose aromas reminded me that I had not eaten since breakfast. The stableman where we rented our horses had provided us with water flasks, but in our haste we had not taken any food. I noted the location of the bakery and promised myself we would sample its delicacies upon our return.

Roberto made no such promises. He let the tempting aromas pull him into the bakery. Moments later he reappeared in the doorway and beckoned us to join him inside where the shopkeeper was busily slathering four thick slices of oat bread with a generous layer of hazelnut butter. My stomach growled in anticipation, quieting only when the first bite passed my lips.

The shopkeeper dismissed me when I offered to pay saying that a visit to his shop by four monks portended good fortune that would not come if he accepted payment from us. We all thanked the shopkeeper for his generosity, but Roberto felt the need to express his appreciation more overtly. Using the same dramatic gestures he had used with the old woman earlier, he blessed the food, the premises, the shopkeeper, his wife, and their apprentice. By the time Roberto had finished his antics Giulio, Federico, and I had left the shop and begun walking the final steps to the central piazza.

The Guardia headquarters consisted of two rooms in the Palazzo del Commune, the city office building, located in the central piazza. On a bench outside the palazzo slumped a disheveled old sergeant who came awake at the sound of our approach. Unlike the old woman we met on Via Cassia, he showed no surprise at having his sleep interrupted by a troupe of unfamiliar monks. Roberto was not moved to offer a blessing to the groggy militiaman, so it was Giulio who adopted the role of an itinerant monk. "My son, we seek the estate of Signor Sporcone. Do you know it?"

The sergeant looked toward a hill a short distance outside the city and pointed. "There," he said

I squinted, unsure whether my eyes truly detected a structure on the far hill or simply a rock outcropping. The old sergeant shifted his aim and pointed to one of the wide roads that angled away from the piazza. "Questa strada... fuori... seconda a destra, this road... outside... second to the right," he said dragging out the words as though merely speaking them took extraordinary effort.

Having discharged his duty, he refolded his arms across his wide belly. It was his indication that we should let him return to his dreams. Such is the life of our civil servants.

The road led us out through the city wall and into the open countryside that surrounds the city. The road continued straight to a sturdy wooden bridge over the Torrente Ombrone river. Upstream a short distance the river forked, and on the bank of the minor fork, a group of boys and girls sat on a cluster of boulders. The writing tablets held by several of them suggested they were students. One of the boys strummed a guitar accompanying a familiar folk tune being sung by the others. The group so enjoyed the pleasant afternoon, the peaceful riverside setting, and each other's company, that they took no notice of us.

The road continued straight. When it reached the base of a range of hills, a narrow road veered off to the right and a short distance later another - the seconda a destra, the second right. That road curved and began a gentle rise from the grassy fields on the valley floor into the forested Apennine foothills. Hardly more than a dirt path, it wound around the backside of a hill taking us out of sight of the town below. We slowed the horses to prevent them from stumbling on the rocks littering the path, and my companions lengthened the distance between them making it harder for them to be targeted by an ambush in the dense forest.

As one who lives in cities, I found the silence of the forest unnerving. Florence is never silent: always people are talking, dogs are barking, carriages are bouncing over rough roads, men complain about their wives, and wives complain about their husbands. Even uncle Nunzio's vineyard outside the city is ever filled with animal sounds and bird songs. But in this forest there were no people, and the thick vegetation absorbed all sounds of any woodland animals. There was only the gentle flexing of leather when I shifted position in my saddle and the rhythmic cadence of our horses' footfalls.

Since leaving the town we had seen neither houses nor side roads. Our climb took us through mixed oak and chestnut forest. We passed only one overlook where a steep drop beside the road gave a view across the valley. To the far north, a high ridge stretched across the horizon. I guessed it to be the mountains known as the Horn, but they were too far, and I too unfamiliar with the region, to be certain.

Gradually the path flattened, and the hardwoods gave way to stands of towering pines, so tall and densely packed that they blocked the sun. The path twisted and turned to wend its way between the burly trunks. Dim light and a thick carpeting of pine needles made it a barren ground devoid of vegetation. With no young plants or other food to sustain them, the woodland animals had no incentive to live there.

I mused that the arrow-straight trunks of the trees with no side branches below their crowns stood like a thicket of reeds magnified to the scale of a colossus. An image unfolded of a young boy ... a toddler ... me, hiding among reeds at the edge of a pond, stifling my giggles so my father, the hunter in this game, could not hear. Father, mother and I had gone to Pisa. I was too young to know why we had gone there, but I know it was Pisa because I can remember how funny the name sounded when my mother stretched the word, Peeeeeeeza. Squatting among the reeds I listened as my father's voice came closer, 'Nico! I'm going to find you!' Finally, his figure loomed above blocking the sun and casting my hiding place into shadow. The child turned and looked upward ... then as suddenly as the memory had surfaced it was gone. I closed my eyes trying vainly to recapture the image, but it would not return. Do all who are orphaned young have such fleeting memories?

With pine needles everywhere there was no longer a road or path to follow. We rode a considerable distance, guided only by markings, simple crosses slashed into tree trunks by an axe, before Giulio, who was in the lead, motioned for us to ride forward and join him. When we reached him, he pointed upward to sunlight shining through the forest canopy ahead and explained, "See that light. There must be a clearing ahead. A large clearing, I think. Maybe the place for a house, Sporcone's house."

Chapter 44

Giulio was correct. When the clearing came into view, we tethered the horses and crept to a position behind thick pine trees that edged the clearing. There we stopped to assess the scene ahead. The large open area immediately in front of us held a covering of pine needles like those we had been riding through. It was spotted with the stumps of large trees that had been felled to create the opening. The clearing ended at a ribbon of rock ledge that formed an outcropping. The sheer drop from the rock ledge afforded an impressive view of Pistoia far below and across the broad valley to a range of hills beyond the town. The outstanding view must be the reason that this location was selected as the site for the house. In the pine-covered clearing not far from the rock ledge were three buildings: a house, a barn, and a structure we judged to be a storage shed.

The buildings were constructed from heavy wooden timbers and round stones that had been gathered locally. I had heard about such techniques but had never seen any structures built in this manner. Other than the meager peasants' houses, all the buildings in Florence are built from quarried stone.

I always considered myself well versed and well-traveled. True, I have not yet seen Paris or Milan or Genoa, but I did grow up in Florence, the capital of the Republic, I have visited Rome, home of the Papacy and our ancient ancestors, and I did attend the world's foremost university for the study of law at Bologna. But this journey, only a short distance from home, was opening my eyes to a very different lifestyle. During our ride along the hillside trail, I had wondered why Sporcone, or anyone else, would want to live in such a remote place. These structures, rustic, and without the comforts we enjoyed in Florence, showed how different, and challenging, life here must be. I vowed that when I returned home, I would ask Alessa about village life in Morocco. The village where she lived as a child is very different from this place, her village is in a desert and this is a forest, but all people with sparse resources must face similar struggles.

We watched for several minutes looking for movement but saw no activity in the house or at any of the other buildings. Finally, Giulio announced, "We leave the horses here and go to the house on foot. They will not see us if we keep the barn between us and the house. At the barn, Roberto and Nico will see if anyone is inside. Federico and I will look for anyone in the shed. Then all of us will go to the house."

Everyone nodded their agreement and we moved out of the pine grove and into the clearing. When we reached the rear of the barn, Roberto and I paused to listen for any activity within. We heard a faint rapping sound as though something were being tapped with a small hammer. Through a crack between two wall timbers we could make out a person, but only a sliver of his back was visible. We were also able to see horses, more than one, but we could not tell how many.

The barn had only one window high up on the end wall. The entrance was on a side visible from the house. To avoid being seen we moved quickly around to that side and entered the barn. Roberto entered first and walked directly toward the center of the building. I stopped just inside the entrance to scan the space.

Horses stood in four of the six stalls along the left wall. I have been in barns that reek of animal sweat and manure, but not this one. It was surprisingly clean with no piles of manure scattered on the floor and no stench. The horses were dry and well groomed.

To my right was a large stack of hay and beyond it a man hunched over a workbench repairing a bridle. He was small and lean with the tight muscles one gets from sustained physical effort. His hands showed the bruises and scars of arduous labor. Streaks of grey in his hair proved he was not young, although his face lacked the creases and wrinkles that come with age.

With his attention captured by his work, the stableman did not notice Roberto moving behind him. Roberto accidentally brushed against one of the stalls prompting a snort from the mare within. At this, the workman turned, startled to see an intruder only an arm's length away. He hesitated upon realizing the figure was a monk, but he quickly pushed instinct aside and grabbed for the pitchfork that leaned against the nearby wall. He swung the tines upward toward Roberto's chest and feinted a jab.

"Who are you?" he squawked in a reedy voice better suited to an older man.

Roberto wasted no time with small talk. "Where is the nun?"

The stableman answered by thrusting the pitchfork forward and striking Roberto solidly in the chest. The sharp tines sliced effortlessly through the soft fabric of the robe but lacked the force needed to penetrate Roberto's armor-like buffalo leather. The stableman stood incredulous that the monk was unscathed, that his flesh was uncut. Could it be that God is protecting his servant?

Roberto took advantage of the worker's confusion and wrenched the pitchfork from his hand. Roberto flipped the tool high above his head and as it fell, he snatched it in midair and held it with the tines now aimed toward the stableman. A sneer spread across Roberto's face, his uneven teeth bared like those of a hungry predator. His tongue swished across his teeth depositing a drop of spittle that dangled from the corner of his lower lip.

The stableman's eyes widened with fear as he watched the intruder transform from a man of God to an angry beast. He turned and bolted for the door. I stood at the entrance but my form did not fully block it, and in his panic, the stableman did not even register my presence. He sprinted toward the open space.

I had no weapon, but I could not let him reach the house where he would alert others to our presence. I stiffened my left arm and as he reached me I arced my straight limb upward and forward, striking the escaping man in the neck with my forearm.

The force of my blow knocked him backward. He lost his footing and fell, striking his head on the hard dirt floor. With an expression that was now more a smile than a sneer, Roberto lowered the pitchfork until its tines rested on the defeated man's throat. Roberto applied no force, but the weight of the tool alone was enough to cause circles of blood to appear around each of its tines.

I bent down and pulled a dagger from its sheath at the man's belt. I lofted it threateningly, pushed the pitchfork aside, and pressed the knife blade against the stableman's throat. I repeated the question Roberto had asked earlier. "Where is the nun?"

With the fight gone from him, he responded to my question. "She is in the house."

Not a very helpful answer.

"Where in the house? Where is she being held?"

He looked confused. "Being held? She is not being held. She can go anywhere in the house, but mostly she has been keeping to her room where she prays."

I looked up and saw that Giulio and Federico had joined us, and they looked as puzzled as I was by the man's statement. I withdrew the knife, pulled the man to his feet, and asked, "What do you mean she is not being held? She is a prisoner here, is she not?"

"A prisoner? No. She was brought here for her protection. I was told there are people in Florence who want to harm her. I do not know why. I was told they might come here to kill her. I think maybe you are the ones... it is possible even monks can be killers."

The three mercenaries and I looked at each other trying to understand who told him that Sister Teresa was fleeing from danger and why.

"We are not here to harm the nun. We are here to protect her. Did Salvatore Sporcone tell you that she is in danger?"

"Salvatore Sporcone? No. Signor Salvatore has never come to this place. I think he does not even know of it. It belongs to his son."

"Alphonso?"

"Yes. Signor Alphonso won it in a card game, but even he rarely visits. He is a city person. He said this place smells funny and that only a barbarian would live here. How could he say that? How could anyone say that? Here it is beautiful and peaceful. The air holds the scent God gave it, not the foul smells of the city and not the stink of money that Signor Alphonso covets. He is pazzo, crazy."

With his fear subsiding the stableman became talkative, and his barrage of words made Giulio impatient. He pressed his face close to that of the stableman and demanded, "How many are in the house?"

"There are two... and the nun."

"The two men in the house, are they the men who brought her here?" I asked.

"No, these men came today, only a short while ago."

"Then who brought the nun to this place?"

"It was another man. He and the nun came yesterday."

"Where is he now?"

"I have not seen him today. Maybe he returned to the town, maybe to Florence. I do not know."

Directing his comment to Roberto and me, Giulio said, "There was no one in the shed, only food drying for winter, animal traps, wood cutting tools, and a small wagon."

The stableman had no more useful information for us. Federico found a length of rope behind the workbench and used it to tie the stableman to a post. Again I pressed the knife to his throat. "If you call out an alarm to the others, you will be visiting Saint Peter."

A nod from the stableman and the fear in his eyes showed that he understood my threat. Turning so he could not see, I winked to Giulio who understood that my threat was hollow; nonetheless, he walked to me and whispered, "I will not want to be accused in a court of law where you are one of the magistrates."

We judged that the stableman was speaking the truth because counting the stableman, the two men in the house, plus Sister Teresa there were four, a match to the number of horses in the barn. Foolishly we did not consider that Sister Teresa might not know how to ride. We were told that she had departed from San Marco church in a wagon so we should have deduced that she also arrived here in a wagon.

Chapter 45

Emboldened by knowing we outnumbered the men in the house, we crossed the distance from the barn to the house without fear of detection. As we approached the house, we heard no sound from inside. The few tiny windows were shuttered, making it impossible for us to see inside. The three mercenaries arranged themselves in a queue at the entry. Giulio, at the head of the line, listened at the door. Hearing nothing, he signaled his readiness by raising a hand. The others responded with a quick nod of their heads. Giulio pushed the door open slowly and the three entered silently.

In a practiced move Giulio surveyed the area of the room directly ahead, Roberto moved to the left and assessed that space, and Federico did the same to the right. The room reflected the rustic simplicity of the building's construction. Instead of smooth white plaster, the walls exposed the wood members of the structure's shell. No paintings or other artwork decorated the walls and no paint covered them. The room was sparsely furnished with crudely fashioned pieces constructed of wood. Five chairs surrounded a table at the center of the room. Another chair, one of its rear legs broken and askew, leaned against a wall.

Federico moved toward an opening to the right that led to at least one other room. Giulio and Roberto went to the left where several other rooms could be seen. Ahead, visible through a narrow opening, was a small space that looked to be a storage area for holding foodstuffs. I went in that direction.

I scanned the shelves to my left along the wall of the narrow storage area. The shelf at waist height held containers of salt, grains, and spices. The one above, at shoulder height, had only a smooth layer of dust. To my right, the lower shelf contained a variety of eating utensils, bowls, and drinking cups, at least twenty of each, a far greater number than the dining table could seat. On the upper shelf sat a stack of serving platters each large enough for a roasted pheasant. I passed quickly through the storage area to the kitchen beyond.

I entered at one corner of the small kitchen. At the opposite wall, a small cooking fire burned in a stone fireplace. Above the fire hung a steaming pot whose aroma told of a hearty soup or stew. A heavy wooden table filled the center of the small kitchen. On it were peelings and stems, the remains of vegetables whose edible parts were boiling in the black metal pot. At the corner diagonally across from where I entered a closed but unlatched door led to the outside. From the doorway a row of wooden pegs stretched along the wall and on one hung a rabbit, skinned and dressed, ready to be cut into pieces and added to the stew. Above the hooks was a long narrow window, the only source of light in the room other than the fire.

Finding no one in the kitchen, I turned to leave and join the others when the door swung open and a pair of black eyes set in a mean face locked onto me. Between the eyes, a pointy nose hooked to one side, a sign that it had been broken in the past and not set correctly. A bald dome topped the face, and a stubby beard framed it below.

The wiry intruder mouthed a single word, "Who." In a flash, he pulled a knife from his belt and swung it toward me in a wide arc, charging around the table toward me. His quickness gave me no time to avoid his strike. The razor-sharp blade slashed the robe across my chest and cut deeply into my left arm.

As he raised the knife preparing for another blow, I looked frantically for something to use as a weapon. The only object within reach was a plate of vegetables on the table. I grabbed the plate and hurled it upward toward his face. Instinctively he turned away and raised his arm to shield his head. The plate was deflected away harmlessly by his upraised hand. It bounced, then skittered across the table and crashed to the floor.

While he was busy avoiding the plate, I backed away around the large wooden table, but a moment later he was advancing toward me, swinging the blade menacingly from side to side. Blood flowed from the cut in my arm, a stain growing on the sleeve of my robe. The knife I had taken from the stableman was in one of the deep pockets of the robe, but I was not able to reach it.

Another step and I felt the heat from the fireplace on my back. I was becoming trapped between a fire behind and a knife-wielding attacker in front. I turned slightly and my elbow bumped into something, the pot of steaming soup. Having only the sleeves of the robe to shield my hands, I lifted the boiling pot away from the flames. The thin cloth of the robe did little to protect my hands from the searing heat.

With agonizing pain begging me to release my grip, I hurled the pot upward in the direction of my attacker. My awkward position and the pain extending up my arms made the throw into a feeble attempt. The pot landed short of my assailant who was now readying for another strike. It struck the side of the table and rolled, spraying its hot contents across my attacker's midsection and down onto his legs.

The scalding liquid soaked his thin clothing and reached his skin. He screamed and dropped the knife. He jumped backward in a fruitless attempt to escape the pain. Then he bent down to brush away the suffering with his hands, but the soggy pants remained stuck to his scalded legs.

I grasped the handle of the pot that now rested on the floor, raised it overhead, and swung the heavy pot downward striking it hard against the side of his bald head. The impact twisted his head to the side with a sharp cracking sound. His eyes fluttered, then closed, and his limp body fell to the floor.

The three mercenaries hearing the commotion rushed into the kitchen to find the intruder on the floor and me leaning against the table gripping my bleeding arm. Federico, the one with medical training, tore the sleeve from my robe and cut a strip which he fashioned into a bandage to stem the flow of blood.

Roberto bent to check the intruder. “He is not breathing.”

Roberto's words pained me more than my wounded arm and burned hands. I intended only to force the man away, not to kill him. My legal training assured me that my action was justified, ‘defense of person’ it is called, but I will never forgive myself for what I did.

Chapter46

Through the open doorway, Giulio saw movement outside and rushed out calling back over his shoulder as he ran, "Roberto, come!"

Roberto leaped over the fallen man and charged out through the doorway in Giulio's wake. Federico informed me, "We found no one in the house." Then he left me leaning on the table as he went to aid his colleagues. I pulled myself up from the table and walked to the doorway to observe the activity outside.

The three mercenaries spread out as they approached two men who were dragging Sister Teresa toward the rocky precipice. When they heard the mercenaries approach, the men threw the nun to the ground and drew their swords.

The two men were similar enough in appearance that they could be brothers. Their light brown hair hung nearly to their waists and was pulled into sheaths resembling horses' tails. Their eyes were blue-gray set deep above strong high cheekbones, and their skin had a ruddy hue unlike that of any Italians. Each wore a necklace from which hung a silver medallion embossed with a pattern that looked like rope twisted into an elaborate knot. Their stance with feet wide apart and the grip on their swords showed them to be experienced warriors. Their faces held no hostility, only determination.

They would have given a good account in an even match, but being outnumbered by the mercenaries gave them no chance at victory. "We want only the nun," Giulio shouted. "Release her! You cannot win!"

The men did not respond to Giulio's challenge. Either they did not understand his words or they felt an advantage because the mercenaries did not carry swords. In unison Giulio, Roberto, and Federico released the maces from their belts. Giulio and Roberto eased forward slowly facing the two men while Federico circled around to position himself behind them.

When Giulio and Roberto got within range, the two men raised their swords high in the air and then swept them downward toward their opponents. Simultaneously the two mercenaries swung their maces upward driving the spiked heads of the maces into the forearms of the assailants. The blows deflected the swords and drew blood from the stricken limbs. Despite their pain, the men did not drop their weapons.

One of the attackers ignored the blood staining his shirt sleeve, shifted the sword to his other hand, and raised it preparing to renew the attack. Few fighters can wield a sword effectively in both hands.

Seeing they were outnumbered three to two, his companion hesitated. The wound proved that the maces had greater reach than his sword and that the opponents were skilled in using their weapons. He concluded that they could not win. He barked words to his companion in a harsh language I did not understand. Intensity vanished from their eyes, replaced by the serenity one might find among people strolling beside the Arno river on a Sunday afternoon. The two lowered their swords in front of them, pointing the blades downward, an indication of resignation - they would not attack again but they were still prepared to defend themselves if necessary. They stepped slowly to the side moving away from the mercenaries. Giulio and Roberto watched but did not follow. Upon reaching the side of the house, the two men sheathed their weapons and walked casually to the stable. Moments later we heard them ride away.

There is a code among warriors that I do not understand. The two who fled were about to throw a nun to her death from the rocky cliff, they attacked the mercenaries with swords, and yet honor demanded that the mercenaries allow their attackers to flee. Vengeance has a place even in the laws I pledge to uphold, but vengeance has no place in the code these warriors follow. They hold no animosity and are quick to forgive, or at least they willingly accept the outcome of a battle.

Federico helped Sister Teresa to the house. She walked easily only cradling her right arm that had been wrenched from her shoulder when the two men dragged her from the house. Federico fashioned a sling to support the injured arm and a strap to hold it immobile against her chest. He escorted the nun from the kitchen to the entry room where she could be seated. I followed.

Throughout her ordeal, Sister Teresa had not spoken. I walked to where she was seated and sat beside her. She recognized me immediately as the person who had spoken with her about Jacopo Sporcone, although she was puzzled by my wearing a monk's robe and being in the company of three monks.

"I am sorry the information I gave to Jacopo brought you suffering. Despite our urging to the contrary, Jacopo did confront Salvatore. To keep the truth from being known, the Sporcones had Jacopo killed." I could have spoken less bluntly, I realized.

Horror registered on her face upon hearing that the boy had been killed. The expression lasted only for an instant then it was gone, and her lips began moving in silent prayer.

"Jacopo must have said that he spoke with you and that is why you too became a target of Salvatore's anger." Sister Teresa did not reply.

Entering from the kitchen with a cup in each hand Federico said, "I could not find any medicines." He handed each of us a cup filled with a warm brew. "I made this from herbs in the storage room. It will help with the pain." He moved closer to me and whispered into my ear so the nun could not hear, "It is the same mixture I give to horses in labor."

As we sat sipping Federico's brew, Giulio announced, "The sun is down below the mountains. The sky is starting to darken.

With no light, we cannot follow the path down the hill. We will stay at this house tonight and return to Florence in the morning."

In the storage shed Giulio had found beans, squash, potatoes, and peppers which he combined with the rabbit that had been hanging in the kitchen to create a tasty stew. Roberto brought our horses to the stable where he untied the stableman. When he returned to the house Roberto secured the doors and window shutters to guarantee that we would not be surprised by intruders while we slept.

Chapter 47 Thursday, August 16, 1464

I awakened in the morning to the ringing of the distant bell tower of San Zeno echoing among the hills. Federico's potion let me sleep undisturbed by any pain from my wound. The others were already awake. Roberto had gone to the storage shed to have the stableman ready the wagon where Sister Teresa and I would ride on the return journey to Florence. As he worked I asked, "The two men who came yesterday. Did they say who sent them?"

"I was working here in the shed. I saw them bring their horses to the stable and then go to the house. They did not come to the shed. They said nothing to me," the stableman replied.

"Had you ever seen them before? Maybe in Pistoia or Prato?"

"I have never seen them before."

"Did you hear them speak to each other? Could you tell what language they spoke?"

"They did say things to each other. Their words sounded like Italian, but in a strange dialect." He could tell us nothing more.

He had been deceived into believing that he was protecting the nun from harm. That was the reason he had attacked Roberto when we first entered the stable. It was a brave act, so we felt no animosity toward him. We bid him farewell and rode away leaving him to return to his bridle repair work that our arrival had interrupted.

The three mercenaries were big men with the strength of bears and appetites to match. During our descent to the valley, they reminded each other of the delicious treats available at the bakery in Pistoia. When we arrived at the shop we were greeted by the shopkeeper's wife, a plump motherly type. She smiled warmly as we entered and gave one last turn to the dough she was kneading. She wiped her flour-covered hands on her apron that was well marked with traces of the confections that filled the display shelves. She came to the shelf where the mercenaries were struggling to choose from the array of delicious looking pastries. She held out a basket filled with pieces cut from a warm peach tort.

"You will like these. Everyone likes them. Everything is fresh. The peaches were picked yesterday from trees here in Pistoia. The honey is from yesterday too. My husband is outside getting more pastries from the oven. He will have them here soon."

She scrutinized Roberto as he sampled the tort. "Do you have someone, maybe a brother, who is a monk? There was a monk here yesterday. He was big like you, with your happy face."

We no longer wore the monk robes. She would not have

imagined that four monks had transformed into three warriors, a wounded academic, and an injured nun.

Roberto deflected her question, "Woman, are you saying that somewhere there is a man of the cloth as handsome as I? That must truly be one of God's wonders."

On the remainder of our return to Florence, I puzzled over who was responsible for killing Jacopo and abducting Sister Teresa. Salvatore Sporcone had reason to keep his past crimes from becoming known, but the stableman told us that Salvatore did not know of the house near Pistoia so he could not have had the nun taken there. The house belonged to Alphonso Sporcone. Would he have reason to want Jacopo killed?

I regretted that we had not detained the two swordsmen to learn who commissioned them.

Upon reaching Florence, we rode directly to the convent of Sant' Apollonia. The same novice that I encountered yesterday was again in the office. Upon seeing us, and especially Sister Teresa, she ran to fetch Abbess Cecilia. Sisters by blood would have embraced at the reconciliation but sisters of God are discouraged from displays of emotion and affection.

The abbess' first words were directed to me. "Bless you for fulfilling your vow by bringing our sister back to us." Her next words were to the mercenaries. "God will reward your kindness and efforts in saving our sister." And then to the novice she said, "Take Sister Teresa to the infirmary and have Sister Clara attend to her wound."

Sister Cecilia asked neither for details of our venture nor where Sister Teresa had been taken. Instead, she provided us with additional information.

"Yesterday, after you departed, a monk came to inquire after Sister Teresa. He was dressed in clerical garb I had not seen before, a coarse black tunic and a black biretta." Almost as an afterthought, she added, "He wore a distinctive silver and gold ring bearing a symbol of the Constantine Cross.

"I told him the sister had been taken from us but that men had gone to rescue her. He said he knew she had been taken and he asked, 'Her liberator, is it Signor Argenti?' I confirmed that it was. How he learned your name I do not know."

"What was his purpose in coming to you, sister?"

"He wanted to assure me that those who had taken Sister Teresa would suffer a lesson."

"Did he say who had taken her? Did he know?"

"He did not say. But this morning we learned that when the Sporcones were returning home yesterday night, three men were pulled from their carriage and beaten. It happened so suddenly that their driver was unaware until he heard them cry out as they were thrown to the ground. One of them had his nose broken and bloodied by the impact. The assailant delivered a warning to them that if any harm comes to the sister of God, they will never walk again."

"The assailant... could the driver identify him?"

"No. It was dark. The driver was surprised and frightened."

Abbess Cecilia assured us that Sister Teresa would be safe in the convent. As we turned to leave, we heard sounds of joy and thankful prayer floating throughout the convent as word of Sister Teresa's safe return spread among the community of nuns.

On the final leg of the journey, from the convent to Donato's house, I sat alone in the rear of the wagon while Giulio drove the horses. I tried to focus on the Sporcone and their motives, but my mind was haunted by the man I had killed. I heard his scream as the scalding liquid blistered his legs; I saw his limp, lifeless body at my feet. Covering my ears did not mask the sharp crack of his neck being severed by the heavy metal pot. How long would it take for those memories to fade?

Chapter 48

Joanna, Donato, Alessa, and Simone were having their midday meal when I entered the house. Joanna was the first to notice my arm wrapped in a blood-stained cloth. "Madre di Dio! What happened?"

Alessa rose from the table and came to where I was standing. She gently touched my arm while inspecting the crude bandage that Federico had fashioned. "Go sit at the table. I will fix this."

Moments later she returned with a basket of medical items. "On the ship I was only a girl, but I was the one who mended all the crew. Ships are dangerous. When the sea is rough men fall from the riggings, and when it is calm they fight with each other. There are always injuries."

Donato and Simone listened as I recounted my exploit and Alessa ministered to my injury. First, she removed the old dressing that Federico had fashioned from the monk's robe. Then she washed the wound and applied a salve to prevent infection and speed healing. Lastly, she wrapped the arm with a clean bandage.

Looking at the makeshift bandage she praised Federico's work. "He did well for you with only these torn pieces of cloth. He had nothing for infection, so you are fortunate there was much blood. Bleeding carries away the dirt." She was correct although at the time I had not felt fortunate to be spilling blood.

"Does it hurt?" she asked.

"No, Federico concocted a remedy that took away all the pain, his secret magic potion," I told her.

When I described the battle with my attacker in the kitchen, Donato saw my regret at the killing. "You have remorse. Your confessor will grant you absolution and that will help to dispel your anguish."

Alessa expressed a different view. "He was a killer. You would not be here if you did not act. You have no blame. Do not bring guilt to your heart." Her philosophy was shaped by harsh memories of the raiders who slaughtered the people of her village who were not fit to be sold at auction.

Bolstered by a second glass of rich Tuscan wine, I continued with an account of our encounter with the two swordsmen. Simone reacted to my description of their medallions. "The medallion is called a Celtic Knot. Several years ago, Venice was visited by an envoy from a place called Ireland. He presented a tapestry to the Doge, and the design at the center of the tapestry was a large Celtic Knot. I do not know if the design has a special significance."

"What is a Celtic?" Alessa asked.

'Celts are fierce warrior people who lived in the North. More than a millennium ago they came over the mountains and conquered tribes that lived in what is now the Republic of Venice. I think they may even have attacked Rome. Now their tribes live mostly in England and Ireland."

"You are correct, Simone," Donato said. "In the very early days of the Roman Republic, the Celts sacked the city of Rome."

Alessa shook her head in disbelief. "You speak of an honor code, but to me it is foolish. Even a child knows not to free his enemy. If you do not cut off the head of a serpent you never know when he returns to strike you from behind."

Again she shook her head, and her expression showed intolerance with our action. "I do not understand this warrior code you speak of. Men came to kill a nun and you failed to learn who sent them. The men of my people in Morocco do not play at being warriors. They do not let attackers go free."

The mercenaries have one philosophy, Alessa has another, and I am somewhere in between. Maybe someday, when I am a magistrate with long experience in tribunals, I will understand how to reconcile their views.

Chapter 49

A visitor was seated with his back straight and rigid, his arms folded across his chest, and looking straight ahead with an expressionless face. He had come to the house to meet with me. His neat simple attire gave no hint as to who he was or his purpose in calling on me. As soon as I entered the loggia he stood straight, let his arms fall to his sides, and addressed me. "I have been asked to offer you my services."

"Who are you?" I asked, startled by his directness.

"That is always the first question."

"Who sent you, and what are your services?" I pressed.

He said nothing but handed me a folded sheet of paper. I took it and read. It was addressed simply to ' P.D.' and it read, 'I am detained in Genoa. See if you may be of service to Signor Nico Argenti.'

It was signed with initials, 'B.S.'

"Am I correct that BS stands for Bartolomeo Scala?"

"Yes. As you see in the note, he asks me to render any services that may be useful to you."

"That answers one of my questions. Need I repeat the others?"

"Who I am is not important. My name would mean nothing to you. As for my services, that is complicated. I provide a variety of services useful to the Chancery and to Messer Scala. A simple answer would be that I am the 'connector.' I connect people together who need to interact with each other, and I connect people with the information they need. I perform other services as well, but that explanation is a beginning."

My visitor stood statue-still while I considered his explanation. I had never heard of a connector being an official Chancery staff position. Seeing my doubtful expression he added, "All Chanceries have agents doing work that is not widely discussed in public."

"Do the Chanceries at Milan and Venice have connectors too?" I asked, while I tried to process this new information.

"Yes, Genoa, Siena, Naples, they all have connectors. We are colleagues who often work together and share information."

His statement and his purpose for being here would be unreasonable were he not sent by Bartolomeo Scala. Nothing is unreasonable for the Chancellor. I decided to test him by asking for information already known to me. "Who is Lo Spruzzatore?"

"Lo Spruzzatore is not a single person. The name applies to all members of the Guild of Assassins who ply their trade using poisons and toxic potions."

His answer not only confirmed what Alessa had told me previously, it went beyond her characterization. She had said nothing about a Guild of Assassins. With a skeptic's voice I asked, "There is a Guild of Assassins?"

"Yes. And like other guilds, it has strict membership requirements. Those who are considered worthy enough to join display their membership with an image of the Leviathan Cross burned into their necks. The guild has officers and governing consuls, but unlike other guilds, it does not answer to the laws of any State. It has members in republics, duchies, and kingdoms across the Italian peninsula."

"Including the Florentine Republic?"

"I am not certain, but it is possible," he answered.

"Even if its members are spread widely, the guild must have quarters somewhere. Where do their consuls meet?"

"Trustworthy reports say their base is in the Kingdom of Naples. Of course, officials of the kingdom deny this, but evidence supports that guild members frequently perform assassinations with outcomes favorable to the King of Naples."

Next, I ventured a question for which I did not already know the answer. "When is Piero de Medici next journeying to Siena?"

"Signor de Medici has no plan to visit Siena."

"Perhaps his plan is kept secret, for his protection."

His eyes flashed in disbelief that anyone would doubt him. "Signor de Medici has visited a physician in Siena who treats his condition. His last visit was twenty days ago. At this time he has not planned a return visit, and he has no other occasion to journey to Siena."

His expression grew more intense as he added, "There are no secrets."

The connector felt confident in his knowledge of Piero de Medici's plans, but his information contradicted mine. Both Jacopo and Francesca heard Salvatore and Alphonso Sporcone proclaim their animosity toward Piero de Medici, and Jacopo heard that the assassin would face his target at Siena.

If indeed Piero de Medici had no intention of leaving his villa, was possible that the assassin had more than one target? I had no clue who the second target might be.

The connector claimed that there were no secrets, and he professed to have extensive information sources. Perhaps he could help me discover whether there was a second target. I asked, "I have learned that Alphonso Sporcone will be meeting with an assassin at an inn near the town of Empoli. Can you find out when such a meeting will take place?"

"That is a more difficult request. I will make inquiries."

When I asked nothing further, the connector rose to leave.

"If I find the information you seek, I will get word to you. If you wish to contact me, tell anyone at the Chancery that you wish to speak with the connector. I will come to you."

When I returned to the atrium, Donato was sitting on a couch relaxing and sipping a glass of wine. Alessa and Simone had finished their meals as well and were preparing to leave.

"I received a message from Messer Bembo," Simone said, "He is returning to Florence from Rome today and he will continue on to Venice tomorrow."

"He planned to be in Rome for two weeks. Did something happen that is causing him to return early?" I asked.

"I suspect so, although his message does not give a reason for his change of plan. It does, however, request that I return to Venice with him."

I gave Simone a quizzical look, hoping he might explain Messer Bembo's request.

"It is a highly unusual request. Not one he would make without good reason so I will honor it. And that leads to another issue."

He turned to direct his words to Donato. "When Messer Bembo was last here in Florence, he invited Alessa to travel to Venice with him to see the city and to meet his daughter. If his invitation still stands then she could accompany us, if that meets with your approval."

Simone's request for Donato's approval brought forth a burst of laughter from both Donato and me. "Alessa is a free woman," Donato replied. "She determines her own actions without needing my approval. My opinion means nothing."

Alessa came to where Donato was seated, stood behind him, wrapped her arms around his neck, bent, and kissed him softly on the cheek. "Your opinion is always important to me, Donato." She placed a second kiss on his other cheek then, "I do have your approval, Donato, yes?"

"Yes, of course you do. I only worry that you will become so enchanted by the city of canals that you will not want to return to a city that offers only cobblestone streets." With drama in his speech, and feigning tear filled his eyes, he added, "Losing you would make me eternally sad. I and all other citizens of Florence could not bear to suffer such a loss."

"I never want to see you sad. I will return. You have my promise." Alessa stood and took Simone by the hand. "I must buy gifts for Messer Bembo and his family. Simone, will you come with me to the Mercato to help me choose?"

After Simone and Alessa departed, I told Donato of my conversation with the connector and how his information implied that the target of the Sporcone's assassin might include someone other than Piero de Medici.

"I cannot offer an alternative possibility. There were no other adversaries mentioned while I was at Palazzo Pitti."

Chapter 50

When I arose the next morning, Simone and Alessa had their travel bags ready and loaded into a carriage sent by the Venetian embassy that would take them to rendezvous with Messer Bembo. Alessa had an additional bag filled with gifts. On Simone's advice, she selected a variety of Florentine silk and woolen specialties. For Messer Bembo's wife Helena and daughter Diana, Alessa found finely crafted silver brooches at a jewelry shop on the Ponte Vecchio. She also selected one for Simone's sister. I decided to ride with Alessa and Simone to the embassy to bid them farewell and also to learn from Messer Bembo what had occurred in Rome that caused him to hasten his return to Venice.

There are three foreign embassies in the city of Florence representing the Republic of Venice, the Duchy of Milan, and the Kingdom of Naples. All three are clustered nearby each other along the Arno River in the Santa Maria Novella quarter. It is said that the three are in close proximity so they can easily monitor the activities of their rivals. The Papal State also has a permanent envoy in Florence, but he resides in the compound of the Archbishop of Florence rather than at an embassy.

The gray stone residence of the Venetian ambassador differed little from neighboring houses except it was taller, surrounded by more massive grounds, and with more colorful flowers in its gardens. If that weren't distinction enough, above the main entrance fluttered the bright red Venetian flag emblazoned with the golden-winged lion of Saint Mark.

Our carriage stopped at the embassy main entrance to discharge us before disappearing around to the back of the building where it would be loaded with official embassy materials and Messer Bembo's personal effects. A young man wearing the colorful uniform of the Venetian navy escorted us to the reception room where Messer Bembo awaited our arrival.

After greeting us, Messer Bembo announced the sad news, "Pope Pius has passed from this Earth."

Simone felt the sadness that grips all the faithful upon hearing of the death of the Holy Father, but neither he nor Alessa understood the full import of Messer Bembo's statement. For their benefit, Bembo explained the significance of the event.

"Pope Pius was instrumental in persuading all Christian states to join a crusade against the Turks. That vow created a unity that keeps the states from squabbling with each other. The pontiff's death casts doubt over whether the crusade will go forward.

"Our merchant vessels in the Eastern Mediterranean are

experiencing increasing pressure from the Turkish fleet. Without aid from other states, Venice will struggle to prevail against the Turks. Lacking a crusade, we must form defensive alliances to preserve the security of our Republic. I have been recalled to Venice to consult with the Council on this matter. The Council instructed me to leave Rome immediately. I did not even have a chance to find gifts for my darling wife and daughter."

Simone said, "I am sure aunt Helena will understand."

Bembo's news cast a pall over the otherwise happy occasion. Simone attempted to lighten the mood saying, "We have overcome other serious problems in the history of our Republic. I'm sure the Council will find a solution to this one." Bembo did not reply.

Messer Bembo, Alessa, and Simone climbed into the carriage. Their luggage had already been loaded onto a rack at the rear of the carriage. In front sat the driver and a member of the Venetian military. Another member of the military mounted his horse ready to escort the dignitary and his entourage.

Florentine laws prohibited anyone from displaying weapons openly within the city, so any weapons belonging to the escorts were stored inside the carriage. They would be retrieved once the military escorts passed through the city gate.

I stood alone in front of the embassy watching as the carriage carrying my friends moved away. I continued watching until they turned onto Via dei Benci and passed out of sight.

Chapter 51

Rain had begun falling by the time I left the embassy. Dark clouds that had barely peeked above the horizon earlier now filled the entire sky casting a gloomy pall over the city. Was this an omen? Florence and Venice have been friends in peace and allies in war. Would Florentines be willing to bear the cost of another war to support her Venetian partner or might Venice be forced to solicit a stronger ally?

I pulled the hood of my oilskin mantello tighter. The long garment was effective at blocking the wind-driven rain, but it also kept perspiration and the heat of my body from escaping. Adding to my discomfort was the hot August air that clung to the mantello and me like a second soggy skin. Days like these drive even the most loyal Florentines from their beloved city to seaside and mountain retreats during August. I hoped the rain and heavy clouds were bypassing Venice so foul weather would not diminish Alessa's first view of that charming city.

Recalling Messer Bembo's explanation for his premature return, I puzzled over the one matter that he had not addressed. What prompted the request for Simone to return to Venice? The reason could be as innocuous as Simone's mother missing her son, or it could be Venetian authorities fearing that unforeseen events might put him in danger. Simone did not inquire as to the reason. If he did not raise the question, then it certainly was not proper for me to do so.

Reflections playing on the wet cobblestone road momentarily distracted my attention. When my focus returned, I recalled a suggestion Donato had made the previous day, to ask Francesca if she heard another name mentioned who might be another target of the assassin. A short distance ahead, at the San Trinita bridge, I crossed the river and wound my way through the narrow streets of the Oltrarno district to Palazzo Pitti.

By the time I reached the Palazzo, I was dripping like a river otter. Rain drenched the outside of my oilskin mantello, and perspiration soaked it from the inside. The two guards who were usually stationed outside the main entrance had the good sense to move inside to escape the steady rain. A servant watching through a lookout port saw me approach and opened the small entrance door when I reached it.

Calling at the estate of a Florentine elite without an appointment was socially unacceptable, so not only was I breaching appropriate etiquette, but I was doing so in sodden clothing unfit for wearing in the elegant mansion. Fortunately, the servant recognized me from my previous visit. On that occasion, Francesca herself had come to the door to greet me, and that consideration established my cachet as a personal friend of Signorina Pitti.

When I entered the anteroom, the servant inspected me with disdain while he summoned one of Francesca's maids, who then raced off to inquire whether her mistress would receive me. Eyeing my dripping clothes, the servant announced in a severe tone, "You cannot roam the palazzo wearing those. Follow me."

I left a trail of wet footprints on the marble floor as I followed him to a service area at the back of the house. The servant studied me briefly estimating my sizes, then pulled a sage green tunic from a shelf.

"Try this one," he instructed.

His selection fitted me well enough, and with its ruffled collar and lace cuffs, the shirt was more elegant than any in my own wardrobe. Next, he handed me a pair of orange breeches. These were sized for a much larger man. When I stepped into them, they billowed out around me as though I were standing in a giant pumpkin. I was about to protest when the servant remarked, "Much better. Now you are presentable."

Adding to my humiliation was the length of the breeches that reached to just below my knees. No properly attired gentleman dons breeches without leggings, but there were no leggings among the garments arrayed on the shelves, so I was forced to suffer the indignity of having my lower legs exposed. Had I expected this treatment I would have had my limbs plucked of hair as some men are said to do.

The appearance of a pumpkin-clad figure returning to the entry hall elicited snickers from two guards who did not even try to hide their enjoyment. When I came into view of the maid, her mouth dropped open. She turned away quickly to hide her astonishment. Whether she too was snickering, or merely embarrassed for me, I could not tell.

"Signorina Francesca will see you. Please follow me." Without looking in my direction, she mounted the stairs and led me to the residence level.

The servant called after me, "Your clothes will be dry when you return."

His voice lacked its earlier edge. I did not look back to observe his expression.

At the top of the stairs, the maid turned right and entered the room with murals depicting scenes of ancient Rome and statues of its greatest leaders. I recalled when Bianca and I had passed quickly through that room on my previous visit to the palazzo.

On a lounge in front of a depiction of the Colosseum, Francesca Pitti sat reading a book. She radiated the elegance of a duchess while I stood before her fashioned as an itinerant French jongleur.

"That is unusual attire for someone hoping to become a magistrate in our esteemed republic," she said smiling.

I spread my arms in mock surrender.

"Armando did this to you, did he not?"

I nodded.

"Forgive him. His life affords him little opportunity for humor."

She motioned to a chair next to her lounge. "Come. Sit here. Tell me, what occasions your visit."

The chair positioned me such that a rendering of Emperor Marcus Aurelius peered over my shoulder, his stony-gray gaze held intent on some distant spectacle now lost in time. Through the sheer fabric of my tunic, Francesca noticed the dressing wrapped around my wounded arm.

"Your shirt does not quite mask an injury. Was it earned during participation in a Ferragosto event?"

I told her of Jacopo Sporcone, Sister Teresa, and my escapade in Pistoia. Then I described my encounter with the connector and explained how his information meant that Piero de Medici might not be the only target of Sporcone's assassin. I asked whether she had heard the name of any other possible victim mentioned during the meeting hosted by her father.

"Conversations with you, Nico, always turn out to be stimulating. If anyone other than you had told me of a mysterious person called the connector, I would not believe it. To answer your question though, I do not recall another name being mentioned. Salvatore Sporcone's ire was directed only at Piero de Medici. Bruttono wanted to include others but his father kept silencing him."

There was no one else I could ask who might know the identity of the assassin's mark. If I were going to solve this puzzle, I would need a different approach. Thinking of this as a puzzle to be solved made me recall the advice of Professor Marsuppini. 'The secret to solving puzzles is in assembling a sufficient number of clues.' I had been hoping to locate someone who had the answer to the puzzle. Failing that, I needed to find more clues by myself.

"Salvatore Sporcone must expect to gain something by eliminating Piero de Medici and the other victim, if indeed there is another victim."

I was thinking aloud and did not expect Francesca to respond, but she did. "Some of those who came here want to end the Medici dynasty so they can replace it with an empire of their own, but that cannot be Salvatore Sporcone's dream. He is just a minor player."

Francesca had voiced a critical piece of the puzzle. I expanded on her idea. "Sporcone is a minor player who wants to move up in status. He is a money changer who wants to be a banker, but the Guild Consuls have rebuffed his petition for elevation to the advanced status."

"The Medici bank holds a consul position," Francesca said. "It has repeatedly refused to conduct business with the Sporcones, so Piero could be expected to vote against them in the future."

"Yes, and if the Sporcones learned of another consul who voted against them, that person could also be a target."

"My father is also a consul of the Bankers and Money Changers Guild so he must know who voted against the Sporcones," Francesca said.

"Consul votes are kept secret. They are not divulged to outsiders, not even to the guild membership."

"Nico, I am Luca Pitti's little girl. I will always be his little girl, and he cannot resist anything his little girl wants. My little girl charm can get him to reveal any secrets. My uncle says that father has made me into a spoiled child. Maybe uncle is right. Do you think I am a spoiled child, Nico?"

"Ah Francesca, why do you always pose such difficult questions? On my last visit you asked if your breasts are sufficiently firm, and now you ask whether you are a spoiled child. I cannot say whether your father spoils you, but I can say that you are a challenge."

"Wonderful! You are learning to speak like a magistrate. They never give direct yes or no answers. Trust in me; I will learn which consuls voted to deny Sporcone's petition. My father is away on a business matter. I will speak with him tomorrow when he returns."

Rising to leave I changed to a different topic. "The painting. The one of Aphrodite and Adonis. Where is it to be displayed?"

"Do you like it? I think it is exquisite. Sandro truly honors his gift when he creates fantasies from the Greek myths. His inspiration for the concept was a rendering that he saw on a fragment of an ancient Greek red-figure vase. I was honored when

Sandro asked me to pose for the painting, although I certainly do not see myself as a goddess. You know little about me, but surely even you agree that my spirit is earthy. As to where the painting will hang, you are asking the wrong person. That painting belongs to Sandro, not to me."

As Armando had promised, my own clothes were dry and waiting for me when I returned to the entry hall. I was happy to be rid of the pumpkin breeches and regain my dignity. I did not ask how he had dried my clothes so quickly. Outside the rain had stopped but the air was still heavy with moisture and had grown even warmer. It was too warm to wear my oilskin, so I carried it under my arm as I returned to Donato's house. I chose a lengthy route along the river, which gave me time to replay in my thoughts the conversation with Francesca.

Chapter 52 Saturday, August 18, 1464

Were it not for the sound from the San Marco bell tower I might have slept past noon. During my undergraduate days at the university, I appreciated the luxury of rising late on days without classes, although I rarely slept this late. By the time I entered the dining salon, Donato and Joanna had gone to the Uccello, and Giorgio was at school. I could only imagine Alessa and Simone looking forward to gliding in a gondola on Venice's Grand Canal. The house was as quiet as a crypt.

I ran a brush through my hair, pulled on a tunic, the same one I had worn the previous day, and I was ready to greet the day. The growling in my stomach grew louder. With no servants and no Alessa to pamper me, I expected that I would need to forage as I had done while living at the university. However, at the university my morning meals consisted of whatever remained from the previous evening, but Donato's house boasted a well-stocked pantry.

I did not need the pantry. Ever-thoughtful Joanna had wrapped a large pastry in a thick cloth to keep warm and set it in the middle of the table with a note alongside that read, 'Nico, enjoy.' Folding back the cloth set free the sweet aroma of figs, almonds, and honey. It is not possible to repay all the kindness Joanna and Donato have shown me. The pastry was so tempting that I could not resist quickly tasting a small piece. Then I refolded the cloth and let the remainder wait until I prepared a drink.

My favorite morning beverage is warm milk flavored with a cinnamon stick. I was introduced to this drink by a university student from Alexandria in Egypt. He claimed, and rightfully so, that it could sooth any stomach suffering from a night of overzealous partying. On the morning following my return to Florence, Simone and I were recounting episodes of our good times at the university when I casually mentioned cinnamon milk. Upon hearing the name Alessa jumped up, said, "Spice milk. I can make that," and she padded off to the kitchen. A short time later she returned with mugs of cinnamon milk more delicious than any I had ever made. Hers had not only cinnamon but another spice that she refuses to divulge. I pray her stay in Venice is not a lengthy one. I miss her joyful spirit already.

Although I always enjoy lively conversations at meal times, the solitude and relaxed pace were a welcome change after the exploit at Pistoia. After licking the last smear of honey from my fingers, my thoughts settled once again on the Sporcones. Francesca would try to learn from her father the possible target of the assassin. The connector was canvassing his sources to discover when Alphonso Sporcone would travel to meet with the assassin. Among the opportunities for me to gather information, a return visit to the Mercato might be promising. There I could see who the Sporcones had found with the expertise to replace Jacopo at their money changer table. I was curious whether the new person would be intimidated by Alphonso as Jacopo had been. More importantly, I could see if Alphonso appeared at the Mercato at all, or whether he had already departed Florence to rendezvous with his hired killer.

Thirty minutes after finishing my meal, I made my way to Borgo degli Albizzi, one of the busiest streets in the city, wearing a clean tunic and shined shoes, and with my hair carefully brushed. Gone from the sky were the black clouds that had gushed rain the previous day. Today the brilliant blue sky held only friendly white puffs. Also gone was the oppressive summer heat. A faint scent of pine hinted that the refreshing cooler air had filtered down from the distant Alps, a rare delight in mid-Summer.

News of the Pope's death was still circulating through the city. Small groups of people, mostly clusters of three or four but some much larger, lined the streets sharing the news. The festive Ferragosto spirit that ruled the city only days ago had given way to a somber tone and contemplation over who would succeed the pontiff rather than one of mourning for him. Pius II, formerly the cardinal of Siena, served for only six years. It came as no surprise that his reign was short because he was known to be suffering from several debilitating maladies at the time of his election. In some respects his selection was a compromise. A French cardinal had received strong support from both the non-Italian bishops and from the French monarchs. Fearing that a French pope might move the papacy to Francia, the Italian electors rallied to support the Sienese cardinal.

In contrast to the crowded streets, the Mercato was nearly devoid of customers. Merchants stood around idly talking amongst themselves alongside tables topped only sparsely with goods for sale. The merchants must have known that everyone had spent heavily celebrating the Ferragosto holiday, so people had no money left to spend at the Mercato. There were no customers at the money changer stalls either. The usually noisy space was uncharacteristically quiet. There too, the workers had nothing to do but chat with each other.

A single person sat behind the table at the Sporcone position. He was neither a small meek person like Jacopo nor an ugly brute like Alphonso. He was of moderate build and medium height, but his somewhat pointy ears, pointy nose, and thin eyebrows gave me to believe that Sporcone blood ran in his veins. Perhaps he was Salvatore's third son, whom I had never met and whose name I did not know.

I observed the stalls for half an hour during which time none of them received even a single customer. Observing them was amusing, for each time a woman passed through the piazza conversation ceased among the money changers and all eyes turned to follow her. It was as if they were all connected to an invisible mechanism that rotated their heads in unison. At first, they only responded to attractive women, but as time passed their standards lowered. I lost interest in watching them when a silver-haired matron with a limp captured their attention.

I approached the Sporcone stall. The man seated at the table was engrossed in reading a document and did not notice my approach. "Is this the Sporcone position? I was hoping to see Jacopo Sporcone. When will he be here?"

Slowly he tilted his head upward to look at me. Most vendors smile as a form of greeting when a customer arrives at their station; he did not. His face remained expressionless as he responded to my question. "Jacopo will not be here. I am Giuseppe. How may I be of service?"

"I am a friend... an acquaintance of Jacopo. I wish to speak with him regarding a personal matter. Do you know when he will return?"

"He has gone away. I do not know when he will return."

"Perhaps his brother Alphonso knows when he will return. Will Alphonso be here later."

"Alphonso is at Prato with his father. I do not know when they will return."

That was his second falsehood. First he said Jacopo had gone away, and then he claimed Alphonso is at Prato. Sister Cecilia told me that both Salvatore and Alphonso already returned from

Prato. Were these lies his own or had someone deceived him? I did want to know whether Giuseppe was the brother of Jacopo and Alphonso, and only a direct question would resolve my curiosity.

"Are you a brother to Jacopo and Alphonso?"

After a suspiciously long pause during which Giuseppe kept rubbing his hands together, he answered simply, "No."

His furtive behavior let me believe this was another lie, although his motivation for lying was not clear. I walked away from the stall and out of the piazza without another word.

I wanted to call upon Sister Teresa to be sure she was settled safely at the convent, but since I was not far from il Pennello I decided instead to see whether Sandro and his artist friends might be there. It was too early in the day for me, or for any reasonable person, to frequent an establishment such as il Pennello, either for a drink or for the other services it offered, but artists move with their own clocks.

From the piazza I turned onto a narrow street and then cut through an even narrower alley where I had to step over someone sleeping off the effects of the previous night. His unpleasant odor, a mixture of cheap wine and fetid cheese, and his loud snoring combined to keep the neighborhood dogs at bay. Puddled near him was a sticky substance that I also carefully avoided and did not even think of trying to identify.

As usual, the lighting was so low inside il Pennello that I had to pause inside the door to let my eyes adjust. Although I could not see anything or anyone, the silence told me that Sandro and his vociferous artist friends were not present. Before long, one of the two women seated on a bench against the far wall rose and advanced toward me. The women working early in the day were not as young or attractive as those who service customers later in the day. The one approaching me smiled, revealing misaligned teeth and deepening the wrinkles at her eyes. I thanked her for her attention and told her I was only looking for one of the artists. She turned without a word and returned to her bench.

Off to my left, Sisi was standing behind the bar. She was the woman who had spoken with Simone and me on my previous visit. She wore no jewelry and only a light touch of color applied to her cheeks. In her hand was a roasted artichoke that she had taken from the plate in front of her. I walked to her and she recognized me immediately.

"You are the one who was too married to enjoy my companionship. I knew you would return. Where is your friend the priest?"

"He had to return to Venice."

"That is too bad. I could have taught him things he cannot learn in Venice."

She offered me one of the artichokes and took another for herself. She continued speaking between bites. "As you can see, I am not prepared to entertain patrons now. The tavern keeper had to be away, so I am only watching the bar until he returns. If you come back later, I will show you a good time, one you will not soon forget, or if you must have your pleasure now one of the other girls can help you."

"I was passing nearby, and I thought that I might find Sandro here," I explained.

"He was here yesterday buying drinks for all of his friends to celebrate his good fortune. I do not know the circumstances, but he said he might need me to pose for him again. He also mentioned Palazzo Medici. Perhaps you will find him there."

Sandro had never mentioned having any interactions with the Medici and that made me curious to learn what drew him to their palazzo. Palazzo Medici, the most elegant estate in all of Florence, was between il Pennello and the convent of Sant' Apollonia; therefore, it was convenient to stop there on my way to visit Sister Teresa.

Chapter 53

For the second consecutive day I arrived at the home of a wealthy influential Florentine family without appointment or invitation. The two occasions differed in that I was known to Francesca Pitti; whereas, I was not known to the Medici, a family mourning the recent loss of their distinguished patriarch. The Medici were buffered by a bevy of servants so there was little chance that my calling at the palazzo would disturb any family members. However, if I presented myself at the main gate, I might accidentally encounter someone entering or leaving the palazzo.

Rather than take that risk, I followed the perimeter of the compound around to the side where a gardener was trimming shrubs. He did not know of an artist named Sandro Botticelli, but he did know there was a boisterous group, possibly artists, in the rear garden. He directed me to a rear entrance used by scholars and artists. That entrance was an opening through a narrow tunnel formed by an arched trellis that led to a vast courtyard. A guard stationed in a cutout midway along the trellis-tunnel informed me that Sandro could be found in the courtyard.

The trellis ended under a portico that bordered the entire courtyard. Two raised flower beds divided the space into three distinct areas - broad strips extending left to right. The archway entrance was at the midpoint of one area. There, immediately in front and to my left, a group of men was having an animated conversation over some characteristic of a marble statue. A circle of empty chairs occupied a portion of the middle area. In the third space, Sandro and two others whom I did not recognize were commenting on a painting mounted on an easel. A small table nearby held a palette and jars of paint suggesting that the painting was yet unfinished. When Sandro noticed me, he detached himself from his companions and came to my side.

"You resemble my good friend Sandro Botticelli," I said, "but you cannot be he as neither your tunic, your hands, nor your face are stained with paint, and your hair has been tamed by a brush."

He ignored my chide, smiled broadly, and clasped me on both shoulders. "Congratulate me," he declared.

"Very well, congratulations."

"Now again."

"You want me to congratulate you again?"

"Yes"

"As you wish, congratulations again. Now, may I be enlightened as to the reasons for my commendations?"

"The first because someone, I know not who, told Lorenzo de

Medici, Piero's son, of my Greek mythology paintings. The young Medici sent a courier to find me with the message that he wished to see my work. I brought Nymph in the Garden, the one you saw at Palazzo Pitti, for him to view."

"You promised that painting to me," I protested.

"It will be yours. I showed it to the young Medici only as an example. He called it 'enchanting,' and said that the time has come for artists to explore other than biblical subjects. He arranged with my patron, maestro Lippi, for me to spend time here working on my own paintings. The Medici provide paint and canvas - everything. They even pay me a small stipend, and they ask nothing in return."

As I opened my mouth to compliment Sandro on his good fortune, he held up his hand signifying that I should remain silent while he continued.

"Wait, Nico, my second news is yet more exciting. The hospital at Siena, Santa Maria della Scala, is expanding and they want paintings for the new building that will raise the spirits of the patients. When they offered a commission to maestro Lippi he declined. He said they need works that are bright, colorful, and inspire imagination. He told them my paintings of the Greek myths are exactly what they need. The hospital directors accepted the maestro's recommendation and offered the commission to me. Along with that news, he said I no longer need to be his apprentice. He recommended that the Company of Saint Luke, that's the guild of painters and artists, elevate me to a master membership."

"That is wonderful news, Sandro, all of it. That news deserves more than just words of congratulation. You must be my guest for dinner at the Uccello to celebrate your good fortune."

"I accept your invitation with pleasure, and I will be sure to record it in my journal," Sandro chuckled. "I will mark it as payment in full for Nymph in the Garden,"

I joined his laughter. We both know that Sandro does not keep a journal.

"The building expansion will be announced at a reception and dinner at Siena. All the influential people involved with the hospital will attend including hospital managers, government officials, bankers who are financing the expansion, and respected physicians associated with the hospital."

"Have you been invited?"

"No, I am just a humble artist who is not fit to dine with the elite. Other than you, dear Nico, all my friends are struggling painters and artisans. My paintings have captured men wearing silk doublets with silver buttons, but I do not own such handsome fashions. As you said earlier, my tunics are adorned with dabs of pigment, unsuitable for a fancy dinner. Fear not though, for dinner with you at the Uccello I will select my least-stained garb."

"Do you know when the reception will take place?" I asked.

"On the day of Ares as the Greek myths would say."

Tuesday. The day of Ares to the Greeks, Mars to the Romans, the god of war, an omen of violence in any tongue.

Chapter 54

I departed Palazzo Medici and walked in the direction of the convent of Sant' Apollonia. Sandro's words replayed in my head: 'All the influential people will attend.' The dinner could be an ideal opportunity for an assassin.

After only a short distance I became aware that someone was following several paces behind me and matching my gait. Without slowing, I glanced over my shoulder to see the connector walking casually and giving no indication that he was following me. I could not imagine how he had found me. He waited until we reached a section of road where there were no others within earshot, then he quickened his step and came alongside me.

While still looking straight ahead he began speaking. "On Monday Alphonso Sporcone will meet someone who is arriving from Genoa or Pisa. My source does not know where the meeting will take place. He also does not know who Sporcone will be meeting and he believes Sporcone may not know the person's name either. The meeting is arranged to protect the privacy of those attending."

As much a question as a statement I said, "This could be the meeting at Empoli that I was told about."

The connector's pace slowed as he considered my conjecture. "It is possible. My source cannot confirm the location of the meeting nor does he know the time of the meeting."

Wondering if the connector had information about the event that Sandro had mentioned, I said, "I understand that a special event will be held at Siena on Tuesday."

"Yes, a dinner reception to announce the new hospital expansion," he confirmed.

Pleased that he knew of the event, I pressed him with another question. "I also understand that bankers will attend the reception. Are any Florentine banks associated with the expansion?"

"I am impressed with how much information you have gathered, Signor Argenti. Three Florentine banks are among those financing the expansion. Representatives of those banks have made plans to attend the celebration."

I had not expected that the connector would have this information readily available.

"Is the project so extensive that three banks are needed?"

"Not at all," he replied. "Any of the banks could provide funds for the entire project with little difficulty. Banks find that their reputations are enhanced by engaging in projects with venerable institutions such as the hospital, so all banks want to be involved. At the same time, to be selected over their competitors they must keep profits low, so each bank keeps its participation small. That is why the three Florentine banks are participating. Banks from

Naples are also involved, but I do not know which ones."

We were walking at a moderate pace. Three young men, walking at a slightly faster pace, passed us. I waited until they were out of earshot before asking another question of the connector. "Will any other Florentines be attending the reception? Guild members or others who are not bankers?"

"Yes, a few Florentine physicians are associated with the hospital. I know that they are planning to attend. Representatives of our distinguished and wealthy families have surely been invited. Some of them are already donors to the hospital. Directors of the hospital hope that invitations to gala events such as this will encourage others to become donors. I do not have the names of all potential attendees at hand, but I can get them."

We continued a short distance without further conversation. When I next glanced in his direction the connector was gone.

Lexia's son Demetrios had overheard that Alphonso Sporcone would be meeting someone at Empoli. The connector confirmed that Alphonso Sporcone will be meeting with someone on Monday. I already knew that the event being held at Siena on Tuesday will attract many prominent people and any of those people could be targets for an assassin. It was unfortunate that the connector could not discover the identity of the assassin. Without having a description, it would be difficult to stop him. The only way to learn his identity was to intercept Alphonoso Sporcone and the assassin at Empoli.

Chapter 55 Monday, 20 August 1464

Travel between Pisa and Florence passed by road and by river. The road was the quickest, and therefore the preferred route for transporting small urgently needed goods that could be carried by riders on horseback or in carriages. The road was also the choice of pilgrims on religious journeys. River barges carried goods such as English wool, metal ingots, eastern spices, and other bulky items upriver to the mills and shops of Florence. On their return, the barges carried finished goods to the seaport at Pisa where they were transferred to ships for delivery to buyers everywhere.

Until the recent heavy rain, the river level had dropped leaving only a narrow channel navigable by the barges. Queues formed at the shallowest sections where the barges were able to pass only in a single file. After the unusual August rain, the river had risen, and its current quickened as bulging mountain streams discharged their copious flows into the Arno. Barge owners took advantage of the higher flow to move goods that had been stockpiled at the town docks.

When space was available the barges welcomed weary travelers and pilgrims whose feet had become blistered from walking long distances. One barge departed from the wharf at Florence early each morning loaded with casks of fresh milk.

Although slower than a horse, the barge would get me to il molo gallegiante, the Floating Dock Inn, at Empoli by mid-morning. From there a carriage ride would get me to Siena by late afternoon or evening. The hospital reception was not being held until the following evening, which should give me ample time to find Alphonso Sporcone and the assassin accompanying him.

Our small barge, with its lower draft, set its course close to the river bank to avoid competing with the larger crafts that claim the middle of the river. I sat at the edge of the deck letting my feet dangle over the side of the barge and watched the bank slide by as we drifted slowly down river.

Three weeks ago I celebrated the successful end of the long and sometimes arduous path to my Doctor of Law degree. I was prepared to begin a career as a magistrate administering justice and the laws of our republic. In the short time since I have become entangled with kidnappers, murderers, and an assassin. I began seeing differences between laws and justice that were not made clear in my university courses. Is this what Bartolomeo Scala expected when he first approached me? 'Gather information' he had said. I felt that the circumstances compelled me to do more. Despite my lack of experience in such matters, I was compelled to make decisions on my own because the Chancellor's guidance would not be available until he returned from Genoa.

Outside the confines of the city, the river passed through mostly empty land dotted with small peasant farms. Because the flat area close to the river flooded regularly, the large farms of wealthy landowners were located on higher ground away from the river.

The slow progress of the barge allowed me time to question whether I was being rash in traveling to Siena alone. I could have asked Orsino or one of the mercenaries to accompany me. Yes, I would have felt safer with one of them at my side.

The connector showed little interest in stopping the assassin. His reluctance might be because the crime would occur, if indeed one were to occur, in the Republic of Siena, not in the jurisdiction of the Florentine Chancery. Or perhaps the connector doubts that my information is correct. He said only that Alphonso Sporcone was meeting someone. It was I who claimed that the 'someone' was an assassin. If there truly were an assassin, and I learned his identity, then I would need to seek help in Siena.

Bianca had mentioned that her brother was a member of the Siena militia, but I could not seek him out directly because I did not know his name. How could it be that Bianca and I had spent hours together talking and I did not learn her surname? Fortunately, the reception was not being held until the following evening so there would be time to find Bianca, who could then lead me to her brother.

We made three stops before arriving at the Empoli town wharf where most of the cargo was discharged. I expected to disembark at Empoli and find other means for getting to the inn located about two miles downriver from the town, but as I rose to leave and thank the barge master, he informed me that his craft would be stopping at the inn so I could remain aboard.

As our barge tied up at the molo gallegiante dock, a group of jovial men was disembarking from another barge that had come up the river. I joined their group on the short walk along the path to the inn. They were physicians from the University of Salerno near Naples who were going to Siena to attend the hospital reception.

"This seems like a roundabout way to travel from Salerno to Siena. Isn't there a shorter route?" I asked one.

"Yes, if you like long carriage rides on bumpy roads. For youngsters like you that may be acceptable, but we tired old men prefer the gentle motion of travel on water. We sailed on a comfortable ship from Naples to Pisa and then relaxed on the smooth river from Pisa. Only on the last part of our journey, from here to Siena, will our bones suffer the ungodly jarring of a carriage ride."

As we neared the inn, I heard one member of the group mention Ferdinand, the King of Naples. I asked the man beside me, "Is the King coming to the reception?"

"No, the King is a benefactor of the hospital, but he will not be at the reception. He has sent an emissary in his stead. In fact, the emissary is already at Siena. The reception is not until tomorrow, but today the hospital directors are meeting to finalize plans for the event. The emissary is representing the King, who is an honorary director."

The inn was situated not far from the river on a rise that kept it from flooding during high waters in the spring. The central section of the building, where the entrance, dining area, and bar were located, was the oldest part of the structure. Its rough-cut stones set it apart from the newer sections constructed of precisely cut blocks. As I reached the crest of the knoll, a stable and large paddock behind the inn became visible. A short distance behind the stable, the Via Pisana, the road to Siena, heads off through a pasture.

The inn's entrance opened into a large room. A massive stone fireplace set into the far wall stood ready to warm guests during the cold months. In the far left corner, a staircase led to guest rooms on the upper floor. Between the fireplace and staircase, a serving tray filled with plates of food had been placed on a serving counter. Tables throughout the room were occupied by distinguished looking men engaged in animated conversation. Other men sat on two long couches positioned in front of the fireplace.

A young woman scurried around picking up empty glasses then carrying them, arms full, into the kitchen through a doorway behind the serving counter. She no sooner disappeared into the kitchen when a man wearing an apron came through the door with another tray of food destined for one of the tables.

My assumption proved correct that the crowd of men enjoying a late morning breakfast were physicians en route to Siena. Some would make the trip by carriage later that day, others would stay at the inn overnight and travel to Siena the following day.

While I stood to survey the room, the young woman returned from the kitchen carrying a cluster of filled glasses. As she sped past toward a table at the far end of the room, she said to me, "Find an empty place if you can, and I'll find you. If you are looking for a room, you're too late. We are full for tonight."

I located one person whom I recognized, a physician from Florence. We had been introduced at the Uccello a few days ago. I walked to his table and was pleased that he remembered me as well. I asked if there were others from Florence who would be attending the reception.

"Dottore Bosco will be there, but he has not arrived yet. I will be meeting him later and we will travel to Siena together. We are the only physicians from Florence who will attend. Many of these gentlemen are from Salerno; some are physicians, and some are professors in the medical school of the university. There is a long-standing relationship between the University of Salerno and the hospital at Siena. As far as I know, the only other Florentine attending today is Luca Pitti."

Seeing my surprise at the mention of Pitti, he added, "Luca is one of the directors of the hospital."

I asked, "Have you by any chance seen Alphonso Sporcone?"

"Sporcone? Here? No. I can't imagine why he would be here."

I did not find an empty chair. I stood leaning against the serving bar contemplating my next steps. I could remain here at il molo gallegiante waiting for Alphonso and his assassin to arrive, or I could travel to Siena and wait for them there. While I puzzled over the options the young hostess called to me as she passed by. "I heard you asking about someone named Alphonso. Someone with that name was here earlier. He was with another person. They wanted to hire a horse."

"Are there horses for hire here at the inn?" I asked.

"A few. Santo, the stable boy, can tell you if there are any remaining that haven't been hired yet."

I rushed outside and ran back to the stable where I found Santo shoveling out stalls. "Did you hire horses to two men earlier? One of them named Alphonso Sporcone?"

"I hired out only one horse. The one called Alphonso paid, but he did not take a horse. The other man took a horse and rode south on the Via Pisana. I do not know what became of the one called Alphonso."

Suddenly the puzzle pieces fit together. The assassin will not strike at the reception tomorrow. He had already left for Siena so he can strike today at the meeting of the hospital directors. His target is the director from Florence who is also a consul of the Bankers and Money Changers guild, Luca Pitti. It must have been Luca who voted against Salvatore Sporcone's elevation from the rank of money changer to banker.

Santo said there were still horses available for hire. At their age, the physicians preferred bumping along in a carriage, as unpleasant as that may be, to thumping along on horseback.

"I want to hire a horse, the fastest one you have," I said.

"No, you do not want the fastest. Siena is far. No animal can run that far."

Santo grabbed a saddle and headed toward a large dark brown mare.

"You want Bia," he advised. "Like the Greek goddess she is named for, she has more power than any other steed in our stable. Keep her at a slow run or a fast walk, rest her when she tires, and she will get you to Siena in the shortest possible time."

Santo gave a short laugh, "Not only does she have energy, but Bia has made the trip to Siena many times. She will get you there even if you fall asleep along the way."

The Via Pisana follows a route first covered by the ancient Romans. There are sections where it passes through woodlands, but most of the way is through open land of brush and high grass. The challenge to travelers, especially those on foot, are the steep uphill grades. The road does not rise gradually to Siena from the level of the Arno river. Instead it visits many of the hilltop towns along the route resulting in long, nearly flat, stretches interspersed with steep uphill climbs. Neither the flat nor the steep sections are smooth, so there was no chance that I would fall asleep.

Chapter 56

The long journey afforded me time to devise a plan. It would have been foolish for me to confront an assassin by myself. Yes, I had done foolish things before, but nothing that might let an assassin send me to greet Saint Peter.

I entered the walled city through the Porta Camollia gate where a city official stationed there gave me directions to the Chancery office. The Chancery building stood out from others surrounding it. It was taller and constructed of sizeable gray stone blocks. On the front facade of the building, the Siena coat of arms was displayed proudly above the entrance. Beyond the unlocked door, the loggia held only a desk for the clerk who greets visitors. The clerk was absent when I entered, so I called out and was soon joined by two men. They both stood looking at me expectantly, waiting for me to state my purpose.

"I need to see the connector," I stated with as much resolve as I could muster.

Both men registered surprise. The older man, his age evident by the gray streaks in his hair, responded, "I am he. Why are you here, and what do you know of connectors?"

I shared with him the information about an assassin having been sent to Siena to target Luca Pitti at the Santa Maria della Scala hospital. He listened patiently as I assembled the many disconnected details into a reasonably coherent story.

"We certainly do not want assassins roaming through our peaceful city, especially if they are targeting a member of the Florentine Signoria, but you must admit that the story you are telling is unlikely, one might even say fanciful. Can you offer any evidence to prove what you say?"

That is precisely what I will be saying to petitioners at tribunals after I become a magistrate, 'Can you offer any proof?'

I had fit together pieces of the puzzle from the knowledge and statements of many different people. Any tribunal would dismiss the story I had just told as hearsay. As a magistrate sitting on a tribunal, I would dismiss it as well. There was only one shred I could offer that might lend credibility to my story. From my pocket I pulled a crumpled sheet of paper, smoothed it, and handed it to the connector.

He read it:

P.D.

I am detained in Genoa. See if you may
be of service to Signor Nico Argenti.

B.S.

"What is this?"

"A message directing the Florentine connector to assist me."

"P D. Yes, I know him. He is indeed your 'connector.' Who is B S?"

"The second Chancellor of the Republic, ..."

Before I could mention a name, he interrupted, "Of course, Bartolomeo Scala."

He turned abruptly, exiting the building at a fast pace. "Come. Follow me," he instructed.

Fortunately, he found that scant piece of evidence enough to be convincing as I had nothing else to offer.

Although the connector was nearly twice my age, he held a steady run to the hospital, which was located on the opposite side of the city from the Chancery. We passed through the central piazza and stopped only briefly at the headquarters of the Minister of Justice to enlist two officers. The four of us then continued to the hospital and went straight to the room where the directors' meeting was underway. The directors were stunned by four men bursting into their meeting room. Such interruption was not acceptable behavior in the staid confines of the hospital. Their surprise turned to fear when we told them of the plot to assassinate one of their members. They assured us that no one else had attempted to disrupt their meeting and none of the attendees had seen a suspicious person lurking around the hospital.

The connector posted the two officers outside the meeting room and advised them that the assassin was marked with the Leviathan Cross. Then the connector and I left the meeting room, intending to return to the justice building to warn other officers about the assassin.

Midway through the long hospital corridor, we passed a steward who was carrying a pitcher of lemon water. I burst out, "The food! The assassin uses arsenic, a poison. Soon dinner will be delivered to the directors in their meeting room."

The connector changed direction and started running along an intersecting corridor that led to the hospital kitchen. Hospital workers shouted at us and jumped out of the way to avoid being struck by the charging connector. I followed close on his heels. We stormed into the food preparation area. Platters of food were arrayed on a long counter ready to be delivered to patients. A single figure hovered over items on a tray at the far end of the counter that was being prepared for delivery to the directors meeting room. The person standing beside the tray wore the smock of a hospital worker, but his hands were covered by dark gloves flecked with a white powdery substance. His open shirt collar revealed a Leviathan Cross design burned into his neck. Seeing us, he scowled and moved away from the counter.

The connector charged forward, arms extended, attempting to grab the assassin, but the assassin jumped backward successfully escaping the connectors' grasp. He dipped into a pouch fastened at his waist, withdrew a handful of white powder, and tossed it into the air in our direction. The connector lurched sideways to avoid the poison cloud, lost his balance, slammed into the counter, and fell forward directly toward the white mist. I dove toward him, put one hand on each of his shoulders, and pushed him down. We both crashed to the floor in a heap, I on top of him. I turned my head upward to witness our peril and, as if time had slowed, I saw the white mist rising into the air and drifting in our direction. In seconds it would change course and descend onto us as a fatal blanket.

There was no time to move from its path. I looked back and forth, scanning frantically for something that might rescue us. A dirty apron hung from a hook on the wall, its bottom hem only inches above my head. I reached up, grabbed, and pulled the garment, but the sturdy fabric would not tear. I pulled harder, lifting myself to put my entire weight on the apron. The hook holding the apron bent then sprang free from the wall and shot across the room. The apron spread as it fell, but its final breadth covered us only from the tops of our heads to our shoulders. I lay still, afraid to move. My arms were bare, and my imagination felt each arsenic crystal settling upon my skin.

"Don't move," the connector warned.

It seemed like several minutes that I lay motionless, listening to my heart and wondering whether each beat might be its last.

Finally, the connector spoke again. "I'm going to remove this cloth. Hold your breath until I have moved it aside."

He slowly lifted the cloth and placed it down on the floor next to us. I could see dots of white powder on my arms.

"Get up. Do it carefully. To be effective arsenic must be breathed or eaten so do not touch your head or face."

I gripped the table and pulled myself to a standing position. The connector did the same, then he led me to the hospital laundry area where we removed our toxic clothes. On our way to the laundry, the connector dispatched hospital workers to deal with the contaminated kitchen area. While we were showering a Guardia officer came to the laundry area to inform us that the assassin had escaped. He fled the city so there was little chance he would be apprehended.

Chapter 57

Bianca and I were having dinner alone in her apartment while her mother and father were at the hospital reception.

"I just learned two new things about you. First, you have your own apartment," I said, looking around.

"Officially, it's my father's apartment. No one will rent an apartment to a woman. Father has accepted my decision to become a fashion designer and not follow his wish that I become a physician. He shows his support in many ways. He not only rents this apartment for me, but he also rents the shop where I operate my dress design business."

"You created the business on your own. Your father has good reason to be proud.

"The second thing I learned is that you are an excellent cook. You learned to play the lute to please your father. Did you learn to cook to please him as well?"

"No. Every woman learns to cook, even society women. Francesca Pitti will never admit that she can cook, but once I watched her make a rabbit stew. She did everything except butcher the rabbits."

Bianca continued, "Speaking of Francesca, I feel truly sorry for her. She's going to be devastated when she learns that her father was the assassin's target."

"It may help ease her distress to know that she provided important information that helped us stop the killer."

We cleared the dining table and carried our drinks to a small couch before continuing our conversation. "What happened to the assassin?" Bianca asked.

"Witnesses reported seeing a horseman riding fast out of the city heading south toward Montalcino."

"So the plot was thwarted and Luca is safe?" She wanted her words to form a statement, but her doubt made them into a question.

"Unfortunately no. The assassins' creed demands that they complete their commissions. He will try again, probably in Florence, not here in Siena. At least now Luca is forewarned. He has a contingent of guards at his palazzo. Both they and the Florentine Guardia have a description of the killer.

"However, there is one detail that the connector and I did not report that could make a difference. The assassin carried his poison in a small pouch at his waist. As he was fleeing the room, the pouch struck the door frame sending a small puff of powder upward toward the assassin's face. Perhaps it was enough to make him his own target."

"What about Alphonso? Will he be punished for his crimes?"

"Again, unfortunately not. There is no real evidence linking him directly to any crime. Little attention was given to investigating Jacopo's death. The official report listed him as an itinerant peasant. If anyone were to identify the body, the claim would be disputed by the Sporcones."

"We never learned who abducted Sister Teresa and held her captive. Although she was held at Alphonso's cabin in Pistoia, there is no proof that Alphonso sanctioned, or even knew about, her abduction. And finally, the only person who can link Alphonso to the assassin is Santo, the stable boy at Empoli. That connection alone is not enough to bring charges against Alphonso.

"If Alphonso is made to pay for his actions it will be at the hands of Luca Pitti. Luca is not a vengeful person, but this incident certainly demands retribution."

For a moment I wondered if retribution might come to Alphonso from the Priors of Constantine.

"What about you, Nico, will you continue your relationship with Chancellor Scala and apply for a position on a tribunal that interacts with the Chancery, or will you choose a less chaotic appointment?"

"I'm not sure, Bianca. What advice do you have for a new laureate?"

ABOUT THE AUTHOR

I hope you enjoyed meeting Nico Argenti as much as I enjoyed introducing him to you. The challenge he overcame in this story sharpened his character and prepared him to cope with other challenges he will face throughout his career.

Nico lived in an exciting place, Florence, during a time when history was being made, the Italian Renaissance. With a little imagination, those of us living today can experience a taste of Nico's world because Florence still echoes many memories of its unique history.

In some places I stretched history to fit this work of fiction. My intent was to do so only with respect.

Florentines were fortunate that their Republic honored the rule of law. In contrast, citizens of certain other city/states suffered under the rule of despots. The next book in this series has Nico using his legal skills to assist a town in defending itself against mercenaries led by a rogue knight.